BLO[illegible]
ON THE
TRAIL

Pinnacle Westerns
BY TERRENCE MCCAULEY

The Jeremiah Halstead Series

BLOOD ON THE TRAIL

THE WICKED AND THE DEAD
(On Sale in August 2022!)

The Sheriff Aaron Mackey Series

WHERE THE BULLETS FLY

DARK TERRITORY

GET OUT OF TOWN

THE DARK SUNRISE

BLOOD ON THE TRAIL

A JEREMIAH HALSTEAD WESTERN

TERRENCE McCAULEY

PINNACLE BOOKS
Kensington Publishing Corp.
www.kensingtonbooks.com

PINNACLE BOOKS are published by

Kensington Publishing Corp.
119 West 40th Street
New York, NY 10018

All Kensington titles, imprints, and distributed lines are available at special quantity discounts for bulk purchases for sales promotion, premiums, fund-raising, educational, or institutional use.

Special book excerpts or customized printings can also be created to fit specific needs. For details, write or phone the office of the Kensington Sales Manager: Attn.: Sales Department. Kensington Publishing Corp., 119 West 40th Street, New York, NY 10018. Phone: 1-800-221-2647.

First Printing: April 2022
ISBN-13: 978-0-7860-4860-1
ISBN-13: 978-0-7860-4861-8 (eBook)

10 9 8 7 6 5 4 3 2 1

Printed in the United States of America

For Richie Narvaez

Chapter 1

"Come on, Col!" Jeremiah Halstead yelled as he spurred the mustang on. "Faster, girl. Faster!"

The Deputy United States Marshal crouched low beside the mustang's neck as bullets from the Hudson Gang cut through the air all around him. High and low and right past him. None of them had found their mark yet. None of them would, if he had anything to say about it.

He knew it was almost impossible to hit a man from the back of a running horse. Returning fire would only be a waste of ammunition. Urging the mustangs to run faster was a much better idea.

The horse Halstead was pulling on a lead rope was also a mustang and Col's sister. She had no trouble keeping up the pace despite the prisoner tied over her saddle like a dead deer. He imagined John Hudson must be complaining something awful. His ribs were probably mighty sore given the pounding they were taking, but the wind in Halstead's ears drowned out the cries of the outlaw.

Halstead could feel Col begin to reach her top speed as the air and blood began to flow through her body. The young mare had been Texas born and usually needed a little bit of time to limber up in the cold Montana weather, but once she did, she was the fastest horse Halstead had ever ridden. He knew he would need every bit of that speed now if he had any hope of out-running the Hudson Gang.

Halstead kept the horses running straight across the flatland in hopes of putting as much distance as he could between himself and the gang.

He stole a quick glance back at his pursuers and saw the group of ten outlaws was quickly falling behind. Halstead knew this was not only because of the speed of his mounts. They were only a few miles out of Rock Creek, and the Hudson Gang's horses were already showing signs of being winded. The animals had spent too much time in the town livery being overfed by the hostler.

The Hudson Gang were overfed, too, but in a much different way. They had managed to cow the sheriff and take over the town of Rock Creek for the past several months. The outlaws had grown soft on whiskey and women. They robbed drunks in alleys and took a share of the winnings at the gambling tables whenever it had pleased them. Easy living in the town they terrorized had made man and beast soft, much to the benefit of Jeremiah Halstead.

But experience had taught Halstead to know better than to take the gang lightly. The Hudsons, as they were known, had a reputation throughout the territory as being a brutal, determined band of stone-cold killers. He knew that even if he managed to get away from them now, these men would continue to stalk him every step of the two-day journey to the federal court in Helena. U.S. Marshal Aaron Mackey wanted to see John Hudson hang in the territorial capital and Halstead had no intention of letting his boss down, especially since this was his first official assignment as a deputy.

After a quick overnight stop in the town of Silver Cloud, he would head on to Helena and see to it that John Hudson received the justice he deserved.

Halstead saw a stand of pine trees in the near distance and steered the mustangs to head in that direction. He was glad the second horse with John Hudson across her back had been able to keep pace with them despite the large prisoner she carried.

Halstead had to crouch even lower in the saddle as he rode among the low-hanging branches of the pines.

He drew his mustang to a gradual halt and brought the horses around to see where his pursuers were now. They had spread themselves out in a line about three hundred yards away and were moving at a much easier pace.

Smart, Halstead thought. *They know where I am. Best to rest the horses while they plot their next move.*

Halstead pulled out the field glasses from his saddlebags and took a closer look at the men. He could see the thick vapor coming from the muzzles of the horses. They were blowing hard and fast in the cold autumn air. They were not used to riding this hard anymore. The speed and distance had taken a toll. They were fat and out of shape and would need a long rest before they were ready to take up the chase again. The liveryman back in Rock Creek had been too generous with the oats, and the lack of exercise had made them sluggish. If the men of the Hudson Gang continued to chase him now, he doubted all of the mounts would make it even halfway to Helena.

Judging by the way they were breathing, he figured at least three of them would come down with pneumonia if they did not already have it. An outlaw was not much of a threat without a horse in open country like this. And since Halstead had their leader tied over the saddle of his mustang, he hoped the remaining members of the Hudson Gang knew enough about horses to know chasing him would get them killed.

But relying on another man's common sense to save his own life did not sound like much of a plan to Jerry Halstead. He had never been much of a gambler as he preferred to make his own luck.

Halstead had bristled at Mackey's orders that all of his men wear all black when picking up a prisoner. He felt like he looked like a preacher or a mortician but did not dare question his friend's orders. Now that he was among the pines, he understood Mackey's reason. Black made for good cover in many situations. At night, for instance, and now among the shadows of the pines. The Hudsons knew where he was, but they could not see him. They were on tired mounts in open ground. All of that was in his favor.

It was time to tilt the odds even further in his favor.

Keeping hold of the rope of the second mustang, Halstead climbed down from the saddle and led both horses to a pair of pines. He slung Col's reins around one of the branches and tied the second mare carrying John Hudson to a tree close by. Col had a tendency to nip at her sister when her blood was up, which it certainly was now.

John Hudson began squirming, but Halstead had bound his hands and feet tightly under the barrel of the mustang too well for him to get free. His prisoner wasn't going anywhere.

Halstead took a knee and took a good handful of Hudson's

hair as he raised his head to look at him. The prisoner screamed through his gag in protest.

"Quit fussing," Halstead told him. "You're not hurt, just uncomfortable. And you'd be sitting upright now if you and your boys hadn't given me so much trouble back in Rock Creek."

Hudson struggled in vain to pull his hair free from the deputy's grip. His fleshy face was red from anger and from riding across the saddle for so long.

"Now, I'm going to have a conversation with your men in my own way. If this turns out like it should, I'll see to it you're riding proper. If it doesn't, then you'll stay as you are until we reach Silver Cloud."

Halstead gripped the hair tighter as he pulled Hudson's head up even higher. "But if you cause me any trouble or try to get away, I'll catch you and I'll drag you all the way back to Helena. Not fast, but real slow so you make the journey." He shook the prisoner's head. "Look at me so I know you understand."

John Hudson did look at him, causing Halstead to smile. If looks could kill, Jeremiah imagined he would be dead. He figured that must have been the same icy glare that had cowed the good people of Rock Creek for so long while he and his gang controlled the town. The same glare that had held them in check until John Hudson had pushed them just a bit too far.

"Don't be angry with me, Hudson. If you hadn't gone and killed the mayor, I wouldn't be here, and you wouldn't be tied over a horse."

Halstead released his grip with a hard shove and left the outlaw to dangle helplessly over the saddle. The deputy had no sympathy for him. John Hudson was a bully and Halstead hated bullies.

He went back to Col and rubbed her neck. The horse had barely broken a sweat despite all the running and seemed content to eat the shoots of grass that had grown up around the roots of the pine trees.

"There's my girl," he said as he dug a carrot out of his saddlebag and fed it to her. He did not dare give her another because he might need her to run again at a moment's notice and did not want her belly too full of food. But he liked to reward a horse as soon as he could following a good effort, and Col had given him her all.

He dug out another carrot and fed it to Col's sister, who he had not gotten around to naming. Both animals had come north with him from Texas and had proved themselves many times on the trail. They might have been smaller than most horses in Montana, but he would put them up against any other mount for durability and speed.

While the animals enjoyed their treat, Halstead slung the field glasses around his neck and pulled his Winchester '86 from the scabbard on the left side of the saddle. He had an old Winchester '73 in his right scabbard but selected the '86 for its range and stopping power. He figured he would need to take these boys at a distance, and the '86 was the right tool for the job.

He walked toward the edge of the trees but remained in the shade. He raised the field glasses and took a closer look at the men following him.

He saw they had stopped completely now and kept their mounts in a straight line as they looked at the stand of pine trees where he was hiding.

"Ten men in the gang and not a brain between them,"

Halstead said to himself as hc looked them over. Then he remembered none of the men who rode with John Hudson had ever been called upon to do much thinking. Hudson had always been the brains of the outfit. All the outlaws had to do was rob what he told them to rob and kill whomever he told them to kill and everything worked out fine. That's the way they had done it for years, or so Halstead had been told when Mackey sent him to bring John Hudson to justice.

The marauders had left a trail of blood behind them that spanned from California all the way to Wyoming and back again. The West was littered with the bodies of stagecoach passengers they had robbed, mining camps they had hit, banks they had held up, and Indians they had massacred and scalped.

As he looked through his field glasses, Halstead saw three of them still had those scalps tied to their saddle horns, dangling from ropes like morbid trophies. A few people had stood up to them of course, but none of them had lived long enough to tell the tale.

That was until John Hudson had been foolish enough to go and kill the mayor of Rock Creek, and the townspeople rallied against him and threw him in jail. The rest of the gang had managed to get out of town before they were lynched and made camp somewhere in the rocks that overlooked Rock Creek, waiting to make their move.

And as he looked them over now, Halstead could tell they were a motley, grimy bunch despite having spent the better part of the past three months in the relatively refined comfort of Rock Creek. The outlaws were of all shapes and sizes and colors. He even remembered some of their names Mackey had given him back in Helena, though he could not tell which outlaw corresponded to which name as he looked them over now.

He figured one of the younger men was probably Hudson's little brother Harry. The others were known simply by whatever title John Hudson had seen fit to call them when they joined his murderous gang. Men with names like Bug and Cree. Pole and Mick. Weasel, Bandit, and Ace. Cliff was the easiest to spot in the group, even from this distance, as he was the only black man in the bunch. The broadest of them, too, with a black patch over his left eye.

Besides Harry, only one of them was said to go by his given name. Ed Zimmerman, who Mackey said was every bit as bad as John Hudson himself. Maybe even worse. He sported two guns, just like Halstead and had acquired a reputation as something of a gunman even before he had joined up with the Hudsons.

Halstead wondered which of the men he was looking at now might be Zimmerman, but there was no way he could tell something like that from this distance. Jeremiah thought of himself as being pretty handy with a pistol, too. He figured he would probably have to go up against Zimmerman at some point between here and Helena. He would be interested in the outcome, especially because his life would be on the line.

He kept watching the men as they maintained a ragged line and although none of them looked at each other, he could see their mouths moving. The small puffs of vapor that rose from them as they spoke confirmed as much.

Halstead did not have to read lips to know they were talking about what they should do next. The lawman had taken their leader into the pines, where there were plenty of shadows and cover to be found. A man could hold off a group their size for quite a while, especially if he knew how to shoot. And they had enough experience to know a deputy marshal knew how to shoot. He might not have his uncle Billy Sunday's eye or his Sharps rifle, but Halstead could still kill a man at a fair distance with his '86.

And the longer they talked, the more he began to wonder if they might not be a bit smarter than they looked.

He hoped not. For his sake.

Chapter 2

Harry Hudson had somehow found himself in the middle of the line, though he had not planned it that way. It was just where he had happened to end up when that damnable lawman rode into the pines with his brother.

Although he was John's brother, there had only ever been one leader of the gang and that had been John. That had always been fine with Harry. He had never been one to make decisions on his own, especially when he could avoid it. He supposed that was why he had followed his brother off the family farm in Kansas and into the life of an outlaw in the first place.

"He's your brother," Cree said to him. The man's dark, swarthy complexion had reminded John of a Cree Indian who had managed to stick a knife in him once. As Harry remembered, Cree was simply a French-Canadian with dark features. "It ought to be your call about what we do next."

Harry was about to stroke his bushy beard as he often did when faced with a difficult decision but stopped himself before he did it. He remembered John's admonishment that the motion made him look like a weak fool. "He might be my brother, but it's all of our hides at stake here, fellas. I think we ought to come to some kind of agreement, don't you?"

"If it was my brother," the red-haired man named Mick offered, "I wouldn't take any chances. We've run that fancy lawman to ground. No shame in that. I say we wait until dark and ride in after him when we're on more even footing."

"What the hell do you know about anything?" Bug said. His wide, wild blue eyes had earned him his name. "I'd bet they don't even have horses in Ireland."

"I was born in California," Mick countered, "same as you, you bug-eyed bastard."

"Simmer down," Bandit told them. He was the best-looking man of the group; clean-shaven except for the moustache he waxed into a tantalizing curl. John had named him Bandit on account of the ease with which he stole the hearts of the ladies he wooed, preferably wealthy widows if one happened to be in the vicinity. "We won't get anywhere with you two barking at each other like a couple of dogs."

"I ain't never been one for waitin'," Weasel offered. He was a pinch-faced man with a long neck that John had thought made him resemble his namesake. "I say one of us distracts him with a manner of peace offerin' while I ride around the side and come at them that way. Sneak up on him and put a bullet in his back, then free John. Best to do it now afore he gets too settled."

"Just like a weasel," Ace concluded. John had called him Ace because he was something of a card sharp. The gang had relied on his winnings in gambling halls to keep them afloat when times were lean. He was good enough that he did not have to cheat all that often. "I say we ride right at him together before our horses get sluggish. Damn it, boys. It's only one man in there."

"One man with a fancy rig," Pole noted. He was the tallest of the group, more than six feet tall by plenty and as skinny as a bean pole. "You see them irons he was sporting in town? A Thunderer on his right hip and another holstered above his belt on the left. Never saw a man with a rig like that. Probably knows how to use them, too."

All of the chatter was giving Harry a headache. He had agreed with every man who spoke as each of them had a point to make. They had been bad men long before they had joined up with John and him. He felt like a fool telling any of them they were wrong and did not want to risk the consequences if he was.

Fortunately for him, not all of the members of the gang had spoken yet. He looked at the large black man at the far right of the group. "Cliff, you haven't said anything yet. What do you think?"

The black man with the patch over his left eye did not speak often, but Harry knew that when he did, the rest of the gang listened. He had gotten his name because John said he resembled a cliff. Anyone who tried to go over him always wound up busted up or dead. He stroked the neck of his horse where the scalps of three dead Indians hung. "Our horses ain't used to this kind of work anymore, boys. They're just about played out. I know mine is and all of yours are, too. I can hear a rattle in Cree's mare, which tells me she's down with pneumonia or will be soon. They might have one good charge left in them, but not much after that. If this Halstead fella takes off with those mustangs of his, we'll be left with a bunch of tired horses and nowhere to ride them." He looked down the line of men looking back at him. "I love a fight just as much as the rest of you boys, so don't go thinking I'm trying to shirk anything. I want John back, too, but we're not outfitted well enough to do it right now. Them's just the facts as I see them is all."

Harry had hoped Cliff would have come up with something better than that, but he was right. The horses were just about done in. His own mount was shivering from the effort of the chase and he imagined none of the other animals were faring much better.

That left him to ask the final member of the gang for his opinion. He also happened to be the quietest and the deadliest among them now that John was out of the way. He looked to the far left of the group at Ed Zimmerman. "Well, we've heard from everyone else besides you, Ed. What do you think?"

Zimmerman had not taken his eyes off the stand of pine trees since they had slowed down. He was looking into them now as he said, "I never thought I'd say this, but every one of you idiots is right in his own way. We're stuck here with tired horses and a target in thick cover." He nodded toward the trees. "This boy isn't just fancy, he's smart. He's packing two Winchesters. One's a '73 and the other's an '86. Saw them when he tied off his horses in front of the jail back in town. That means we're already in his range, depending on what he's got it loaded with."

Harry was glad he could finally contribute something to the discussion. "It only holds if we stand still, Ed, and there's ten of us. If we rush him, he's bound to miss most of us."

"But not all of us," Zimmerman told him. "And I won't

count on him being the type to panic. I watched how he handled himself in town. He's about as cool as they come, and I'd wager my share of the money that he's every bit as good as he thinks he is. He's a fighter and we can't buffalo him like some homesteaders on a wagon train."

He pulled up one of the four scalps dangling from his saddle horn and began to feel the hair between his fingers, as if it might tell him something. For all Harry knew, it just might. Ed had always been the strangest man in their outfit.

Harry hung his head. He had asked the question, hoping someone would have an idea they could all agree upon. But everyone had a different opinion on what they should do next.

"That didn't help much."

Zimmerman cleared his throat and spat over his horse's head. "I say we play it Weasel's way for once. That'll mean one of us rides out there and tries to talk to him. Can't hurt. We can't scare him off, but maybe we can buy him off. We've got enough to spare. A man in his position might be willing to take the money and let John go. You can tell him we'll ride on and away from Rock Creek if he wants. Tell him we'll ride clear out of the territory. Promise him the moon. We can always kill him later after we get John back."

Ace cursed. "No way in hell I'm giving up Rock Creek. The only reason why we left was because they had John. I'd rather see that place burn than have them say they rode us off."

"Then we'll burn it," Zimmerman said, "because even if we get John back, we're going to have to kill that deputy who has him. Halstead doesn't strike me as the kind of loose end you leave untied."

"So what?" Bandit said. "Won't be the first lawman we killed."

"Won't be the last," Pole added.

"He'll be the last we kill in Montana," Zimmerman told them, "because once word gets out that this Halstead fella is dead, Aaron Mackey will come looking for us. And believe me, boys, you don't want to still be in Montana when that happens."

Weasel was far from impressed. "Hell, I heard all them same stories you have, Ed, and I don't believe the half of them. What's one man against the ten of us? Eleven if we can get John out of this."

Zimmerman continued to stroke the scalp in his hand. "I'm not going on any rumors or fairytales. I'm going on what I've seen, and I can tell you Aaron Mackey's worse than anything you've heard. If we kill Halstead, he'll kill all of us. That's a fact."

"I don't care about Mackey right now," Cree said. "I care about that half-breed whose got us pinned down in there."

"He's not a breed," Zimmerman said. "His father's white and his mother's Mexican. Heard them talk about it in The Railhead last night."

"I don't care what he is," Cliff said. "He's in our way, and someone's got to do something about it."

Zimmerman finally took his eyes off the stand of pine trees and looked at Harry. A shiver went through Hudson when he did.

"I say one of us needs to ride out to talk to Halstead," Zimmerman said, "while Weasel flanks him from the right over there. I'd prefer to send more, but if too many of us disappear, Halstead's likely to notice. It's not perfect, but it's the best plan we've got, given the circumstances."

Harry swallowed hard as he felt the eyes of every man in the gang on him. They did not have to say what they were thinking. Harry was smart enough to know they doubted him. They thought he was weak and stupid. They thought he had lived his life in his brother's shadow. What's more is that he knew they were right.

He also knew it was up to him to decide what needed to be done.

He tried to keep the quaver out of his voice as he said, "Sounds like a good idea to me, Ed. I'll ride ahead a bit to get into shouting distance of him while Weasel here works his way around the right side." Giving orders like this made him feel a little better about what he was about to do. Put a little iron in his backbone. He only hoped he didn't catch any iron in his belly for his trouble. He picked up his reins and urged his horse forward. "No time like the present. Just be ready to back me up, whatever happens next."

The men grumbled their encouragement to him as he walked his horse at a steady pace. But the closer he got to the pines, to the chance of death hc knew was waiting for him in its shadows, the more his courage began to wane. He even thought about turning back and having one of the other men do it. But kept on moving.

He feared his own men might shoot him dead if he did anything else.

Chapter 3

Halstead dropped to a knee beside a pine tree when he saw one of the men break away from the middle of the line and begin to ride toward him. His pace was slow and deliberate. It did not feel like the beginning of an attack.

Halstead raised his field glasses to get a closer look at the approaching rider. It was clear now that it was John Hudson's younger, thinner brother Harry. The front of his beard was thinner than the rest of it, more scraggily as if he had spent a considerable amount of time pulling on it. It was a nasty habit for a grown man to have. It showed weakness.

Halstead lowered the field glasses when Hank stopped his horse about a hundred yards from the pines. He pulled them off his neck and leaned them against the tree as he brought his '86 up to his shoulder. It would be an easy shot from this distance. One hundred yards was practically point-blank range for his Winchester, especially since there was no wind to complicate the shot.

He moved his finger next to the trigger while he aimed his front site just to the right of Harry's chest. Legally, he was within his rights to kill the man right then. He had been part of the gang that had not only chased him but had shot at him all the way from Rock Creek to here. That broke about half a dozen laws Halstead could think of and probably a few more he did not know about.

But killing Harry would serve no purpose at present. At least not until Jeremiah knew what the man was up to. He could always kill him later.

Harry cupped his hands to either side of his mouth and yelled, "Hello in there. Deputy Halstead. John Hudson. Can either of you hear me?"

"What do you want?" Halstead yelled back. He was careful not to say too much or else the men might know his position.

"I want to talk about how we can all get out of this alive and still get what we all want."

Halstead watched one of the nine men behind him ease his horse out of the line and ride off. Probably trying to flank him. Some of the trees in front of Halstead's position blocked his shot, otherwise he would have easily brought the man down.

He readjusted his aim back on Harry Hudson. "How so?"

Harry thumbed over his shoulder. "You see that man who just left? He's heading back to where we've got our gold stashed. He's going to be back here in an hour or so with more gold than you've ever seen in your life. And it'll be all yours if you'll just agree to let my brother go."

Halstead grinned behind the rifle. Harry was a rotten liar. "And here I was thinking that skinny runt was riding around trying to flank me."

"Not at all, friend," Harry assured him. "There's been enough shooting for one day, don't you think?"

"I should," Halstead yelled, "seeing as how I was the one getting shot at."

"Well, that's all done with now," Harry said. "There's no reason for any more shooting. Not from us. Not from you, either. What I propose is simple. I get my brother back. You get rich, and no one else has to get hurt."

"Except for that mayor your brother killed." Halstead heard a branch snap somewhere close. The skinny man was fast. He was coming toward him from the side.

So much for becoming a rich man.

Halstead had grown tired of Harry's banter. "How much were you planning on offering me to hand over your brother?"

Harry seemed happy to get an easy question for once. "We've got five thousand in gold if you're of a mind to end this peacefully. You can tell your boss in Helena that we jumped you if you want. Hell, mister. With five thousand in gold in your pocket, you can just ride off and never go back to Helena at all."

Halstead heard another branch snap on his left, only this time it was closer. Weasel was making progress.

He decided it was time to draw the show to a close. "Never been much of a fan of gold, Harry. I prefer to deal in lead."

Halstead fired and the .45-70 round slammed into Harry's chest, sending him tumbling backward and out of the saddle.

He levered in the next round and took aim at the rest of the Hudson gang that had already begun to turn and ride the other way. He aimed at the middle of the line and fired. The gang was about three hundred yards away and Halstead had rushed the shot. His bullet hit one of the horses in the side of the head, killing the animal immediately. The rider managed to fall out of the saddle on his right as the horse collapsed to its left.

Halstead heard another branch snap, followed quickly by another. The skinny man was in a hurry now and running toward him through the pines.

Halstead leaned his rifle against the tree and pulled the Colt Thunderer from his belly holster just as the man broke into the clearing. He had spotted John Hudson hogtied to the mustang and, for a moment, froze where he stood.

That moment cost him his life as two shots from Halstead's pistol hit him in the chest and cut him down.

Halstead remained quiet against the tree, listening for anyone else who might be approaching on foot or horseback. But the only sound he could hear was the quiet whimpering of John Hudson through his gag.

Halstead looked back out at the grass beyond the pines. The gang had regrouped some five hundred yards away or more and did not look like they were in any hurry to charge his position. Their horses looked more winded now than before.

The rider who had escaped being crushed beneath his dying mount had managed to reach Harry's fleeing horse and was already climbing into the saddle.

Only one man had held his ground through the ordeal. Halstead picked up his field glasses to get a closer look at him. It was the same man he had seen at the very end of the line. A tall, broad man in a torn black coat and a rumpled black hat whose crooked brim shielded his eyes. His beard had been thinner than that of the others, as if he had only started growing it a few days before. He rode a dappled gray. The rifle under his left leg remained in its scabbard, and Halstead saw him patting one of the four scalps that dangled from his saddle horn as if it was a cat. It was difficult for him to see if the man was smiling, but Halstead imagined he was.

That's him, Halstead thought. *That's Ed Zimmerman.*

He could not see if the man was looking at him directly or just at the pines in general, but that did not matter. He had shown the lawman and the gang who he was. When everyone else had run away, this man had held his ground. While two of his men had died, he lived.

Halstead saw one thing clearly. Zimmerman was the new leader of the Hudson Gang now. And John Hudson's life had just become a lot less valuable.

Halstead holstered his Colt and picked up his Winchester as he rose to his feet. He carefully aimed at Zimmerman, who seemed to sense he was being targeted and reluctantly wheeled his horse around to join the others.

Halstead knew the man was still within range, but he did not want to risk taking the shot. He did not want to give Zimmerman the satisfaction of missing. He had no doubt that he would have to kill this man someday, but not on this particular day. He had no doubt that they would face each other again some day.

Halstead picked up his field glasses and brought them back to where he had tethered Col and the other mustang. He slid the field glasses into his saddlebag and took two .45-70 rounds and loaded them into his rifle before tucking it back into the scabbard.

John Hudson's whimpering was getting on his nerves. He slowly walked over to where the skinny man had fallen as he pulled the Colt in his belly holster and opened the cylinder. "This one the man you called Weasel?" he asked Hudson.

The bound prisoner struggled to lift his head to see where Halstead was. Hudson stopped squirming and began to weep.

"I figured as much." Halstead dumped out the empty shells on Weasel's body, plucked two fresh rounds from his belt, and slid them into the cylinder. He gave the wheel a good spin and snapped it shut.

"Your brother Harry is dead." Halstead tucked the Colt back into his belly holster as he went back to Col. "Weasel tried to sneak up on us. He's dead, too. Your gang is down to eight now and their mounts are about done in. They won't be coming for us any time soon, and they sure as hell won't be catching up to us before we reach Silver Cloud. Of that, you can be certain."

Halstead walked back to his prisoner and took another handful of Hudson's hair and forced his head to raise. The outlaw's eyes were red, and his gag was soaked from spit and tears. The good nuns down in El Paso had done their best to instill some compassion and Christian love into their charge when they raised him. He liked to think their lessons took, at least most of the timc.

But not where John Hudson and his men were concerned. Where someone else might feel sorry for this man tied over a mustang's saddle, Jeremiah Halstead only saw the fear in the faces of the countless men, women, and children Hudson had killed over the years. Instead of Hudson's whimpering, he heard their screams and begging and sorrow. He heard the tears of the loved ones they had left behind.

Jeremiah Halstead did not see a man when he looked

at John Hudson. He did not even see a prisoner. He saw a package that needed to be delivered to Marshal Aaron Mackey in Helena, Montana. A piece of meat that would soon be swinging from a noose. Hung by the neck until it received the death it had earned in life.

"No one's coming for you," Halstead told him. "Zimmerman's in charge now, and the last thing in the world he wants is you telling him what to do again. You remember that as we ride to Silver Cloud."

Halstead let the prisoner's head drop and untied the mustang's tether from the tree. He led the animal over to Col and kept a good grip on the lead rope as he climbed into the saddle.

He unwrapped the reins from the branch and brought the animals about.

"Come on, girl," he said to his mare. "Let's see if we can't make Silver Cloud by dinner time."

Chapter 4

Zimmerman eyed each of the remaining members of the Hudson Gang who huddled around the large cook fire they had built. They had just finished a delayed breakfast of coffee and biscuits as there had been no time to eat before Halstead had tried to sneak Hudson out of Rock Creek at just before dawn that morning.

There had been ten of them then, Zimmerman recalled. There were eight of them now. He was surprised the men still had appetite enough to eat so much. He supposed even outlaws had to eat sometime.

Night was fast approaching, and the men had settled in for another cold night in the highlands of Montana. Zimmerman wondered how they would handle a night spent out in the elements. The whole gang, including himself, had grown soft in the three months they had occupied Rock Creek. They had grown accustomed to three hot meals a day, shelter from the elements, and the warm company of women whenever they had sought it.

Zimmerman had not been immune. He found himself

missing Bridie's down bed and plush blankets as the cold crept its way into his bones.

He was sad to see all of the remaining men were as uncomfortable on their bedrolls as he was. He was sad to see what they had allowed themselves to become. The Hudson Gang had once been a group of hard-riding, hard-killing men. Their time in Rock Creek had reduced them to a bunch of gun-shy old men pining for the comforts of hearth and home, even if that home had been a whorehouse.

Zimmerman noted that none of the men had said much since the last pistol shot had echoed out from the pines several hours before. There had not been much to say. Their horses were exhausted and needed rest. Halstead had ridden off with their leader, probably headed for Silver Cloud, the next town between here and Helena.

Harry Hudson was dead. His body was still a heap on the ground in the same place where it had fallen. Zimmerman and Bandit had ridden into the pines after they figured Halstead had ridden on. They found Weasel on his back with two neat holes in his heart and two empty shells next to his corpse.

The ground had already frozen over, so burying either of the men was out of the question. They could have found rocks to cover them with, but they all knew it would only be a matter of time before wolves or coyotes dug them out and had at their remains anyway.

Besides, the remaining members of the Hudson Gang were well acquainted with death. They had little honor for the sanctity of life and saw no reason to protect the dignity of the dead.

But as quiet as they may have been, Zimmerman could

sense something stirring in the men that had only grown stronger as the sun began to set below the western mountains that surrounded them.

Of all the men, he was surprised Cliff was the first to break the silence by chucking a rock into the fire. "Damn it, boys. If none of you are man enough to say it, I guess I will. Letting that bastard ride off with John after killing Harry and Weasel doesn't sit well with me. Doesn't sit well at all."

Pole was mindlessly making designs in the dirt with a stick. "I've been thinking the same thing. Just don't seem right that we're letting that damned half-breed get away with killing our friends, even if he's the law."

"Sets a mighty bad precedent, boys," Bandit added. "Mighty bad."

"President?" Mick repeated. "What the hell does President Harrison got to do with any of this?"

Zimmerman enjoyed the puzzled looks Bandit drew from the other men. "Not president. Precedent. You know, like a rule or an example. Letting Halstead live after killing us will make us look bad when word gets out is what I meant."

"Then say what you mean next time," Bug yelled. "Don't go using no ten-dollar words when talking to men without a nickel's worth of education."

"Speak for yourself, bug-eyes," Mick said. "I've had my share of schooling. I can even read Latin, by God."

"Lot of good it's done you," Cree said as he pulled his poncho closer around his shoulders. "All that learning, and you're still dumb enough to be out here freezing your ass off like the rest of us."

Ace said, "Brains have nothing to do with this, boys.

Mick can read Latin. I've heard Cree speak Spanish and French. Bandit's got charm and the rest of us have our own skills. Mine happens to be cards. None of that matters much now. Weasel and Harry are dead and John's going to hang." He looked down in his cup and swirled his coffee. "Just bad luck is all."

"Luck?" Bug glared at him. Zimmerman thought his eyes looked even wilder in the flickering light of the fire. "What's luck got to do with it? And since when have we ever needed luck to get what we wanted? We didn't get to be the Hudson Gang by luck. We got it by stepping on anyone who got in our way."

Zimmerman was glad Ace was cool-headed enough to not rise to Bug's bait. "And what would you call John shooting the mayor like he did? Good fortune?" He looked at the other men in turn around the fire. "How many times did that old boy give John a good ribbing with never a crossed word between them? Must've been dozens of times by my count. John just went along with it and gave it back to him. Nothing but laughs all around. Hell, he had the mayor in his back pocket, so what did he care if he joshed him around a little? We ran that town. What did words matter? But just look at what happened. The mayor told him he had a face only a mother could love on the very anniversary of Mama Hudson's death."

Ace looked at all the men around the campfire again. "Out of all the things he could have said and all the days he could've said it, he just happened to say that on the wrong day to the wrong man and John took it bad enough to drill him for it." He held up a finger to prove his point. "You boys might not call that bad luck, but I sure do. And now we're here, and John's on his way to hang." Ace drained his coffee and grabbed the pot to fill his cup. "That's all there is to it."

Zimmerman sat in silence, watching the men absorb everything that Acc had told them. They were brutal, violent men. Among the worst sort Zimmerman had ever ridden with save for one man. That man had taught him the importance of cunning, and it was cunning that made him keep his silence now. He did not want to offer his opinion like the others had. He wanted to be asked for it. Only then would he be able to begin to put his plan into action.

Cree was the first one to look at Zimmerman and say, "What about you, Ed? You're the only one who ain't said anything yet."

Zimmerman waited to speak until he saw every man looking at him. "I didn't know I was riding with a bunch of philosophers all this time."

The remark made the men laugh and ease some of the tension that had settled over the group. The outlaw who had been his mentor had used humor in times like these and with the same affect. "Every one of you has a point in your own way. Cliff is right. We should've run Halstead down and probably caught him, too, if our horses hadn't been half dead. But I didn't see any of you in a hurry to charge into those pines after old Harry hit the dirt. Didn't see anyone in a hurry to go in after we heard that last shot that killed poor Weasel, either. I'm not chastising you boys. I didn't ride in there blasting, either."

"No," Bug said. "You just stood there. Frozen in fear like a damned deer."

Zimmerman did not allow the notion to sit too long in the minds of the men. "Not frozen and not fearful. I stayed put and watched. I observed. I wanted to see what all of you would do. I watched you run. Even Bug here ran when he got his horse shot out from under him and grabbed Harry's."

He leaned forward closer to the fire so the men could get a better look at his face. "But I wasn't just looking at you boys. I was looking at Halstead, too. Or rather, I was looking where I thought he was. I wanted to see if he was going to take a shot at me after he killed Weasel. He could've done it. I was no further away from him than Bug had been when his shot killed his horse. He could've drilled me right then and there. He knew he'd rushed the first shot at Bug, but he had plenty of time to aim at me. Probably could've hit me square between the eyes if he'd taken the time to try. But he didn't try."

"Why do you think that is?" Cliff asked.

"I don't know," Zimmerman admitted. "I can only explain why I did what I did. I stayed where I was because I was studying the man. I wanted to see what he'd do. In a way, he told me something about himself. He didn't shoot me because he didn't have to. That showed me he's not some mad-dog killer with a star on his chest. This man's a thinker. He's got control."

"So?" Cree asked.

"So, you can't go after a thinking man the way you would, say, men like us. You've got to go after him carefully or you'll end up like Harry and Weasel and who knows how many others he's put a bullet in. I'd say quite a few, seeing how he handled himself out there today."

"Jesus, Ed." Bandit took a pull on his flask. "Almost sounds like you admire the son of a bitch."

"Not admire," Zimmerman said, "but I do understand

him. Or at least I'm beginning to understand him." He looked into the fire as he decided to share a bit of information that might help his cause. "Had a run-in with his father a while back. Bet you boys didn't know that. Silent Sim Halstead they called him. He was quite a fighter in his own, quiet way."

The men now all traded looks. Zimmerman could almost taste their intrigue.

"What happened between you and his old man?" Cree asked.

"You kill him?" Bug added.

Zimmerman shook his head. "No, but one of the men I rode with did. I had already separated from the group by then, but my impression of the man has stuck with me all this time. And if the son is anything like his father, which I believe he is, then I think I know how we can beat him."

A great chatter rose up from the group as they all began to ask him the same question in their own ways at the same time. All of the babble boiled down to a single word. "How?"

Zimmerman was all too glad to tell them. "By killing him the same way my friend killed his father. By using his sense of duty against him."

The outlaw smiled as he watched the notion sink in with them. Some reached the conclusion faster than others, but in the end, the decision was the same. If Zimmerman knew how to defeat him, then he was probably the best one to lead them.

Which was what Zimmerman had wanted all along. He could not take command of men like this by force. It had to be their idea or else it would never stick.

And that thought was sticking with them now.

Bug asked, "Think we can still get John sprung free?"

Zimmerman could not have cared less about what happened to the mindless thug, but for now, he served a purpose. "That's why we're out here, isn't it?"

The assurance settled over the men as the possibility of success reached them.

Mick looked at him from across the fire. "Seeing as how you're the only one whose got an angle on this Halstead fella, I guess that kind of means you're in charge now, don't it?"

That was when Zimmerman knew he had them eating out of his hand. His mentor, Alexander Darabont, would have been pleased. "If you insist. And I happen to have an idea about how we could begin to pull him down this very night."

Cliff squinted at him with his remaining eye. "How?"

Zimmerman pointed at the gambler. "It involves Ace. Now, let me tell you what I'm thinking."

Chapter 5

Dusk was already coming to an end by the time Halstead reached Silver Cloud. He had been able to see the town for a good mile or so away, but the dying light prevented him from making out much detail.

He could tell the town was comprised of one long stretch lined with buildings of every type on either side of the street. The only discernable feature was a clock tower that rose twice as high as any other building in town. He figured it was either a church or a bank since time seemed to be a preoccupation of the faithful or the wealthy.

There did not seem to be much of the town beyond that main thoroughfare, though it was too dark for him to be certain. By then, just the only things he cared about were a jail to house his prisoner, a livery to stow his horse, and a place to sleep for the night. If he managed to find a place where he could get something to eat, all the better. But if not, it would not be the first time Jeremiah Halstead had gone to bed on an empty stomach.

He was glad to see the sign for the County Sheriff's Office & Jail at the edge of town. He had been in the saddle for most of the day with only one break since his run-in with the Hudson Gang, so the sooner he could walk on his own two feet, the better.

He noticed the jail was across from a saloon that sounded like it catered to a lively crowd. The hand-painted sign on the window said it was The Green Tree Saloon, and he was glad it was in close proximity to the jail. He had never been much of a drinker, but he figured a quick whiskey or two might be just what he needed after such an arduous journey.

Halstead ignored the looks he and his prisoner drew from the few people on the boardwalks on both sides of the thoroughfare as he wrapped Col's reins around the hitching post in front of the sheriff's office. After securing the reins of the second mustang to the rail, he produced his father's Bowie knife from the back of his pants and easily sliced the rope binding Hudson's feet and legs together beneath the horse. He tucked the knife away as the unconscious prisoner slowly slid back along the saddle until his feet hit the ground. His legs gave way and the rest of him hit the compact dirt of the thoroughfare with a heavy thud. Halstead had not intended for his prisoner to fall but did not care that he had.

Some of the curious townspeople who had been watching him gasped when the bound prisoner hit the ground like a side of beef. Halstead heard the murmurs among the crowd as he nudged Hudson with his boot to get to his feet. The outlaw flailed on the ground as he tried to get up on his own power. Halstead grabbed him by the collar and jerked him to his feet, steering him up the stairs and throwing him through the open door of the sheriff's office.

The bits of chatter he heard from the crowd was nothing he had not heard before.

"Who does that half-breed think he is, handling a white man like that?"

"Why, it's a shame what these Indians think they can get away with these days."

"Wipe 'em off the face of the earth, I say. They're savages. All of them."

Halstead heeled the door shut behind him. Such words had lost their effect on him long ago.

He was surprised to see both desks empty since the front door had been open. "Hello? Anyone here?"

Hudson was trying to say something, but still had the gag in his mouth. While still holding him by the collar with his right hand, Jeremiah pulled down the gag with his left.

Hudson flexed his jaw now that it was finally free of the gag that had bound him since morning. "Looks like you picked a great place to hole up in, marshal."

Jeremiah pushed Hudson toward one of the chairs against the wall and, by some miracle, he managed to sit in it without falling down. "Keep your mouth shut, Hudson, or the gag goes back on. And I'm a deputy, not the marshal. You'll be seeing him soon enough at your hanging."

Normally, he would not have allowed a prisoner to sit without being tied to the chair, but Hudson was so dizzy from spending the day slung over a saddle that Halstead knew he was in no shape to go anywhere.

He walked to the door that he figured led back to the cells. He tried to open it, but found it locked. He looked through the small notch cut in the door to see if the sheriff or his deputy might be back there tending to a prisoner, but the cells were empty. A ring of iron keys hung on a nail next to the door.

Where is everyone?

He got his answer when a voice behind him said, "Don't you move a muscle, chief, or I'll blow you right through that door."

Halstead cursed his foolishness. It served him right for turning his back to the front door, even if it had only been for a second. Mackey would have been mighty sore about the oversight. Uncle Billy, too.

Halstead did not hold up his hands but held them away from his sides in plain view. "My name's Jeremiah Halstead, and I'm a deputy United States Marshal."

"So, you say. How do I know for sure?"

Halstead did not turn around. "You Sheriff Boddington?"

"What if I am?"

"Then you must've gotten a telegram from Marshal Aaron Mackey telling you that I was coming and bringing the prisoner John Hudson with me."

"Maybe I did and maybe I didn't," Boddington said. "So how about you turn around real slow, chief, so we can get a better look at you?"

Jerry complied and turned around as slowly as he could manage. He made sure he kept his hands away from the Colt on his hip and the other holstered above his belt. He stopped turning when he faced Boddington fully. The silver deputy marshal star was clearly pinned on the lapel of Halstead's black coat.

He saw Sheriff Barry Boddington aiming a shotgun at

his belly. He was a stocky man in his late thirties or early forties. He sported black hair and a thick black moustache. His brown duster coat was filthy with coal dust, and his brown shirt looked as if it may have been white once upon a time. If it had not been for the sheriff star pinned to his vest, Halstead could have easily taken this man for a member of the Hudson Gang.

A fat, pink-faced deputy stood in the left side of the doorway behind Boddington. His gunbelt hung well below a massive stomach, and his pistol was aimed at Jeremiah's head.

A crowd had gathered behind them. Men and women pressed their faces against the glass to get a good view of what was happening inside the jail. Why a jail would have such a large window was beyond him and a question to be answered later.

Boddington let out a low whistle as he looked over Halstead. He took his time taking him in. The black pants and the black coat and the flat brimmed black hat that shielded his eyes. But it was the silver handles of the Colts on his hip and belly that drew his admiration. "You don't look like no marshal I ever saw."

"And just what's a marshal supposed to look like?"

"Not like you." Boddington kept his eyes on Halstead as he spoke to the fat deputy on his left. "What do you say, Tim? Think this dusky fella here is the genuine article?"

"Don't know," the round man said. "That telegram didn't say nothing about him being a breed."

Halstead shook his head. He was getting awfully tired of repeating himself. All of his years in Texas, no one had ever once accused him of having Indian blood. He had never even been mistaken for Mexican. But Montana was a long way from Texas. It felt like it got a little farther every day.

If he had cared enough about what people thought, he might have considered wearing a sign. But Jeremiah Halstead did not put much stock in the opinion of people. Not since El Paso, anyway.

Boddington kept looking him over as he said, "How do I know you're not some road agent who jumped this Halstead character and took his identity? That star's as easy to take off as it is to pin on."

"And took his prisoner, too? Rode him all the way into town out of a sense of guilt?" He was growing tired of the sheriff's nonsense. "I've got paper on John Hudson right here in my coat pocket if you want to see it."

Halstead could tell Boddington believed him, but he was not done having fun at the younger stranger's expense. Boddington spoke to a shorter, thinner man on his right. "What do you say, Dan? Think we can trust him?"

"Can't rightly say," the second deputy allowed. "He looks awful dangerous with them fancy guns poking out at all them odd angles. And it don't hardly pay to trust a breed."

Halstead decided it was best to keep his mouth shut. He could see the sheriff and his men were town tough. They were used to buffaloing braggards and drunks who could not handle their whiskey. They broke up the occasional bar fight and cracked a couple of heads a month and thought themselves to be dangerous men. It was obvious that they were not gunmen, at least it was clear enough to him. The sheriff had not even cocked the hammers on his shotgun, and the pistol trembled just a little in the fat deputy's hand.

Boddington and his deputies were like most of the law

he had seen time and time again in towns like this. Bullies with badges and nothing more. If this came down to shooting, guns aimed at him or not, Halstead knew he could peg all three before the little deputy even thought about clearing leather.

But he hoped it would not come to that. Mackey would give him hell for killing these men on the first assignment when he got back to Helena.

"Which pocket is the paper in?" Boddington asked.

"Inside left," Halstead told them.

Without waiting for instruction, he kept his eyes on Boddington and his deputies as he pinched the front of his coat with his left hand and slowly opened it so they could see it. The top half of the warrant was sticking out of the pocket and he slowly pinched it with his right hand and took it out. He held it up for them to see.

Again, without instruction he walked over to the large desk he took to be the sheriff's and placed it on top of the other papers that littered it.

He was now also within arm's reach of the shotgun Boddington was aiming at him.

Halstead stood beside the desk and faced the lawmen. "It's all right there in black and white, sheriff. Plain as day for anyone to see."

"I can see paper, but not what's on it." It was clear Boddington was playing to the crowd who was watching the show through the jail's window. "How about you hand it to me? And do it real slow like you've been doing, chief." He held out his left hand and grinned. "There's a good redskin."

Halstead snatched the shotgun out of Sherriff Boddington's hand and slammed the stock hard into the fat deputy's arm. He let out a yelp as the pistol dropped from his hand.

Halstead smacked the stock of the shotgun into Boddington's nose, knocking the sheriff back into the crowd that had gathered behind him.

The skinny deputy named Dan slapped at the pistol on his hip, but Halstead slapped him across the temple with the butt of the shotgun, sending him down to the boardwalk beside his boss.

The townspeople screamed as they scrambled away from the jail but did not run away.

The fat man sagged to the boardwalk as well, cradling his busted arm. Halstead kicked the pistol to the side just to be safe. He had already made one mistake that night. He did not want to take any chances.

Halstead broke open the shotgun as he stepped onto the boardwalk. The sheriff was covering his shattered nose when Halstead stood over him and dumped the shotgun shells on him.

He eyed at all of the people who looked back at him in horror as they watched a stranger take down the entire three man sheriff's department without much of an effort. He saw the fear in their eyes. *Good.* He wanted their attention for what he was about to say.

He held the open shotgun by the barrel at his side as he said, "I'm Deputy United States Marshal Jeremiah Halstead. Anyone still standing here in sixty seconds will be placed under arrest for loitering. Best get on home if you don't want to spend the night in jail."

The men and women scattered into the coming night like a flock of frightened birds with not so much as a glance his way.

Halstead left the lawmen where they were as he went back in the jail. He tossed the empty shotgun aside and did not care where it fell.

John Hudson was still in the same chair where he had left him, giggling hoarsely to himself. "Good ol' Jeremiah Halstead. Making friends wherever he goes."

Halstead snatched him out of the chair by his collar and shoved him hard toward the door that led back to the cells. He took the ring of keys from the peg on the wall and tried each one in turn until he found the one that opened the door. When he found the right one, he opened it and pushed Hudson inside.

There were six empty cells and stuck Hudson in the one in the back right-hand side. He slammed the iron door shut and the first key he tried locked it.

"Best get used to that sound, Hudson," Jeremiah told him. "You're going to be hearing it for the rest of your life."

Halstead did not jump when the outlaw charged the door and grabbed hold of the bars. His hands were still shackled together. "You think this is the end of it, Halstead? You think my boys will stop just because Harry and Weasel are dead? Well, you're wrong. You don't know my boys. They won't give up trying to get me out of this. Not even right up until the day I'm supposed to hang." He let out another low giggle. "You'll see, half-breed. You'll be the one who swings long before I ever do."

Halstead shut the door and locked it. He was glad it was thick enough to block the prisoner's screams.

He hung the key ring back on the peg and leaned his back against the door. Finally, a little peace and quiet for the first time all day.

Boddington and his deputies were still lying flat on the boardwalk and no one had dared tend to them yet. They were just beginning to recover, and Halstead saw no reason why he should help them.

He realized he had not had the chance to look around the jail properly until now and decided to see what there was to see.

A cast iron stove was tucked against the wall next to the sheriff's desk. A pot of coffee was on top of it, reminding him that he had not eaten or had any coffee all day. There had not been time when he decided to hit the trail with Hudson before dawn. And his run-in with the Hudson Gang made food the furthest thing from his mind.

He walked over to the stove and picked up the pot. It was still warm and more than half full. He swiped a cup off the sheriff's desk, dumped the stale coffee inside it on the floor, and poured himself a cup.

He was about to sit down when he noticed the mess of papers on the desk were stacked at an odd angle as if something was buried underneath them. More curious than concerned, he shoved the papers aside and discovered a large box of cigars beneath it. He flipped open the lid and found it was filled with long, dark Havana cigars, which happened to be Halstead's favorite. He liked his cigars as he liked his coffee. As dark as night and strong as hell.

He glanced out at Boddington, who was trying to sit up as he cradled his shattered, bleeding nose. "Ain't you the Fancy Dan," Halstead said to him. "These are expensive sticks, sheriff. Where'd you get the money to pay for these?"

Boddington was in no shape to answer and Halstead had not expected him to. But he made a mental note to ask him about them later. The answer was probably an interesting one.

He noticed the skinny deputy was no longer on the boardwalk next to his boss. The halfwit had probably regained what little sense he had and had gone to fetch a doctor. Or raise a posse to come back and try to gun him down. Halstead was ready for either one.

He took a fistful of cigars and stuck them in the same pocket that had held the warrant before selecting an additional one to smoke. He bit off the end and spat it in Boddington's general direction. He dug a match out of his pocket, thumbed it alive, and brought the flame to the cigar until he got a good burn. He waved the match dead and flicked that at Boddington, too.

With coffee and cigar in hand, he lowered himself into the sheriff's seat and put his feet up on his desk. He closed his eyes for a moment and breathed in deep. It was the first moment he'd had to himself in three days. And, in his experience, there was no better way to end a day of violence and bloodshed than with a cup of coffee and a cigar.

He took a sip of coffee, ready for it to be horrible, but was pleasantly surprised that it was not half bad. It was not as good as the stuff Uncle Billy brewed, but it was more than passible. He hoped Deputy Tim was not the coffee maker of the outfit, as that busted arm he had given him would put a crimp in his method. He hoped it was the skinny one instead. Halstead hoped that deputy was the least banged up of the three and, since Halstead did not know how long he might be in town, he knew he would need a good cup of coffee now and then.

Halstead whisked his feet off the desk and got to his feet when he saw a flame dancing outside the window. He drew his belly gun when he thought it might be a mob carrying torches. *Skinny didn't waste any time, did he?*

But he quickly relaxed when he saw it was not a mob, and the flame was not from a torch. It was just an old man moving about town lighting the lamps in front of each building. The old man stepped over Boddington as if he was nothing more than a dead dog in the street.

Halstead called out to him, "Hey, old man. Come in here."

The stooped old man with the heavy white beard complied. He stood in the doorway with the end of his staff burning. His face as open as if he hadn't a care in the world.

"Yes, sir?" the man said as if he had known Halstead all of his life. If he was bothered by a stranger sitting behind Boddington's desk or the sight of the lawmen on the boardwalk, he hid it well.

"You know if the telegraph office is still open?"

The old man looked at the clock on the wall across from the sheriff's desk. "Should be. It's six o'clock now and it don't close until seven. Or at least it ain't supposed to close until then."

Halstead was glad to hear it. He wanted to get a telegram off to Mackey to let him know all that had happened. "Where is it?"

The lamplighter gestured to the right. "Way down Main Street here. You could walk it, but if you've got a horse, I'd take it instead. Town's mighty dangerous come nightfall.

A man can see things better from atop a horse, or at least the horse can see better at night."

He was beginning to like the old-timer. "Thanks. Now, where's the best food in town?"

The man gave it some thought. "You looking to eat or are you looking to have fun?"

"Just a meal. A good one."

"Then you'll be wanting Maddie's Dining Hall. Best stew you'll ever have. You'll find it across from the telegraph office."

Halstead thanked the old man, who stepped over Boddington again to resume his duties. He called out to him one last time before he was gone. "Aren't you going to ask about what happened here?"

"Nope," the old man said as he kept going. "I've got plenty of troubles of my own and it don't pay to be nosy."

Halstead laughed as he sat back in Boddington's chair and took a healthy pull on his cigar. *Now there goes an intelligent man.*

Chapter 6

After finishing his coffee, Halstead tucked his cigar in the corner of his mouth and walked out of the jail past Boddington, who had finally managed to sit up on the boardwalk.

He ignored the curses and threats the fat deputy hurled at him as he removed his Winchesters from their saddle scabbards and saddlebags from Col and placed them under the cot in the farthest cell from Hudson.

He locked the cell door, then the door leading to the cells, and took the keys with him. He ignored another round of curses and threats from the fat man as he climbed into Col's saddle and took the spare mustang with him on his way to find the livery. The fat man was already beaten and had a busted arm. Halstead saw no reason to make him feel any worse.

As he road along Main Street, Halstead passed the skinny deputy and a man carrying a medical bag hurrying toward the jail. Jeremiah noticed the deputy was more than a little unsteady on his feet, probably the result of the crack in the head he had just received. Both men seemed too concerned about getting to the jail to pay him much mind, which was just fine by Halstead.

He was glad he had taken the keys with him before he left the jail, just in case Boddington and his men decided to release Hudson out of spite. He knew he would have to deal with these lawmen until Mackey allowed him to leave town. It would be best if he trod lightly around them for the duration of his visit.

He also figured he would be in a better mood on a full stomach. He remembered what the old lamplighter had said about Maddie's and he looked for it as he rode the long thoroughfare of Silver Cloud.

He had to admit that the place looked pretty in the flickering lamplight along the boardwalk. He would have feared the notion of so many open flames in a town made of wood, but upon noticing the heavy glass covers surrounding the lamps on the tops and sides, he figured the risk was minimal.

He had never seen a town with such a long, strange layout, but it certainly made things easier to find. No side streets to look for and only a few dark alleys to watch as he rode by. A few townspeople that he passed did not pay him any notice, but most of them did. They huddled together and stole glances up at him as he rode by. He imagined his actions down at the jail were the topic of conversation and probably would remain so for the next couple of days. It would likely grow in scope and gore with each retelling. El Paso might be a long way from Silver Cloud, Montana, but all towns were alike when it came to gossip.

He found the telegraph office where the lamplighter

had told him it would be, almost in the center of town. Next to it was the Silver Cloud General Store. Maddie's Dining Hall was directly across the thoroughfare from them. The stone building with the large clock tower he had seen on his way into town sat next to Maddie's and was called The First National Bank of Silver Cloud. A man named Emmett Ryan was listed as President of the Bank on a plaque nailed into the stone beneath the carved letters of the bank's name on the façade. Halstead had not been told to be careful of Mr. Ryan, but any man who had his name on a bank building deserved attention. Halstead would keep an eye out for him.

He found The Silver Cloud Livery, Stables and Blacksmith at the end of Main Street, several stores past a grand-looking building of the Spanish style called the Hotel Montana. The Silver Cloud Feed Store was directly across from it.

The livery was the least-attractive building he had seen in town. All warped wooden planks and crooked beams. Its roof was dented and crooked, no doubt the result of many harsh Montana winters. It looked as if it had been painted once, but the paint long gone, and the wood dried out by the equally harsh Montana summers. It looked like it was still standing out of habit and spite, which was just fine by Halstead. As long as the place did not cave in and kill his horses while he was there, he would be a happy man.

Halstead pulled his horses to a halt and climbed down from the saddle. A wiry, bowlegged man of about forty came toddling out of the darkness. He was pulling on a pair of wire-rimmed spectacles.

"Evenin', young fella. Lookin' to board your horses for the evenin'?"

This was a much warmer reception than he had received down at the jail. "Maybe a few evenings, actually. I won't know how long until I hear back from my boss in Helena."

The liveryman peered up at Halstead and squinted at the star on the lapel of his coat. "You one of them new crop of marshals they just swore in over in Helena? One of Mackey's Chosen Men?"

Halstead had read that description in the papers and hated it as much as Mackey had. Monikers had a way of making a man memorable and a target all at the same time. "I'm new if that's what you're asking."

"Don't make no difference to me." The man held out his hand. "The name's Wheeler. Ralph Wheeler, Deputy Halstead. I knew your daddy some. Knew old Pappy, too, in Dover Station when I was there for a time. Both were good men. This territory is for the worse without them and I hope you'll accept my condolences."

Halstead had not expected Wheeler to know who he was, much less know about his father and Mackey's father, Pappy. "How'd you know it was me?"

Wheeler laughed. "Word of what you just did down at the jail reached me in about a minute flat. Only saw the end of it myself, and by that, I mean you standin' in front of the jail and announcin' yourself to the town. Couldn't hear what you said, but the gossips wasted no time in letting me know your name."

Halstead had not thought of that before he did it. As the nuns had taught him in El Paso, rash decisions often had unintended consequences. "Guess I'm not too popular in town right now."

"Far from it," Wheeler told him. "Boddington and his deputies had it coming. Their names are the Upman brothers, but since the sheriff made them deputies, we've taken to calling them the Uppity Brothers. The three of them are just about the worst bullies you could hope to meet. We've just been waitin' for the right man to come along and take them down a peg or two. I couldn't be happier than to see it was Sim Halstead's own flesh and blood to be the man to do it."

Halstead decided to test the man to see if he really knew his father. "Guess you and Sim spent many a night in long conversation."

"On paper and in letters, sure," Wheeler said. "But they didn't call your daddy 'Silent Sim' for nothin'."

Halstead was glad the man had passed the test. His father had taken a vow of silence after his second wife and son had been murdered. "Sim sure had an elegant hand, didn't he?"

"Made readin' his letters such a pleasure," Wheeler said. "I'd imagine you must be mighty hungry after haulin' that human trash all the way here from Rock Creek. Boddington get around to telling you about Maddie's before you knocked him on his ass."

Halstead grinned. "No, but the lamplighter did. I plan on heading there now. I'll be needing to keep them here at least for tonight but I won't know how long you'll need to keep them until I get word from Helena."

"Take your time, young man," Wheeler said. "I've got plenty of room and we can work it out when you're ready to leave. Just be sure to do yourself a favor and keep an eye on Boddington and the Upmans. They're a nasty bunch and they'll put the spurs to you if you give them the chance."

Halstead promised he would as he crossed the thoroughfare and began walking toward the telegraph office. He normally preferred to ride wherever he went and would have stopped off at the telegraph office as he rode past it earlier. But that day had been far from normal, and he knew the mounts needed a rest. It was an idea that had been drilled into him when he had been a boy with his father's cavalry troop. "Take care of your horses, son, and they'll take care of you." He figured the animals needed rest and oats while they could get it. If Mackey ordered him back to Helena at first light, they would need to be as fresh as possible.

The telegraph office was deserted except for a beetle-eyed clerk with a green visor huddled over the counter. He looked up when he saw Halstead and, for a moment, the deputy thought the man might run out the door.

The clerk swallowed hard instead and stammered, "Y-yes, Marshal Halstead?"

Halstead closed his eyes. "So you heard, too, huh?"

"Nothing bad, I assure you," the clerk said eagerly. "How may I help you."

Halstead went to the pad on the desk and began writing his message to Mackey. "I need this sent to Helena as soon as possible with all urgency. Request an urgent reply. Can you do that for me?"

"Of course," the clerk said as he watched Halstead write out the message. "I'll stay here until a reply arrives."

Halstead finished writing and turned the pad so the

clerk could read it. Since he was paying by the word, he had made sure to keep it brief:

REACHED SILVER CLOUD. KILLED TWO HUDSON BOYS. HUDSON IN JAIL. AWAITING ORDERS.—HALSTEAD.

The clerk repeated the message aloud so there would be no mistake in transmission. He told Halstead the cost and the deputy paid it.

"Bring the reply over to Maddie's as soon as you get it," Halstead told him. "I'll be there having supper. If you don't get a reply beforehand, I'll come back here. Don't bring it to the jail under any circumstances." He looked at the clerk. "Understand?"

The clerk stammered again that he did, and Halstead left him to his business. He did not particularly enjoy people being afraid of him. In fact, he preferred it if they did not notice him at all. But fear could be a useful weapon if wielded properly. Halstead made a mental note to not let it go to his head.

When he finally made his way over to Maddie's, Halstead selected a table at the back of the place and sat facing the door. No one could come in or out without him seeing them.

The dining hall had about four other groups in the place, all of them older. He drew some cautious glances from the other patrons but did his best to ignore them. He could see they were looking him over like a prized bull at an auction.

The women looked him over head to toe and spoke in

hushed tones about what they saw. The men who glanced his way focused on the silver pistol butt sticking out above the table. Aaron Mackey had warned him against wearing the rig the day he had picked it up from the leatherworker in Helena. "You're going to get an awful lot of attention sporting a two-gun rig like that."

"I can handle the attention," Halstead had told him, "and any man who wants to try me."

He'd had it custom-made based on the one another man had worn back in Dover Station. A bad man who was now dead. It was a shoulder holster attached to his gunbelt. One of his Colts faced butt-out above his belly, which made for an easy draw while on horseback or sitting. It attached to the gunbelt that he wore around his waist and the other Colt he had on his hip. Every inch of leather was used to store bullets for the Thunderer pistols he wore.

If he had learned anything from the horrors he had witnessed during what had come to be known as The Fall of Dover Station, it was that two guns were better than one. And if people found the new rig intimidating, all the better.

Halstead imagined his fellow patrons had already heard about his run-in with Boddington and his deputies, but he did not trouble himself with their opinions. He had just finished a fine cigar; he was enjoying a glass of passable red wine and the promise of a good bowl of stew coming his way.

He looked up when the telegraph clerk entered the dining room. Halstead waved him over and took the envelope he offered. He did not wait for a tip before scurrying away and Halstead had not offered one.

He quickly opened the envelope and began reading Mackey's response.

GOOD WORK. REMAIN IN SILVER CLOUD UNTIL FURTHER NOTICE. SEND DAILY TELEGRAMS—MACKEY

Halstead folded the telegram and stuck it in the inside pocket of his coat. He wondered why Mackey had ordered him to hole up in Silver Cloud instead of heading straight on to Helena after sunrise the next morning.

They had agreed that the most dangerous part of the trip would be between Rock Creek and Silver Cloud when Hudson's men and horses were at their most rested. The trek to Helena was a little more than a day's ride away. He could even make it before sunset if he pushed Col and the other mustang hard enough. They were a couple of sturdy three-year-olds and more than up to the challenge.

Waiting in Silver Cloud simply did not make any sense.

But Halstead dared not question Mackey. Aaron might be an old friend, a man he had admired since childhood, but he was no longer the young lieutenant who used to ruffle his hair in the fort in Adair, Arizona. He was no longer the sheriff of Dover Station, either. He was responsible for the entire Montana Territory now. He had a lot on his mind.

Halstead's uncle, Billy Sunday, had seen the question on his face when Mackey gave him his orders and followed him out into the street to talk it over with him.

"I know you've got questions," the black man had said, "and thanks for keeping them to yourself for now. Aaron's got a lot of things on his mind, and he's still in an awful lot of pain over losing his daddy like he did. Just do what he told you exactly like he told you, and we'll figure it all out later."

That had always been Billy's gift; smoothing over the ruts Aaron left in the ground behind him.

Billy's advice was the reason why he did not question the clothes Aaron had ordered him and the other deputies to wear. All black except for a white shirt. The color of his lapel was tougher to keep clean on the trail, but the star definitely stood out against a dark background.

Something different had come over Aaron since they had all returned from the ruins of Dover Station. A certain darkness that had not been there before. A darkness that concerned everyone around him and Halstead in particular. He had grown up idolizing Aaron, just as Aaron had idolized Jeremiah's father Sim. Jeremiah had known Aaron before he had become the Hero of Adobe Flat and had met him just after he had become the Savior of Dover Station. He had known the man beneath the acclaim and had done his best to grow up to be just like him. Halstead imagined he had fallen short several times along the way, but Aaron Mackey had always been the kind of man Jeremiah Halstead aspired to be.

And if a man like Mackey could give into the darkness of hate, Halstead wondered what hope there could be for men like him to avoid it.

He was pulled out of his own swirling thoughts when the aroma of beef stew reached him. He saw the bowl being placed before him by a slim elegant hand. "Your dinner, sir."

Halstead followed the hand to the bare arm of a young woman with alabaster skin in an obscenely green dress. The powder and rouge she wore was meant to make her look better, but to Halstead's eye, it only took away from her appearance.

"Thanks," he told her. "I take it you're not the cook."

She stood up and put her hands on her hips. "Do I look like a cook?"

"Can't say that you do. And I know you're not my waiter. He was wearing a blue dress."

The woman giggled, which drew side glances and frowns from the rest of the customers in the dining hall.

She gestured to the chair across from him. "Mind if I sit down?"

Halstead did not consider himself to be a man of many weaknesses, but the few he had involved forward young women. "As long as you promise not to try to kill me. I've had enough of that for one day."

"So I've heard," she said as she sat down and leaned forward at a tantalizing angle. It was a clear invitation for him to look at her cleavage, which he refused to do. He knew what her game was, and he was in no mood to play.

"I'm Cassie," she continued. "Cassandra if you want to get fancy all about it, but Cassie will do."

"And I'm hungry," he told her. "You're more than welcome to sit there and watch me eat, as long as you're in the market for a one-sided conversation."

"Go right ahead." She tucked her hands under her delicate chin and smiled. "Don't worry about me. I like to see a man enjoy a good meal, and Maddie makes the best stew in town, maybe even the territory."

One forkful into the meal and he was inclined to agree with her. In between bites, he said, "I guess you already know who I am."

"Jeremiah Halstead, Deputy United States Marshal. At

least that's what I heard you say in front of the jail a bit earlier." She smiled. "Can't say as you look like any marshal I've ever seen."

"There's a lot of that going around," he said. "What's a marshal supposed to look like, anyway?"

"Grizzled," she said. "Old. Paunchy. Mean." She looked him over again, but only from the waist up. "Not like you."

"Guess that's because I'm only a deputy marshal," he said as he swallowed his food. "I've still got plenty of time to work up to being paunchy."

"No, not you," she observed. "You'll only get better as you get older, unlike me. Girls in my line of work don't stay pretty for long."

He gladly took the cue to look her over. She was obviously a working girl, there was no doubt about that. She was prettier than most he had met, and he had met plenty in his day.

But he could not figure out why she was here instead of one of the many saloons he had seen when he had ridden along Main Street.

"You seem to be holding your own for now," he told her. "But if you don't like what you're doing, why not change it?"

"Oh, I'm working on it, believe me," she said. "I've got plans. Great big plans with lots of bows on them."

He smiled as he remembered something Pappy had said once. "There's nothing in this world quite as long or pointless as a whore's dream." God, how he missed that old man.

"What's so funny?" Cassie said. "Don't you believe me?"

"I don't even know you." He tried to change the subject.

Arguments were bad for his digestion. "You sore at me for what I did to Boddington and his men back at the jail?"

"Not especially," she teased. "Barry's a bully and so are those two mutts who follow him around all day long. No, I'd say what you did makes you even better looking to me. Maybe even a little dangerous. I like dangerous men. Guess that's why I'm a whore."

A bit of the gravy from the stew went down the wrong way, causing Halstead to cough. His eyes began to water as he gulped down a bit of wine to clear the pipes. "You're certainly not shy about it. I'll give you that."

"No reason to be," she said, clearly enjoying his discomfort. "I do it for money. Everyone does something for money in this life, don't they?"

He thought that over as he continued to chew. "You've got a point there."

"Besides," she went on, "I'm not just any whore. I just happen to be Barry Boddington's whore."

Halstead stopped chewing. He rested his fork on the bowl. His right hand was less than a quarter inch away from the handle of the Colt on his belly. "That so? I thought you just called him a bully."

She shrugged. "Doesn't mean I like him. He sure likes me, though. Tells me how I'm his favorite. I know he goes with other girls when I'm otherwise engaged, but he swears up and down that I'm his favorite."

"Lucky you." He swallowed another morsel. "I guess he sent you to talk to me, didn't he? Deliver a message for him. Maybe find out more about me?"

"God, no." Her eyes went wide as she waved her hands. "He'd beat the hell out of me if he knew I was here with you now, especially after how you showed him up just now. I said I was his whore, not his lover. I can't stand him and if you ask me, you gave him a beating that was a long time coming."

Halstead had been lied to plenty of times in his life and not only by pretty women. He had developed a knack for being able to know when most people were lying or telling the truth. And just as he had seen with old Wheeler up at the livery, he could tell Cassie was telling the truth now. "Seems to be a lot of people in town who think that way."

"A lot of people have a lot of opinions about Barry," she told him. "If you're on his good side, Silver Cloud's your Elysium. But if you're on his bad side, it's closer to the fifth ring of hell."

She certainly had a better vocabulary than most of the working girls he had known. "So why are you here with me now? Sounds like you're risking a lot for a little conversation."

Another shrug of her slender shoulders. "Guess I'm curious about you is all. And maybe I've come to give you a bit of a warning. Not from him and not a threat, of course. More like a bit of friendly advice to a man who's new in town."

Halstead began to relax a little and went back to his stew. "Let me guess. Boddington is a dangerous man. He's a stone-cold killer. This is his town and anyone who crosses him winds up dead. The cemetery's loaded with men who've crossed him." He looked at her and smiled as he chewed. "That what you came here to tell me?"

"No. I came here to tell you're going up against more than one man when you go against Boddington. And I'm not talking about his deputies, either. The Upman boys have never added up to much. But Mr. Ryan runs Boddington. He's the man who controls all of the mining around here. Gold, mostly. Some coal, too. And in his spare time, he even got around to founding Silver Cloud, if you can believe that."

Halstead set down his fork on his bowl and closed his eyes. Yet another town with another rich man pulling the strings. It was beginning to feel like Dover Station all over again.

"Let me guess. This Ryan's got an army of gunmen to back him up."

"Mr. Ryan?" She laughed. "He doesn't need gunmen. He owns the town. He might hire on gun hands to help move his gold for him, but that's only once in a while. Everyone in Silver Cloud works for him in one way or another, even the saloons in town. All of our customers work for his mines. He tells them a place is off limits, it doesn't stay open long."

"He live in town?" Halstead asked.

"He's got a place here, but he prefers to live in a shack up by his mines," she told him. "He says he likes to keep an eye on things."

Halstead went back to eating. "Good. Means I'll probably be gone before he even hears about me."

"Oh, I'm sure he's already heard about you," Cassie told him. "Not much goes on in Silver Cloud that he doesn't know about. But just because he doesn't strut around with a bunch of armed men wherever he goes, he's still mighty powerful. He might even be able to make trouble for you with your boss in Helena."

Halstead enjoyed more stew. He imagined he would already be in plenty of trouble with Mackey for hitting the sheriff in the first place. He doubted this Mr. Ryan could make it any worse.

"Thanks for the warning."

She bit her lip as she looked at his pocket. "Couldn't help but see Mr. Warren, the telegraph clerk, come in here earlier. Guess he was here to see you."

Now Halstead was beginning to understand why she was there. "Maybe."

"He doesn't make special deliveries this time of night unless they're mighty important," she pressed. "Must've been pretty important if he gave it to you. What did it say?"

He kept chewing. "Why do you care?"

"I don't." She shrugged. "Just curious is all."

But Halstead could see she was lying, and now it all made sense. He left his fork in the stew as he said, "That's why you're here, isn't it? You want to know who I telegraphed just now. Why? What's so important about it?"

"I already told you I don't care," Cassie tried. "I was just making polite conversation."

"Why? Who are you planning on telling?" He had no sooner asked the question when he figured it out. "You're working for this Mr. Ryan, aren't you? You know he'll be looking for information on me, and you want to give him the whole picture. Earn yourself a little money for the effort. You're his eyes and ears around here, aren't you?" The more he thought about it, the more it made sense. "Sure. Pretty girl like you. You probably get lots of good dirt you can turn into gold."

She looked down and began tracing something on the tablecloth. "He's going to find out one way or another anyway. I figured I might as well be the one to tell him. What's wrong with that? I *am* a working girl after all."

He admired her for at least being honest about it. "Tell him not to worry about me. Whatever he's got going on around here is none of my business. I'm only stopping through with my prisoner. John Hudson's my only concern. I'll bc gone in a day or two, and he'll never hear from me again. Unless he breaks the law and Mackey gives me paper with his name on it. You be sure and tell him that." He picked up his fork again and dug into his stew. "You be sure to tell him if he's got any questions, he can ask me himself."

He knew he should have felt bad about the way she got up and walked away from the table. And as he watched her walk toward the back door of the dining hall, he noticed she looked the very picture of rejection. She even held a handkerchief to her mouth as she left as if she might begin to cry, though her eyes were dry as a bone. She was simply performing for the other diners in the hall, just as Boddington had been playing to the crowd at the jail.

Cassie was a clever young woman, that much was clear. He might never know the real reason why she had come to his table. He just hoped he was long gone from Silver Cloud before he had to find out.

At least she had not called him a half-breed.

Alone at last, Halstead finished the last of his stew and set the bowl aside.

Why *did* Aaron want him to remain in Silver Cloud until further notice? What was so special about a town he had never heard of until Mackey had ordered him to bring Hudson there? Before leaving Helena, Halstead had heard that Judge Forester had been hunting the Hudson Gang for years. Hanging John Hudson would be one of the proudest moments of his time on the bench. Why would Mackey want to delay it? He could have Hudson in a Helena cell by this time tomorrow night.

Something else had to be at play here. Just like Cassie's visit to his table, there was another purpose to all of this.

He supposed he would just have to wait and see what it was.

The waiter approached his table to take the bowl away. "Anything else?"

"How about an explanation for dessert?" Halstead said. "Why'd you let that woman deliver my meal?"

"Cassie?" the waiter asked. "She does things like that, especially when we have a customer she wants to meet. Never saw any harm in it before. Men kind of like her."

Halstead was sure they did. And he bet they probably did not like the trouble that followed one of her visits. "I'll take a coffee and the bill, and I want both right now."

The waiter cleared the table and went off to get Halstead what he had asked for. He hoped the coffee was good and strong. He had a long night ahead of him.

Chapter 7

Halstead took his time walking back to the jail. He enjoyed walking around a new town at night. He found he got a better sense of a place that way, when the sun was down, and the lamp lights came on. Sometimes, he could learn more about a town from its shadows than from what happened in the light of day.

The saloons he passed were loud, but not to the point of being rowdy. Each of them had a tinny piano and the sounds of men playing cards. A whiskey or a glass of beer would feel good right about then, but he decided against it. He did not know how many friends or enemies Boddington might have in town, and a saloon was the wrong place to find out.

If Cassie was to be believed, a fair amount of people might not have liked how he had treated their sheriff. People might not have liked Boddington, but they were apt to disapprove of a stranger beating the hell out of one of their own. Especially when that stranger looked like Halstead.

As he approached the sheriff's office, he saw no sign of Boddington or his deputies on the boardwalk. He figured that meant they must be inside the jail getting their wounds tended to.

He looked in the jailhouse window and saw the deputies in various states of recuperation. Deputy Tim Upman's right arm had been bandaged and set in a new sling against his chest. Deputy Dan Upman had a bandage wrapped around the top of his head. A small spot of blood had already seeped through the dressing on the left side.

The doctor Halstead had passed on Main Street was tending to Boddington. The sheriff was pitched back in his chair while the doc tended to his nose.

Halstead pushed in the door and walked inside.

The two deputies got to their feet when they saw Halstead. Dan had gotten up too fast and almost fell against his heavier brother. Halstead figured that blow to the head had rattled his brains some.

The doctor held Boddington down in his chair to prevent him from getting up. That did not prevent the sheriff from glaring at Halstead with reddened eyes. "You've got one hell of a nerve coming back here."

Halstead heeled the front door shut and walked to the back where the cells were. "Of course, I came back. I'm sleeping here."

The fat deputy moved to block his path. "No, you're not. You can sleep in the livery with the rest of the animals if you want to, but not here."

The coffee at Maddie's had been weaker than Halstead had hoped, and he was tired. Too tired to deal with the deputy's nonsense. "Take a seat, fat boy, or I'll break your other arm."

Tim looked over at Boddington who gestured for him to sit, which he did.

Halstead unlocked the door to the cells and found Hudson was already asleep, snoring his head off. The empty bowl of stew was on the floor just outside the iron door. The fork was there, too. Hudson had been a prisoner enough times to know he would have checked had it been missing.

The two deputies remained standing as Halstead walked back into the office and went over to the stove to help himself to another mug of coffee. They eyed him carefully as he sat in a chair against the wall across from the sheriff's desk.

"What's the prognosis, doc?" Halstead asked. "He going to live?"

The doctor was a lean man with gray hair and spectacles. A neatly trimmed gray moustache gave him a capable look. "He will. He won't be as pretty as before, but he'll have a busted nose to talk about."

"I'm sure Cassie will find him as appealing as ever." Halstead drank his coffee. "Yep, I believe she will."

Boddington shoved the doctor aside and pitched forward in his chair. "Just what do you know about me and her?"

Halstead shrugged. "Just what I heard. That you two are quite an item. You know how town gossip goes."

The doctor urged Boddington to lean back in his chair and the sheriff reluctantly complied.

Boddington said, "You've got some mouth on you, breed. It'll get you killed one of these days if you're not careful."

"Hasn't happened yet." Halstead looked at the two deputies who were still standing. "Don't think it'll happen here in Silver Cloud, either. And, for what it's worth, quit calling me a half-breed. My old man was white, my mother was Mexican, and I was raised in a Catholic mission down in El Paso. I don't much care if you call me names as long as they're the right names."

"A damned Papist," Boddington sneered. "That explains the arrogance."

"And the flair for the dramatic." Halstead smiled. "Us Catholics love to put on a show."

The doctor stopped working on Boddington's nose and turned to face Halstead. "It just so happens that I'm Catholic, too, mister, and none of what you did to these men tonight would have been sanctioned by any church I know."

"You'd be surprised, doc. Texas is a different place."

"Well, you happen to be in Montana now, marshal. And you'd better learn the difference."

Halstead normally did not tolerate rebuke, not even from a doctor, but he liked the man's fire. "What's your name, doc?"

The man went back to applying a bandage on Boddington's nose. "Doctor Mark Mortimer. And if there's any justice in this world, I'll be patching you up soon."

Halstead sipped his coffee. This sawbones had spunk to spare. "What's that oath you boys take when they make you doctors? 'First do no harm' or something like that?"

"I didn't say I'd be the one to do it," Mortimer said.

"Good thing you didn't."

"But there's nothing in the Hippocratic Oath that says I can't hope someone gives you what you deserve. Tim over there has two broken bones in his arm right above the wrist and Dan's got a cracked skull and probably a concussion. Sheriff Boddington's got a busted nose and a crack above his nasal cavity. That's a pretty raw way to treat your fellow peace officers, Halstead."

"They held me at gun point and tried to make me look like a fool in front of the town," Halstead told him. "I don't like people aiming guns at me for no reason, especially when they know better. I only hope they're smart enough to know it could've been a whole lot worse."

Tim cursed and went for Halstead but stopped when Halstead looked up at him.

"Keep pushing, fat man, and I'll finish what I started."

"Enough!" Boddington pounded the arm of his chair as the doctor kept working. "What's done is done. No sense in keeping on hammering away at it. Just make damned sure you and your prisoner are out of here come first light tomorrow."

Halstead sipped his coffee. "I hate to break the news to you, sheriff, but I've got orders to stay here until further notice. That comes straight from Marshal Mackey in Helena. I don't like it any more than you do, but there's not much we can do about that, now is there."

Doc Mortimer finished with the bandages and helped Boddington sit up straight in his chair. The sheriff said, "I'd like to see those orders."

Halstead took the telegram from his inside pocket, got up, and handed it to the sheriff. "I just got it a little while ago after I told him I was here. Read it for yourself."

The sheriff snatched the telegram from him and read it. He had to blink his eyes several times and hold the paper at various lengths before he could focus enough to read it.

Doc Mortimer told him, "Your vision might be blurry for the next day or so." He looked at Halstead. "Thanks to the marshal here's good efforts. Same goes for you, Dan. You took a nasty blow to the head, so you'll be a might dizzy for the next day or two. Might even get sick to your stomach, so you'll want to keep a bucket handy just in case."

Halstead grinned at Tim, enjoying the anger he felt coming from him. "What about our prosperous friend here?"

"I set the breaks as best I could," the doctor said. "With any luck, he'll have use of his arm again in about a month or two."

Halstead decided not to goad the deputy any further and looked away.

Boddington finished reading the telegram, then crumpled the paper and threw it on his desk. "Damn."

Doc Mortimer began placing his bandages back in his medical bag. "So, as you can see, Mr. Halstead, you've done quite a bit of damage in your brief time here in Silver Cloud. I hope you're happy."

"I'm not happy about any of this," Halstead told him. He even meant it.

"I'd advise the sheriff and Tim here to go home and get plenty of rest. Sleep helps the healing process, especially with their kinds of wounds. I'll be back here first thing in the morning to check on everyone's conditions." The doctor shut his case and took his coat from one of the chairs. "I'd appreciate a word with you in private, Mr. Halstead. Outside. Now, if you please."

Halstead could feel the eyes of the three lawmen burning a hole in his back as he followed the doctor out onto the boardwalk. Even when he shut the door behind him.

Now that they were alone, Doc Mortimer's tone changed. "Was all of that really necessary?"

"Yes, it was," Halstead told him. "All day long, people have been trying their damnedest to kill me, doc. Boddington and his men knew who I was and why I was there. They even admitted it. But they decided to play to the crowd because they wanted to have a little fun at my expense. I'm the law, same as them, and I don't deserve that." He tapped the star on his lapel. "This badge deserves respect even if they don't think I do."

"Boddington and his men also happen to be the law in this town," the doctor reminded him. "The only law we've got."

"Then they should've set a better example for the people they serve," Halstead told him.

Doc Mortimer let loose with a heavy sigh. "Well, at least your pride is intact. I guess that counts for something." He smiled as he said, "I only hope you realize you've bitten off more than you've bargained for."

Halstead did not like the medical man's tone. "Meaning?"

"Meaning that there's a sign in the general store that tells customers, 'You break it, you bought it.' Well, you've broken our entire sheriff's office tonight, deputy. Looks like you're just about the only functioning lawman we've got left. I'm glad you're going to be sticking around for a couple of days because you'll have the chance to pay for some of the damage you've done."

Halstead did not think so. "I'm a federal marshal. What goes on in Silver Cloud is out of my jurisdiction."

"You might be a federal lawman, but you're a lawman first. You're duty bound to help us out if we need it and

I intend on holding you to that. You'll find Silver Cloud isn't a peaceful place as the name might imply. Sheriff Boddington and his men are bullies, I'll grant you that, but they're that way for a reason."

"Never saw a good reason for bullies. Never liked them much, either."

Doc Mortimer smiled as he pulled on his hat. "You'll change your mind in a few days, Deputy Halstead. You'll see." He looked down at Halstead's guns. "I hope those things aren't just for show, because I've got a feeling you'll be putting them to good use before your time here is through. And don't worry about your boss having any objections to you pitching in around here. I intend on writing the good marshal a letter to that effect this very evening. It'll make the morning post and should reach him in a day or so. And you may rest assured my letter will be much more detailed than any telegram you send him."

Halstead did not care what Mortimer wrote. He just wanted sleep.

The doctor touched the brim of his hat. "Get a good night's sleep, Mr. Halstead. You're going to need it."

As he watched the doctor walk along the boardwalk to wherever his office was, Halstead could not doubt the sense of dread he felt creeping in his belly. He had always been pretty good at knowing when someone was telling the truth, and he knew the doctor was not lying now.

He pitched his hat farther back on his head and scratched his temple.

What the hell have I gotten myself into?

He decided it was best if he went back into the sheriff's office. He had nowhere else to go.

CHAPTER 8

Halstead settled into a chair as he continued to drink his coffee. The tension in the jail was beginning to give him a headache, and he knew he had to do something to cut it.

"Are we going to spend the rest of my time here glaring at each other or are we going to let bygones be bygones? I'm fine with either one."

Boddington glared at him from behind his desk. The two deputies were sitting but at the edge of their chairs, like dogs waiting for a command from their owner. Halstead had to admire their grit, as banged up as they were.

Boddington said, "That depends. You going to apologize?"

"No. But I'm sorry it had to happen the way it did."

Boddington looked like he wanted to say more but stopped himself. "Yeah. I guess we all are." He gestured at the crumpled telegram on his desk. "Anyways, it looks like we're going to be stuck with each other for a while. Any idea on why Mackey wants you to stay here? What makes Silver Cloud so special?"

"I don't know," Halstead admitted. "When he sent me

out to bring Hudson back from Rock Creek, he told me to stop overnight here in town. It made sense, since it's on the way to Helena and we figured I'd have Hudson's gang on my tail. But he never said anything about wanting me to stay here for a couple of days."

"And did you have any trouble from the Hudson Gang on your way here?"

Halstead was too tired to get into the details. "Nothing I couldn't handle."

"That's not what I asked," Boddington reminded him. "Because if you *did* have trouble with them, I need to know that. You've left us kind of in something of a predicament here, deputy, seeing as how you've busted up me and my men pretty good. If trouble's following you here, I want to be ready for it."

That was the problem. Halstead did not know if the Hudson Gang had given up or if they were going to keep on coming. Either way, he figured Boddington had earned the truth. "They chased me and Hudson as soon as we hit the trail from Rock Creek. They tried to hit us in the flatlands, but I managed to make it to a stand of pines and fought them off. Killed two of them, including John's brother Harry. I think they've got themselves a new leader now. A man named Zimmerman. Ed Zimmerman."

He noted the look of recognition flash in the sheriff's bruised eyes. "Ever hear of him?"

Judging by the way Boddington looked over at his deputies, Halstead could tell the name meant something to them. "We've gone up against him and his kind before. I guess you could say he's ridden a bit of the road with every outlaw gang that's passed through the territory for the past five years or more. Never stays too long with any one gang in particular but sticks around just long enough to pick up a few things, make some money, and move on."

Halstead had not been in Montana all that long, so the idea that he had never heard of Zimmerman or the Hudson Gang did not bother him. But Boddington's reaction to the man did. "Sounds like you've gone up against Zimmerman more than once."

"More than once," the sheriff told him. "He rode with a nasty bunch a couple of years ago who actually tried to hold the town hostage, if you can believe that. Lucky for us, someone got word out to a cavalry patrol that was in the area and they scared them off. Called themselves The Devil's Cut of all things. Oddly enough, they pulled the same stunt a few months later against your boss Mackey back when he was the sheriff of Dover Station. And, as I remember it, there was another man named Halstead who fought alongside of Mackey and the townspeople."

"Sim Halstead," Jeremiah told him. "My father."

Boddington sat back in his chair. "I just put that together this very moment. Hell, son. Had I been listening better, you and me never would've had a crossed word between us. I knew your daddy a little. More by reputation than in the flesh. He was a mighty fine man."

Jeremiah would have to take his word for it. He had only grown up knowing his father from the letters he wrote. Sim had always made it a point to write him several times a month, even when Jeremiah was in prison. But you could only learn so much about a man by his handwriting. He wished he had been able to spend more time with him than circumstances had allowed.

"Unfortunately, we're not here to talk about good men,"

Halstead reminded him, "only the bad. You and your deputies know what the rest of the Hudson bunch looks like?"

"Can't say as we do," Deputy Tim Upman said. "We don't even know what Zimmerman looks like."

"We've got a general idea," Dan added, "but it's not like any of us have been formally introduced."

Boddington said, "You know it's awful easy for a man out here to change the way he looks. He can let himself go or with a few scrapes of a blade look like a completely different man." He picked up a handful of the wanted posters on his desk. "These things aren't much to go by. More times than not, they resemble the man who drew them, not the man we want."

Boddington would get no argument from Halstead on that score. He knew John Hudson's picture looked nothing like the sketch drawn on the poster. He was beginning to learn that marshaling, at least on the federal level, would be done more by feel than by fact.

"That'll make our jobs tougher," Halstead told them, "because his bunch is apt to try to free John while he's here. And the longer I'm here, the more likely that possibility becomes."

"You said you had a run-in with them on your way here," Boddington said. "You get a look at them?"

"Only through my field glasses, which wasn't much. I saw the outline of the man I think is Zimmerman, but that's only a gut feeling. He could probably walk past me on the street and I'd never know it."

Boddington chewed it over. "Guess that means we'll need to be ready if and when they do," Boddington concluded. "And we will be. That I promise you."

Halstead took a quick glance at the two deputies and

the sheriff and regretted the sorry condition he had put them in.

Boddington seemed to know what he was about to say next. "Don't let appearances fool you, Halstead. Out of the three of us, I got the worst of it. Tim's arm hurts pretty bad, but he knows how to handle himself. Dan just had his bell rung a little and his head is sore, but he'll be fine." The sheriff gestured to his broken nose. "And you're not the first man who ever broke my nose. It'll take more than this to keep me out of a fight."

Halstead knew the amount of damage he had inflicted on these men. He doubted they were as fit as they claimed to be, especially if that fight came in the morning. But he went along with them anyway. "Guess you were just playing up your injuries before to make me feel bad about laying into you like I did."

"Can't blame us for having a little fun with you." Boddington and his men smiled. "Did it work?"

"Not really." He finished his coffee and went to the stove to pour himself some more. "Which one of you will be here overnight?"

"Me," Dan said. The bandage around his head was still seeping blood. Halstead knew that much was not a fake. "Doc Mortimer doesn't want me falling asleep tonight on account of my head being hurt anyway, so I'll keep an eye on things until tomorrow morning."

"I'll pass the word to the saloons and hotels to keep an eye out for strangers," Boddington added. "What do you say you and me take a ride around town tomorrow? Maybe in the area surrounding it. See if we can find a trace of any Hudson boys around."

Halstead was not sure how much good it would do

besides perhaps mending things between him and the sheriff. Since it looked like he was stuck in town for a while, it was probably worth the time. "I'll look forward to it. And now, if you boys will excuse me, I'd like to grab some sleep."

"In the cells?" Deputy Tim asked. "Why most of the marshals we've had through here either take a room over at The Green Tree or sleep in the stables with their horse. You'd find the stables a lot more comfortable than the cots in the cells."

But Halstead had no intention of leaving John Hudson alone. It felt like he had patched up his differences with Boddington and his men, but he knew how spiteful a man could be in the middle of a long night. He did not want to risk one of the deputies letting Hudson go. If someone had beaten him as badly as he had beaten Boddington and his men, he might be tempted to do the same.

"Thanks," Halstead said as he took a half a cup of coffee with him as he headed toward the cells. "But Mr. Hudson here requires special attention. Since all the other cells are empty, I'll keep watch on him right here."

He took the iron key ring from his coat pocket and opened the door to the cells. He held up the key ring for the men to see. "I'll keep these with me if you don't mind. "I know we're friends and all, but it'll make me feel better if I hold on to them. If you need them for another prisoner, just wake me and I'll give you boys a hand."

He walked back into the cell and locked the iron door behind him. He set his cup on the floor as he sat on the cot. It was not the worst mattress he had ever felt, but it was far from being the most comfortable.

John Hudson was still snoring his head off two cells

down, which Halstead imagined would last the rest of the night. He shrugged out of his pistol rig and laid them on the floor under his bunk, then began removing his boots. The freedom he felt as he set them aside almost made him pass out.

He laid back on the bunk and was grateful that there were no windows in this part of the jail. No shadows to be cast along the walls and ceilings for him to study on a sleepless night. No hint of what was going on in the outside world just beyond the walls.

Nothing to distract him from the time he was being forced to do here in Silver Cloud.

For this was not the first time Jeremiah Halstead had slept behind bars.

It was just his first time sleeping in a jail as a lawman. For one time, not too long ago, Jeremiah Halstead had also been an inmate.

He fell asleep as soon as his head hit the flattened pillow. The darkness enveloped him, and the old horrors quickly returned. The endless screams of the condemned that sounded like they came from the depths of hell, perhaps because they did. The whimpering of new convicts calling for mothers long dead or just as powerless to help them. The endless rattle of chains and the slamming of iron doors still echoed in his soul.

And beneath it all, the terrible knowledge that he was in prison because he had been a fool. He had been lied to. He had been used. The only thing that had kept him alive during all those endless nights was the notion that every single day he survived had brought him one day closer to freedom and to the moment he would exact justice on the man who had put him here.

The howls of torment in the darkness of his dreams gradually gave way to the memory of fire. The empty horror he felt as he had no choice but to watch Dover Station burn to the ground. A town that had taken decades to build had been reduced to rubble in a single night. A town Mackey had ordered him to protect. A town he had protected the best way he could, but his best had not been near good enough.

He remembered the doubts and the helplessness that had brought him to his knees in the middle of the thoroughfare that terrible night when he had been too late to save Mackey's father. The heat and the smoke and the flame had repelled him like a living, angry force and he had no choice but to watch a good town burn.

A town Sim Halstead had once defended with his life, but Jeremiah Halstead had been unable to save. He had been unable to do much of anything at all, except barely manage to get himself trapped in the jail like a cornered rat until Mackey and Billy had rescued him.

The memories of the prison and Dover Station bled into each other as they had every timc hc darcd to sleep. The howls of the condemned prisoners swirled together with the flames that had consumed the town he had failed to save. The knowledge of his own weakness and mistakes only made the flames grow higher in the black sky of his mind as they burned away all they touched. The howls of the damned drowned out every other sound, and there was nothing he could do to stop any of it from happening. The flames fed on wood and tar and despair. They fed off him and his own failings, burning hotter and brighter until . . .

. . . Until he shot upright and when he realized someone was tugging his foot as they called his name.

The echoes of the forsaken men of the prison he had once called home still echoed in his ears as he heard Boddington say, "Wake up, Halstead. Wake up. There's been trouble."

It took the deputy a moment to realize that this was not the stuff of nightmares. It was all too real. Hudson's jagged snoring proved that and anchored him back to reality. "What is it?"

"Get your boots and gear on and come see for yourself," Boddington told him. "No need to bring your rifles with you but those Colts might come in handy."

He found himself pulling on his boots before he realized he was doing it. He got to his feet and shrugged into his gun rig. The closeness of the leather and gun metal always felt reassuring. "What happened?"

"Like I said, it's best if you see it for yourself," Boddington told him. "Looks like someone's killed Cassie."

The mere mention of the whore from the night before was enough to stop him cold for a moment, before he grabbed his hat and coat from the edge of the cot.

Chapter 9

Halstead followed Boddington across Main Street, through the crowd that had filled the alley between the dress shop and The Green Tree Saloon.

The sheriff shoved people out of the way so he could get through to where the body had been found. Halstead would have simply gone through the saloon and out the back door of the place, but Boddington did not strike him as a man who did things the easy way. He did them his way.

When they had finally made it through, Halstead saw several of the women weeping over the body that was clearly Cassie. Her yellow hair and green dress told him it was her. One of the women was on her knees in the mud, cradling her body to her breast as she wept. Someone had placed a white sheet over her that was now filthy from the mud of the alley.

"Leave her be, Daisy," Boddington told the woman. He looked at the rest of the crying women who had formed something of a circle around their fallen friend. Halstead could tell by their faded makeup and hard appearances that they were in the same line of work that Cassie had been in.

"It's all right now, ladies," Boddington told them. "All the crying in the world won't bring her back. You girls best be on about your business and let me do my job."

Halstead watched some of the women start moving back into the saloon but taking their time about it.

The crowd in the alley had begun to thin out, too, though not by much.

Boddington took a knee beside the woman he had called Daisy, who still cradled Cassie's body in her arms. "Come on, old girl. Let her go."

But Daisy would not budge, and her tears kept flowing. Her dark curly hair fell over Cassie's face. "How can I let her go, Barry?" she wept. "She was beautiful. She really was. She was the best of us. Better than the whole house put together. She didn't deserve this. She didn't deserve this life. She had plans. She was getting out of this life. Out of Silver Cloud. She had dreams."

Halstead remembered Cassie had told him as much the previous night in Maddie's dining room. He had known many a girl who had promised to leave the brothel, but only one or two who had actually left it on their own terms. He decided to keep that opinion to himself while he watched Boddington work.

He watched the gruff sheriff tenderly ease Cassie's body from Daisy's grip. He was glad the sheriff did not force the issue. There were still a fair number of people in the alley taking in the spectacle. If Daisy set to screaming, some of the men might be tempted to come to her aid in the hopes it might lead to a free roll in the hay at some point in the future. He had seen riots break out over less, and the cramped confines of the alley were a bad spot for Halstead and Boddington to be in.

Boddington looked up at Halstead, his own grief and frustration easy to read on his face. Halstead gestured for the sheriff to ease the sheet farther down from the body and Boddington complied.

From the way Daisy was holding her, Halstead could only manage to see Cassie's back and the bullet hole on the left side of her dress. The same green dress she had been wearing when she had interrupted his supper the night before.

Halstead moved around to the other side and looked over Boddington's shoulder to see her body from the front. He saw a smaller hole just above her left breast.

Halstead had seen enough shootings to know someone had shot her from the front and the bullet had gone clean through the back. The only thing that had gotten in the way of the bullet was her heart. It was a small hole, likely from a .22. The kind of gun a girl like Cassie might carry to protect herself from a customer. The dangerous kind she had admitted she liked.

He went to examine the sheet when Daisy almost bit his arm off. "Get away from her, you demon. Don't touch her! Nobody can touch her. My poor, poor Daisy."

But Halstead did not withdraw his hand and examined the sheet that had been used to cover her instead. He had expected to find it bloody where it had covered her, but except for some minor staining, it was fairly clean.

"How did you find her?" Halstead asked her. "Where was she, exactly?"

Boddington glared up at him. "There'll be time enough for questions like that, Halstead. Now ain't it."

"It is if you want to find whoever did this," Halstead told him.

"He's right, sheriff," said a balding, skinny man with a pockmarked face who had been sitting on the wooden steps leading up to the building next to the saloon. "I found her crumpled on her side about a half an hour ago. Thought it was an old blanket or shawl someone had dropped in the alley. But when I got closer . . ." It was all the man could say before he dropped his head back into his hands.

Halstead left Boddington to tend to Daisy and Cassie and went over to speak to the man. "Who are you?"

"Lester Greenly," the man said. "I own The Green Tree Saloon. Who the hell are you?"

"Deputy Jeremiah Halstead. I'm from Helena." Given what had happened, such details seemed petty now.

"Halstead," Greenly repeated as if trying the word on for size. "I've heard of you. You're the one who raised that ruckus last night at the jail, ain't you?" He looked over at Boddington. "You're the one who did that to Barry's nose and busted Tim's arm for him."

Halstead had no interest in stirring up that nonsense again. "We're talking about what happened to Cassie now. Tell me how you found her."

"What difference does it make?" Daisy shrieked. "She's dead, damn you. Someone killed her. Who cares how she was found? Stop asking so many fool questions and find out who did this or shut your mouth!"

Boddington consoled her as she broke into a complete crying fit as she continued to cradle the dead woman's body.

Halstead propped his leg on the stairs next to where Greenly was sitting and spoke to him quietly. "Tell me when you found her."

Greenly sneered up at him. "Why should I?"

"Because if you don't, I'll come back later when it's quiet and kick the holy hell out of you until you do. You saw what I did to Boddington and his boys and you're not half the man he is. I don't like mouthy sheriffs, but I hate pimps. So a little conversation now will save you a whole lot of pain later. Tell me how and when you found her. I won't ask again."

The sneer disappeared. "I already told you. On her side I guess."

"Right or left?"

Greenly gave it some thought and twisted his body a bit to mimic what he had seen. "On her left. Slumped over like she was asleep in bed. I even thought she might be asleep until I turned her over and saw the hole. Her eyes were all empty, and I knew she wasn't living anymore."

Halstead was not done with his questions. "When you rolled her over, was she stiff or loose like a rag doll."

"She was—" Greenly stopped, reliving the event in his mind. When he curled up his right arm, Halstead knew he had his answer. "Come to think of it, her right arm was sticking up like it had been on the ground. She stayed like that when I turned her over." He looked at Halstead. "I hadn't really thought about it until you made me. What does it mean?"

He knew it meant plenty but figured it would be up to Doc Mortimer even more. "You find her an hour ago?"

"Less than that," Greenly told him. "I don't know. Half an hour, maybe."

Halstead would remember that detail. "Someone send for the doc?"

"I sent one boy to fetch Boddington and another to get the doc," Greenly said. "Say, what does her hand being like that mean, anyway?"

"Best tell the doc everything you saw as soon as he gets here," Halstead told him. "Where's Cassie's crib?"

The owner of The Green Tree looked like he had just been slapped. "This ain't Arizona, mister. I treat my girls right. They've got proper places to sleep and earn a living. They don't have cribs. They've got rooms." He jerked his thumb up the stairs he was sitting on. "Cassie was one of my best girls. She had her own room upstairs above the dress shop. She catered to a certain type who preferred their privacy."

Halstead looked up the long staircase that led to a single door. "Interesting."

But Greenly did not hear him. He was looking around Boddington at Daisy cradling Cassie's body instead. "Damned shame if you ask me. Brought her all the way out here from Wichita. She'd just finished paying off what she owed me, too. We were gonna make a lot of money together. I had big plans for that girl. Now I'll get nothing." He dropped his head into his hands again.

Halstead stepped around him as he made his way up to Cassie's room. God, how he hated pimps.

Halstead found the door to Cassie's room unlocked so he went inside. It was less of a room and more like an attic. The steep pitch of the room made it difficult for him to avoid bumping his head anywhere except in the middle of the room.

The room was nothing fancy. Lace curtains were hung over the windows to give the place a better look than it deserved. The four-poster bed was in the farthest part of the room away from the door. A silk topping matched the rise in the pitch of the roof. Two small bedside tables had oil lamps, neither of which was lit.

Interesting, Halstead thought. A quick examination of the table on the right side of the bed held perfume and powders, the tools of her unfortunate trade. A trunk at the foot of the bed had a lace pillow on top of it, which made it suitable for sitting.

The bed was still made. The harsh red cover had been pulled up and the pillows fluffed.

Halstead began putting it all together in his mind.

The lamps were unlit, and the bed was made. She was still in the same clothes from the night before. She had been found just after sunrise. Had she been here at all when she had been killed? Or had she been dumped in the alley?

They were small details when considered separately but might help him figure out who killed her and why.

He spotted a large wardrobe near the door that stood half open. The door creaked as he pulled it open farther and he found what he had expected. Gowns and dresses and lady's things of varying colors. Each of them were as loud as the green dress she had worn. The last dress, as it had turned out, that she would ever wear.

The top shelf had several powdered wigs and hats she could wear depending on the occasion or the customer. He imagined Cassie would have looked pretty in all of them.

He searched the wardrobe for anything else that might

tell him more about the woman who had called the place home but found nothing. No letters. No hidden compartments. No mementos of who she had been or what she had done before she had come to Montana.

He walked over to the bed and felt it. Too soft for his taste, but comfortable. He pushed down on the bed a couple of times and did not hear any springs. Interesting. He wondered if she had charged her clients extra for a quieter coupling.

He sat on the right side of the bed and examined the powder and perfume beside the lamp. The lamp still had plenty of oil in it, and the wick was cool to the touch. He opened the drawer of the table, but all he found were ribbons for her hair.

As he went to lift the pillow to see if anything might be hidden beneath it, his boot heel slipped and struck something beneath the bed. He took a knee and pulled up the ruffle at the bottom of the mattress and found he had knocked over a small pile of books Cassie had stashed there.

He gathered them up and placed them on the mattress to take a closer look at them. They were old, well-worn tomes of various sizes bound in leather. Although the nuns down in El Paso had taught him how to read and write, none of the titles of these books meant anything to him.

The Prince. The Communist Manifesto. Utilitarianism. Leviathan.

He began to leaf through the pages of the books and saw someone had made notes in the margins in pencil. Some sections had been underlined, and the corners of some pages pulled down as if they meant something to the reader. Whoever these books belonged to had read them from cover to cover several times. Was it one of Cassie's clients who had left them behind?

It was not until he accidentally flipped to the first page inside the cover of *Leviathan* that he saw the following written in pencil:

From the library of Cassandra Browne.

It was in the same handwriting as he had seen in the margins of the books.

Halstead looked at the books for a long moment. Why would a woman in Cassie's profession want to read thick old boring books like these? Ladies' catalogs and women's journals, maybe, but this was heavy reading and not just because of the weight of the volumes. What little he had read in each book had been enough to make his eyes cross.

He remembered some of the references she had made at dinner and how he had remarked on her vocabulary. Was it due to reading books like these?

"What were you up to, Cassie girl?" he asked the empty room, but the room held its silence.

He stood up to check the left side of the bed for more clues when he heard heavy footfalls coming up the stairs in a rush. He figured Boddington was on his way up to check on him.

That was why he was not surprised to see the sheriff step through the door.

But he was surprised to see him aiming his pistol at him. His eyes were red and wet. "Don't move, Halstead. You're under arrest for the murder of Cassie Brown."

CHAPTER 10

Halstead allowed his right hand to rest on his belt. The Colt on his belly was less than an inch away and could easily be pulled if he had to.

And judging by the dark look on the sheriff's face, he figured it just might come to that.

"You've got a real bad habit of pointing guns at me, Boddington."

"I've got good cause. Now throw up your hands."

But Halstead did not move a muscle. "Mind telling me why? We both know I didn't murder that girl."

"Damned right you did," Boddington said. "You didn't tell me you had words with her last night. You didn't tell me she ran out of Maddie's crying hysterically after you insulted her or that you followed her back here and shot her dead when she wouldn't take you upstairs."

He saw the pistol tremble in Boddington's hand as he seethed. "I knew there was something about you I didn't like, Halstead. And now I know what it was. You killed my Cassie."

Halstead remained very still. "I didn't kill her, Boddington. I left Maddie's long after she left and when she left, she was fine. I didn't see her again until you and I walked into that alley just now. Together."

"I got a witness that says different," Boddington said. "Says you two argued, she ran out of the place hysterical and you tore after her." The sheriff's reddened eyes narrowed. "You hurt her. You made her cry. Why'd you do that? To get back at me for riding you a little? Is that it?"

"Ask the people who were in Maddie's last night," Halstead told him. "I didn't storm after anyone. After she left, I had coffee, paid my bill, and went right to the jail. Passed a couple of people on Main Street or whatever you call it as I walked back. Someone's bound to remember seeing me. I was in the jail all night. Dan can vouch for that. I don't know who killed her, but it wasn't me. Think, Boddington. You saw me right after supper. Did I act like I'd just killed someone, much less a woman?"

"Your type doesn't show much," the sheriff said. "You're as stone cold a killer as there ever was. I can tell that just by looking at you." His mouth opened a little as he began putting things together. "You talked about town gossip last night when you talked about her and me. She told you about us at Maddie's, didn't she? Told you that she was my special girl. You killed her to get back at me, didn't you?"

"Your witness tell you all of that, too?"

Halstead could tell by the look in Boddington's eyes that he had. A twitch that told him he had struck just a little too close to the truth.

Halstead decided to keep pushing the truth. "Greenly said Cassie was stiff when he found her, the way bodies get after they've been dead for a few hours. You heard him say so yourself."

Boddington blinked. "So?"

"So I've been in the jail since before nine o'clock," Halstead told him. "If I'd killed her then, she wouldn't have still been stiff. You've seen enough dead to know I'm right."

Halstead paused long enough for the words to sink in a little before continuing. "Whoever told you I killed her is using you, Boddington. Using you in the hopes you'll do exactly what you're doing right now. Shoot me in a rage over Cassie."

Boddington began to slowly lower his pistol. "But why?"

"I don't know," Halstead admitted. "Might have something to do with why Cassie got killed in the first place. Someone killed her for a reason. It's up to us to figure out how and why. You and me. Together."

Boddington's failing nerve returned. "I know who and how. You shot her dead in the alley like she was a dog."

Halstead shook his head slowly. "No, I didn't. You saw the bullet hole. She was shot with a much smaller gun than I carry. And she didn't die in the alley. She was shot up here and dumped down there."

Boddington's eyes went wide and wild. "And just how would you know that if you weren't the one who did it?"

"Because I've got two good eyes is why," Halstead said, "only I didn't see it until now. You're standing on the proof. It's right under your boots."

The sheriff looked down at the bare floor beneath his feet, then quickly looked back up at Halstead. "There's nothing to look at."

"But there used to be something there, wasn't there?" Halstead pushed. "You've been up here plenty of times, haven't you? I'll bet there was a rug right there where you walk in. I can see the outline of it on the floor."

Boddington kept the Colt aimed at him as he took another, closer look at the floor. "You're right. There *was* a rug here. A big one. Too big for the space. Used to bump up against the sides of the room. I was always tripping over the damned thing. I told her to get rid of it a million times, but she never did." He looked around the room now. "Where is it?"

Halstead could tell he was beginning to make some progress with Boddington. "I don't know. Maybe the killer wrapped her up in it and carried her down the stairs. He unfolded it and left her in the alley. That's why she was curled up like she was asleep. Greenly said he found her like that before he turned her over to see she was dead."

Boddington's gun sagged as he struggled to make sense of everything Halstead was telling him. "She was shot up here?"

"Probably fell on the carpet the killer used to carry her in. Took the carpet with him from the looks of it, though I can't tell you why. Can't tell you why he moved her, either, only that he did. There's not enough blood on the ground out there to show she died in the alley. And that sheet Daisy or whoever put on her didn't have much blood on it. That means it was dry. The fact she was stiff when Greenly found her means she's been dead since I've been in the jail."

Halstead pushed the point further by pointing at the bed. "Look at the bed, Boddington. It's still made. The lamps haven't been lit and they didn't burn out. Whoever it was probably wasn't a customer, and it wasn't a trick gone bad. It was probably someone she knew. Someone she trusted. And that's not me."

Halstead could practically see all of the facts bumping up against each other in Boddington's mind.

"But it doesn't make any sense," Boddington said more for his own benefit than Halstead's. "Why would someone she knew kill her. Everyone loved her."

"Somebody didn't," Halstead said. "At least, not in the moment when they killed her."

Boddington looked like he wanted to lower his pistol but did not. "Everything you're saying, everything you've told me sounds like the truth. I guess you're right, but how do I know I can trust you?"

Halstead drew his pistol from his hip, cocked it, and aimed it at Boddington before the sheriff realized he had done it.

He enjoyed the stunned look on the sheriff's face. "Because you're still alive."

He un-cocked the pistol and slid it back into the holster. "Besides, I had no reason to kill her. But someone did. And if I were you, I'd talk to the man who told you otherwise."

Boddington scowled as he slowly holstered his Colt, too. "I intend on doing that right now. Come with me."

Halstead scooped up the four books off the bed and followed Boddington downstairs. His head began to throb, and he desperately needed coffee.

But he needed answers more.

Chapter 11

Halstead leaned against the back of The Green Tree Saloon as he watched Boddington hold the old drunk's head in the rainwater barrel until he finally let him come up for air.

The man's hair and craggily beard were sopping wet. "This is how you treat an old friend, Barry?"

Boddington dunked his head back into the barrel. "Old friends don't lie to each other, Cy. Not even when they've got a snoot full."

Halstead watched two big bubbles break the surface of the rainwater before the sheriff pulled the man up again and pushed him away from the barrel. Halstead was surprised the man had managed to stay on his feet.

"What'd you lie to me for, Cy?" Boddington pointed at Halstead. "Why'd you tell me you saw this man fighting with Cassie?"

The drunk shook his head clear and pawed away the water from his eyes with a sopping sleeve. He took a good look at Halstead, and at the pile of books on the ground beside him.

Cy saw the books and said, "Who are you? Some kind of teacher?"

"In my own way." Halstead hauled off and gave Cy a hard kick to the groin, which brought the man to his knees. "There's your first lesson. Don't frame people for murder, especially when you've never seen them before." He brought his leg back as if he was going to kick him again. "Ready for the second lesson?"

"No!" Cy moaned as he held up one hand to block the blow while the other cradled his sore groin. "I've never been one for much schoolin'."

Boddington grabbed the man by the collar and jerked him back up to his feet. "Then you'd better start talking, or I'll let him teach you a lesson you won't soon forget. Why'd you lie to me about him killing Cassie?"

"Because I was paid to!" Cy yelled. "That's why."

"Who?" Boddington shook him. "Who paid you?"

"I don't know his name," the drunkard said. "Some Fancy Dan I've seen in the Tree from time to time. We ain't exactly what you'd call friendly, but I'd never known him to cause trouble, neither." He looked up at Boddington. "And I never said I saw your friend here do it. I told you I heard tell of him doing it. That someone else saw him, not me."

Boddington balled a fist, but Halstead stopped him from following through. "How much did this fancy man give you?"

"Ten whole dollars," Cy said proudly, "and a bottle of fine Texas Lightning he was totin' in his saddlebags. You want some? I still got it inside. It'll take the varnish off them fancy guns you're totin'."

Halstead passed on the offer. "What did this man look like."

Cy blinked hard as he tried to wring out his brain from the booze that had pickled it. He looked Halstead over. "I guess he was about your size and frame; except he was sportin' a moustache all curled out to here. Always fiddling with it while we was playing cards like he was proud of the fact he could sprout hair under his nose. Good card player, though. Kept the game movin'. Seem to remember he was apt to winnin' a lot, too. Picked most of the boys clean. I'd like to say he was cheatin', but I wouldn't want to tear down a stranger like that, especially one with such a kindly disposition."

"Ain't that grand?" Boddington snatched Cy by the throat and pinned him to the saloon wall. "But hanging a murder on a man doesn't bother you, does it?"

"I took the man's money!" Cy gurgled. "What'd you want me to do? I was honor bound."

Halstead eased Boddington off the man's neck. "This man tell you where he was staying?"

"I was watchin' him and the boys playin' cards, mister. Not socializin'." Then Cy thought a moment. "But he had his saddlebags with him, so he probably liveried his horse. You might want to check with Wheeler at the livery. Or Greenly. Maybe he knows where he's stayin'."

Halstead figured they had gotten as much out of the old sot as they were liable to get. "If you see this man again you don't talk to him. You don't thank him for the Lightning. You don't do anything except come straight to the jail and tell one of us where he is. You got that? Because if you don't, we won't be as gentle next time we meet."

Boddington pulled Cy off the wall and gave him a swift

kick in the pants to send him on his way. The old drunk teetered a bit but managed to keep his footing as he ran into the back door of the saloon like a rat back to its nest.

As Cy ran off, Boddington fumed. "Lousy no-good drunk." He shook his soaked sleeves as if he might be able to dry them that way. "Caused all that trouble for a bottle of rot gut hooch. Ruined my good shirt in the process."

Halstead glared at Boddington until he realized it.

"What?" the sheriff asked as he continued to try to shake himself dry.

"You almost shot me," Halstead said, "because of what that thing told you. The town drunk."

"I've known Cy my whole life," Boddington protested. "I've never known him to lie to me like that before."

"You'd better get better at picking your friends before it gets one of us killed." Halstead scooped up the books from the ground and walked into the back door of The Green Tree Saloon. "Come on. Let's see if anyone else knows about who this Fancy Dan is."

By the time they were done talking with the bouncer at The Green Tree, Doc Mortimer was ready to take Cassie's body back to his office for preparation for burial. For in addition to being the doctor for Silver Cloud, he also served as the town mortician and coroner.

With Cassie's body in the back of a flatbed wagon drawn by a single horse, Boddington led the slow procession along the town's back street Halstead heard called South Street to Mortimer's workshop near the livery. Halstead brought up the rear.

Daisy had trailed behind the wagon bearing Cassie's

body for a while until she trailed off and was comforted in her grief by a couple of the ladies who worked with her at The Green Tree.

There were not many people watching the body being taken to Doc Mortimer's shop, something Halstead had expected. People enjoyed the spectacle of death when it first happened. The shock of the discovery. The gory details of the manner of death. The bloodier, the better.

But the aftermath of death held little interest for them. They tended to shy away from the pained loved ones left behind. He imagined they also did not like to think about the embalming practices or the grave digging or what happened to a body once it was lowered into the ground.

South Street was not much to look at. It was simply the back doors of all of the buildings that faced Main Street. A few dwellings had sprung up along the way, the type not suited for the main thoroughfare.

When the wagon reached the back of Mortimer's office, Boddington and Halstead helped carry Cassie's body into an old barn where Mortimer prepared the bodies of the deceased for burial. A single table sat in the middle of the barn for this macabre purpose.

Upon placing her body there, the doctor said to Halstead, "Barry here tells me you had made a remark about when rigor set in. Used it to determine an approximate time of death. Most impressive, deputy. Do you have any medical training?"

"Just a lot of experience around dead bodies," Halstead told him. "But I was assigned to carry the bandages and medicine when I rode with the Rangers for a while in Texas."

"Ranger, lawman, marshal," Doc Mortimer listed. "You've

covered quite a lot of ground for such a young man. I'd imagine you're not even thirty yet."

And convict, Halstead thought but did not say. Enough people already knew about that part of his past. He did not see the benefit in spreading the word around. "Was I right about the rigor being important?"

"Yes." Doc Mortimer looked at Sheriff Boddington. "Deputy Halstead was already in the jail when Cassie was shot. And by a much smaller caliber weapon than the guns he carries." He looked down at the blanket covering the young woman's body. "Did she carry a derringer, perhaps? For her own safety, I mean."

Boddington gave it some thought. "She did from time to time. Especially when she was expecting to be out and about at night. Why? You think someone took it from her and shot her with her own gun?"

"I don't know if I'll be able to prove anything like that for certain," the doctor admitted. "All I can promise you is a full examination and a feasible conclusion based on the facts. And after that, I'll do the best job I can to make her beautiful for burial."

When he heard Doc Mortimer clear his throat and shuffle his feet, Halstead knew they had finally reached the part of the discussion that talked about money. "Barry, about my fee. As you know the stipend for the coroner work does not cover the mortician fees. I was wondering—"

"Send Greenly the bill," he said sharply. "If he don't cover it, I will. But don't tell him I said that or that louse will stick me with the whole thing."

With his fee settled, Halstead could tell the doctor was ready to get to work. "Well, if you gentlemen would excuse me, I have quite a bit to tend to."

Halstead was in no hurry to leave. "Just one quick thing before we go." He handed him the books he had found in her room. "Cassie had these under her bed. Any idea on what they're about? I've never heard of them before, but don't go by me. I've never been much of a reader."

"So that's what you were carrying as you walked behind the wagon. I thought they might be Bibles or prayer books or something. I have to say it added a certain solemnity to the grim proceedings. I might pay someone to do that from now on."

Halstead frowned. Cassie had been right. Everything boiled down to making a buck.

The doctor's eyebrows rose as he began to look the books over. "You're sure she was reading these? They weren't propping up a chair leg or a mirror or something?"

"Cassie could read as well as you or me," Boddington argued. "She was a good girl who was always looking to improve her mind."

Doc Mortimer held out the books to him. "Then I suppose you could explain what these are about and why she was reading them."

The sheriff looked away. "Can't say as I can. My mind's as improved as it's likely to get."

Mortimer went back to examining the books. "This is some mighty dense reading for anyone, especially a woman in Cassie's line of work." He held up each of them in turn as he discussed them. "I believe *The Prince* is about how to manipulate others for one's own gain. *Leviathan* is another book about power. Justification for the king of England as sovereign, if memory serves. This book says it all in the title. It's about communism."

Halstead had absolutely no idea what he was talking

about. And judging by the blank look on Boddington's face, neither did he.

Doc Mortimer indulged them by saying, "Communism is a political theory, but unlike the other two, it pits workers against the ruling classes." He handed the books back to Halstead, who reluctantly took them.

Mortimer continued, "It's all rather heady stuff and beyond my interest or expertise. I've always been far more content with setting bones and prescribing medicine than setting the courses for nations and prescribing solutions for the fates of men. Politics has never held any power over me, and I count myself the better for it."

Mortimer would get no argument from Halstead on that score. Politics had cost him three years in prison and burned Dover Station to the ground.

But he wondered why Cassie would be reading books like these. It was not for conversation. Men usually hired women like Cassie for one purpose and it was not to discuss literature. He imagined every whore wanted an edge over her client, even a mental one, but a derringer or knife under the pillow usually did the trick.

He looked down at the heavy books in his hand and wondered what she had been up to. He wondered if it had gotten her killed.

Chapter 12

They thanked the doctor and shut the barn doors behind them when they left.

Boddington swore as he pushed down the bandages on either side of his nose. His eyes were wet, and his tears were not from his broken nose. "Damned thing is a nuisance. Won't stay on."

"It got wet when you were dunking Cy's head into the rain barrel," Halstead reminded him. "I'm not the one with a busted nose, but I'd say it was worth it, him telling us about his Fancy Dan and all."

"A Fancy Dan the bouncer doesn't remember and the bartender who might remember already went home," Boddington said. "You think the man who lied to Cy might be the same one who killed Cassie?"

"Could be," Halstead said as he kept walking. "You keep your horse in the livery?"

"Town pays for it," Boddington said as he struggled to keep up with Halstead. "Why?"

"Because I've got my horses there, too, and it's about time you and me take that ride you talked about to see what we can see."

Boddington asked, "What are we going to be looking for?"

Halstead did not dare say it now. But Cy's drunken ramblings had got him thinking. His details about the man with the fancy moustache were beginning to add up.

He decided to keep his ideas to himself. He did not want to risk looking like a fool if it turned out to be nothing. "The kind of thing we'll know if we see it. And I've got an idea of where we might be able to find it, too."

Boddington squinted at him. "You're getting to sounding as thick as them books you've been holding."

Halstead hoped that was not the case. Because if he was right, he would need a lot of clear thinking ahead.

Boddington's brown and white paint had no trouble keeping pace with Halstead's mustang as they rode the trail toward Rock Creek.

Halstead had always enjoyed his own company and had never minded the silence he felt on the trail. He even dreamed less when he slept out under the stars and had developed a strange preference for being on his own.

But after being in the saddle for only a mile or so out of town, it was painfully clear that Sheriff Barry Boddington was a talker.

"You ride that mustang all the way up here from El Paso?"

"Had her shipped up here on the railroad," Halstead told him. "Her sister, too. That's the horse that carried John Hudson here. They were together when I bought them, and I felt bad about splitting them up. Dumb, I know, but I've always been a bit sentimental when it comes to horses."

"Only a fool would be any other way." Boddington patted the paint's neck. "My girl here's named Mary. What's yours called?"

"Col."

"Col?" Boddington's face soured as he chewed the name over. "What kind of name is that for a good-looking mare like her?"

"Long story," Halstead allowed.

Boddington gestured to the open land around them. "We've got time, Halstead. You see anything else we should be doing besides talking?"

Boddington's gestures had caused Halstead to look around and led him to catch a glimpse of something in the trees. "As a matter of fact, I do. Come on."

He dug his heels to Col's sides and rode in that direction. Without asking questions, Boddington followed close behind.

Halstead reined in Col when they got into another clearing that gave him a better view of the sky. He did not need to explain to the sheriff what he had seen, for they could both see it plain as day.

Three vultures were flying in a lazy arc high above something about a mile away.

"That what you expected to find?" Boddington asked.

"That's what I was looking for," Halstead admitted. "Now let's see if I'm right."

He put the heels to Col and the horse responded immediately. Boddington and Mary followed close behind.

They slowed their pace to a trot as they found themselves in the middle of a stand of trees. Given his experience in a similar circumstance with the Hudson Gang the day before, he was particularly careful. "Hang back and keep an eye out for anything that moves," Halstead told Boddington. "Cut loose with a whistle if you hear anything that doesn't belong. There's a good chance we might not be alone out here."

Boddington pulled his Winchester and held it across his lap while Halstead weaved his way through the trees to get a closer look at what had caught the attention of vultures.

He found it about fifty yards into the stand of trees. A dead horse flat on its side.

The smell of death made Col skittish and Halstead climbed down from the saddle. He wrapped her reins around a tree up-wind from the dead animal.

He approached the fallen horse on foot, closely examining the ground for tracks as he went. He saw the dried foam on the horse's mouth and noted the neat bullet hole at its temple. The saddle was gone, but a quick look at the hooves told him all he needed to know.

He placed a hand on the horse's barrel and it felt cold, but it had not frozen over yet. He kept his hand there and closed his eyes as he said a quick prayer over the animal.

He had no idea if prayer even worked, much less a prayer for a dead horse, but if any creature deserved the pleasures of a hereafter, Jeremiah Halstead figured a horse would deserve it most.

He called Boddington over with a whistle as he untethered Col and climbed back in the saddle.

The sheriff winced when he saw the dead horse. "I hate seeing that. Looks like the poor old thing was ridden into the ground. At least whoever rode it into that condition had the decency to put it out of its misery."

"Was the least he could do, seeing as how he caused it," Halstead reminded him. "You much good at tracking?"

"I've done my share, especially in these parts. Why?"

He pointed down at the footprints that led away from the horse. "Because we're tracking a man carrying a saddle, saddlebags, and at least one rifle. And unless I'm wrong, he was headed in the direction of Silver Cloud. A man who rode his horse to death in the hopes of catching up with me. He did it at night and in pitch darkness and I'd like to know for certain where he went, though I've already got my suspicions."

It did not take Boddington long to catch on. "You think that's the Fancy Dan who Cy was talking about," Boddington said. "The same one who put him up to lying about you."

"I think it could be," Halstead cautioned as he brought Col about. "Might be someone else, but Cy said this man had his saddlebag with him and had a fancy moustache. That matches the description of a man from the Hudson Gang. A man who goes by the name of Ace. Him being a card sharp and all, it stands to reason he might be the one Cy watched playing cards. The one who paid him to lie about me killing Cassie."

Boddington gripped his Winchester tightly. "Maybe the one who killed Cassie, too."

"One step at a time, sheriff," Halstead cautioned. "Let's track him as best we can and see where it leads. No one knew where Cy's man was staying, but it's got to be somewhere in town. Especially because he was on foot. Let's see where these tracks take us and decide what to do when we know more."

He let Boddington take lead as he looked over the side of his horse, watching where the footprints led. Halstead was a fair tracker himself. His uncle Billy had taught him how to read trail sign as soon as he was old enough to set a horse. He had no doubt he could track Ace—or whoever it was—without Boddington's help.

But the sheriff had not had an easy time of it since Halstead had come to Silver Cloud. A busted nose, some wounded pride, a dead woman he was fond of, and the betrayal of an old friend could hurt a man deeply, especially the kind of man Boddington seemed to be. The sheriff needed to feel useful again, and half-drowning the town drunk was not likely to be enough to set him right.

But tracking a dangerous man might just be the medicine Boddington needed to feel like a lawman again. Besides, Boddington was no good to Halstead if he was doubting himself.

As they followed the tracks back toward town, Halstead was glad to see Boddington was doing a pretty good job of reading what the ground was telling him. Perhaps there was more to Barry Boddington than just being a bully.

"If he killed Cassie," Boddington said as he read the tracks, "I'll kill him. No trial in Helena. No hanging. I'll kill him with my own two hands."

Halstead did not doubt he would try. "Just read the signs, sheriff. We've got to find him first."

Chapter 13

Emmett Ryan sat on the bench in the mining shack that served as his office and listened to Earl Perkins, his foreman, repeat the story a third time. He still could not believe what he heard.

"And you're sure this Halstead character busted up all three of them?" Ryan asked. "Boddington and Tim and Dan?"

"Yes, sir," Perkins confirmed. "I was standing in the crowd watching it all while it happened. I wouldn't be telling it to you now if I hadn't seen it with my own two eyes. That marshal feller moved faster than I've ever seen anyone move. Busted Tim's arm, broke Boddington's nose, and brained poor old Dan like it was nothing. Those boys had him dead to rights, too, but they never stood a chance against the likes of him."

Perkins shook his head at the memory of it. "One of the damnedest things I've ever seen."

Ryan took that as quite a testimony considering the source. Earl Perkins was a lean, powerfully built man who easily forced his will on others and did not hesitate to use force on his men when the occasion called for it. Emmett Ryan needed such a man to run his mines for him. Perkins's brutality was matched only by Ryan's own and may have even surpassed it.

It took a strong man to work a mine and an even stronger will to keep him in line. Culling ore from the earth was a dangerous enough profession as it was. The risk of cave-in or disaster always tugging at your elbow. One act of carelessness, one distraction, and an entire crew could be lost in a matter of seconds. Perkins had been his foreman for two years now and had performed every task Ryan had assigned him.

But this business with the new marshal was troubling. "And you said this man's name was Halstead. Jeremiah Halstead?"

"That's what he said it was," Perkins confirmed. "I'd never heard of him before, but when I was bending an elbow over at The Green Tree afterwards, I heard some of the boys talking about him. He looks like a breed, but he ain't. His father was white, and his mama was Mexican. He's close with that new U.S. Marshal they've got in Helena. Mackey, I think his name is, but he grew up with some nuns in Texas. El Paso, I think they said."

Ryan had heard that the governor had hired himself a new marshal for the territory but had paid little attention to it. He did not bother with anyone other than the governor of the territory and whomever he needed to know in Washington.

Dealing with underlings was far from beneath him. He had flakes of mine dust embedded in his skin. The dirt under his nails would never be cleaned out, and he would not have it any other way.

But a mining man was a man concerned with time. How long before the mine played out? How much time before the air ran out? Should he bring his lode to market or wait until the price rose? Should he hire on more men now or wait until a new vein was found in the ground.

Time was as important a commodity to him as the gold and silver and copper he dug out of the ground. He took his concerns straight to the men he could buy to get him what he needed. They could never give him what he needed most—time—but sometimes they could alter it to his advantage.

That was why he did not waste his time on inconsequential men outside of Silver Cloud like marshals. Men like Mackey or this Halstead fellow. He made his own law out here, far enough away from the prying eyes of Helena but close enough to influence it when he wanted to. He did not even care whether or not statehood ever came to Montana. The gold and silver and copper would still be in the ground no matter what happened in the world above it. Someone would have to dig it out, and Ryan intended the Silver Cloud Mining Concern to take more than the lion's share.

That was why the actions of this Jeremiah Halstead character bothered him so. He had brought the troubles of the outside world with him to Silver Cloud. The town was his. He did not like outsiders meddling with it.

"Can't say as I've heard of this Halstead myself," Emmett Ryan said, "but he's obviously a rough customer. You told me he brought in John Hudson all by himself?"

"Saw him ride into town with him lashed over the saddle like a dead deer," Perkins reported. "Handled him kind of rough, too, and you know Hudson's no walk in the park himself."

Ryan had no sympathy for Hudson or his gang. They had harassed his miners in the western part of the state and robbed the pay wagons for his men. He did not like his employees to be bothered by outside forces. He wanted them to fear only one man in this world and that was Emmett Ryan. If he could not protect them, they would not fear him, and he could not have that.

He had been thinking about putting a bounty on the heads of the Hudson Gang, especially after he had learned they had taken over Rock Creek.

Now, it looked like this Jeremiah Halstead had done that for him. And if there was one thing in the world that Ryan liked better than making money, it was saving himself from an unnecessary expense.

But Halstead had also made a mistake. Boddington and the Upman boys were Ryan men, too. And just as he could not allow a threat to his miners to go unanswered, he could not allow anyone to injure the lawmen who served his interests.

"And what of this dead whore you mentioned," Ryan asked as though it was an afterthought. "The one you said they found in an alley somewhere?" Though he knew exactly where. And he knew the whore, too.

"That happened just before I came back here," Perkins explained, "which is why I'm so late in getting back here."

Ryan liked to treat Perkins to a night in town when he sent him down to Silver Cloud to deliver a message or run an errand. It gave him a chance to let off some steam and check in on his interests in town. Perkins reminded everyone that Ryan might spend most of his time in the mines, but the town was still his.

This particular trip had been to deliver a message to the town's merchants association but had quickly turned out to be much more than that. "Tell me about this dead woman. Spare no details."

According to the way the shadows slowly crept across the floor of the shack, Ryan estimated Perkins had spent a good fifteen minutes relating the discovery of Cassie's body in the alley between the dress shop and The Green Tree Saloon. How she had been shot once through the heart and how they had blamed Deputy Halstead for a while, but not for long.

The story amused Ryan. "Sounds like the new deputy hasn't exactly gotten a warm welcome from the people of Silver Cloud, has he? Mocked by the sheriff and now accused of murder. Who's the one who charged him?"

"Cy," Perkins told him. "I heard it turned out to be hogwash, but Sheriff Boddington looked like he believed it for a while when he stormed up to Cassie's room to get Halstead."

Ryan caught that. "What was Halstead doing up in Cassie's room?"

Perkins shrugged. "Afraid I can't tell you that, Mr. Ryan. I was too deep in the crowd to have heard his reasonings. I saw him talking to Greenly for a bit before he walked up the stairs to her room above the dress shop."

Ryan had not needed Perkins to remind him where Cassie's room was. He had spent many an enchanted evening there. Always in secret, of course. "Did you see what happened after Boddington went after him?"

"No," Perkins said, "because Doc Mortimer had arrived by then and told all of us to clear the alley on account of him needing to get his wagon inside. We all knew it was nonsense because there's plenty of space for him to bring the wagon along South Street, but everyone was anxious to be about their business anyway. That's why I hung around the saloon for a while to see if I could pick up any information for you." The foreman shrugged. "Sorry it wasn't more."

Ryan hid his curiosity about Cassie's death from his foreman lest he show his hand too much. He had grown fond of the soiled dove during their couplings and, despite his better judgment, had developed feelings for her. Feelings he had not allowed himself to understand until that very moment. The woman was a whore. A means to a carnal end.

She was also a distraction that had slowly crept further into his thoughts just like those shadows he watched across the rough-hewn floor of the shack. In the back of his mind, he had entertained wild ideas of making her into something more. Perhaps marrying her and giving him an heir. At fifty, he knew he was too old to entertain such notions, but they were pleasant enough to think about. And he had found himself thinking about them more and more each day until Perkins delivered his news this morning.

Distractions were a luxury a miner could ill afford.

Halstead was proving to be a distraction of a completely different variety. He was an unknown entity. He was a troublemaker, even if he had no idea who Emmett

Ryan was. Men like that were not predictable. They were not easy to buy off.

That would be bad for Ryan and even worse for Halstead.

"What's the matter, boss?" Perkins asked. "You're not looking too good right now."

"I'm fine," Ryan lied. "But I have to admit that this Halstead has me curious."

Perkins held his hands at his sides. "Want me to handle him? As tough as he is, no man is bulletproof. I can make him disappear whenever you tell me to."

Ryan waved off the notion. "I said I was curious, Perkins, not concerned. I don't want him harmed." Perkins was a tough man, but from what he had heard about Halstead, his foreman might not be able to handle him so easily.

Perhaps it would not need to come to that. "Let's do something that keeps my curiosity from becoming a concern. When are you supposed to head back into town?"

"Whenever you say, Mr. Ryan."

Ever the pliant lad. "If your regular duties at the mine won't suffer, I'd like you to find Mr. Halstead and invite him up here to a meeting at his earliest convenience. Whatever time he wants. Invite Boddington along, too, while you're at it. Can't hurt to have another friendly gun around in case the good deputy begins feeling forceful."

Perkins told him to consider it done and asked him if there was anything else he wanted to discuss before the foreman went back to the men. They discussed a few matters concerning the mines, after which he told Perkins he could be on his way.

As soon as he knew his foreman was out of sight, he pushed himself away from his desk and walked out the back door of his shack and took in the town of Silver Cloud below. This was his part of the world. This side of the mountain was his, by God and by law. So was the other side, though he'd had neither the time nor the inclination to mine it yet. He had resisted the calls from his partners and his colleagues to go full bore into the excavation of ore from the rich mountain and dig both sides at the same time. This mountain had been good to him, better than he had deserved, and he had no intention of abusing his good fortune.

He was already richer than any son of Wexford County had any right to expect. He knew better than most that luck was a finite resource that came in waves as regular as the ocean tides.

It was bad luck that had swamped his native land and killed the potato crop and most of his family over several years. Some blamed the British, others the Almighty Himself, but Emmett Ryan never placed much stock in blame. Whenever trouble comes to darken his door, a man has a responsibility to look it in the eye and see it for what it is. He must then decide whether it's something he can fight, something he can outlast, or something he should flee.

Emmett Ryan, at the tender age of twelve, did not know if the famine was caused by the British or by God, but knew he could not defeat either one. So he fled to America, where he had heard the streets were paved with gold and there was a fortune to be made by anyone who wanted to work hard enough for it.

One glimpse of the hell that was Manhattan's Five Points told him his fortune, if a fortune was to be had at all, would lie in the countryside where he was more comfortable. The fewer the people, the better.

Which was how he had found himself in Montana tending bar at various mining camps around Helena. When he was sixteen, Tom Robinson, the owner of one of the gambling houses nearby, needed a man to help deal blackjack. He offered the young Ryan a piece of the table's winnings if he would come work for him. Ryan gladly accepted and, on his first night at the table, took an old miner's claims on Silver Cloud Mountain on a final turn of the cards. The old man begged for his claims to be returned to him. Begged as Ryan had never seen a man beg before, not even in the lowest depths of hunger.

But when the owner had the old miner thrown out of the place, the old man staggered into the middle of the street, pulled out his gun, and shot himself through thc head.

His boss had wanted to split the claims fifty-fifty, but Emmett Ryan cut a deal to keep the claims in exchange for forgoing a week's salary. His boss had thought him mad and gladly took the bargain. But Ryan had a feeling that there was more ore in that mountain than anyone had ever dreamed. The old man had foolishly gambled his claims, but young Ryan was no such fool.

Emmett Ryan spent the next several years saving his money and buying up parcels and pieces of businesses all around town. And by the time he was twenty-five, he had amassed enough money to hire men and material to work the claim himself. He built a shack on the site with his own two hands and helped the men search for ore in the ground.

"Mad Emmett Ryan" was what they had called him then. Until he found silver, then lead, then copper, and finally, gold. The few people in town who were still around from those early days called him "Mr. Ryan" now. He had seen to that.

He looked down now at the ramshackle mining camp that had become Silver Cloud. There was not much to it at first glance, but anyone who took the time to look around the place found a grand town indeed. Saloons where his workers could quench their varied thirsts. A claims office where men could come to find their own fortune as he had found his. A bank where hard-working men could rest assured their earnings were secure and growing. Some of the best food in the territory from chefs he had brought in from San Francisco and Colorado to cook the meat from the ranches he had financed. Hotels that catered to every taste and budget and gambling halls where a man could count on a fair turn of the cards every time.

He had made sure Silver Cloud had all of these things and more out of a sense of gratitude. Luck had played a hand in bringing him to Silver Cloud, Montana. Luck had played a hand in causing that old miner to bet his claims and lose. Luck had smiled on young Ryan and made him now, at fifty years of age, one of the wealthiest men in the territory.

But despite all of his success, he had never forgotten that luck ebbed and flowed for everyone, and he was far from immune. Was this Halstead character a sign that his luck was beginning to ebb? Had he come to town with one task in mind only to take up another? One that threatened all that he had spent the best years of his life trying to build.

Cassie. Cassandra, as he preferred to call her in their times together.

He would not allow the death of a whore to threaten all

that he had built. All that he planned to build in the future. Nor would he allow Halstead to challenge him. Others had tried. Claim jumpers. Bank robbers. The Celestials with their cursed opium. All of them had found more than they had bargained for at the bottom of Old Mary.

Perhaps Mr. Halstead would find what he was looking for down there and move on.

And if not, Old Mary would be receiving another guest.

Chapter 14

Halstead could see Boddington had already worked himself up into a state as they followed the tracks to The Green Tree Saloon.

"I knew it," he yelled. "I knew these here tracks would lead us straight here. As soon as I saw that dead horse back there, there wasn't a doubt in my mind."

Halstead remained calm. The footprints they had followed had certainly led them back to town, but the ground had become too scared with wagon tracks and hoofprints to be able to read the sign clearly. The rider now afoot could have easily passed by The Green Tree as gone into it, though Cy's account convinced Halstead that the man had, indeed, gone there.

Boddington pointed down at a jumble of footprints in the thoroughfare. "It's right there, as plain as the nose on your face. Tell me I'm wrong."

Halstead tried his best to break it to him gently. "We haven't been able to read a clear track since we reached the edge of town. But it matches with what Cy told us about his Fancy Dan."

"You're damned right it matches," Boddington said as

he practically jumped down from the saddle and tethered his horse to the hitching post in front of the saloon. "And I aim to get to the bottom of this right now."

But Halstead was in no such hurry and remained in the saddle. "Wait."

Boddington was already on the boardwalk of the saloon. "Wait? What for?"

"For you to calm down. You running into that saloon all fired up the way you are won't do anyone any good, least of all me." He checked the clock in the bank tower in the middle of Main Street. It was already half-past four. "Let's see if the bouncer from last night is around so we can ask him about Cy's fancy man. See if he knows where he's staying."

Halstead looked at the sheriff for a long moment, willing him to calm down. "That sound about right to you?"

Some of the red had left Boddington's face. "Yeah, sure. Sounds right. Robinson's probably working the bar by now. He was working last night, so maybe he could tell us something."

Halstead slowly climbed down from the saddle, flipped Col's reins over the hitching rail, and joined the sheriff up on the boardwalk. "Best let me go in first. I'm a little calmer than you."

"I already said I was calm, damn it!" Boddington yelled, but the pain that webbed through his nose made him regret it.

Halstead grinned as he walked past him and into The Green Tree. "Stay here. I'll come get you if I find out anything."

* * *

The Green Tree Saloon was lively for a late afternoon. The bar had a fair number of men in attendance, about ten or so by Halstead's count, and they all seemed to be getting along just fine.

The gaming tables were also doing a good business with almost half of them full. A quick glance toward the back told him there was another game going on there, though he could not make out the faces of the players.

A couple of the saloon's sporting ladies were flitting among tables like butterflies in a garden, though their hearts did not seem to be in it. After what had happened to Cassie, he could hardly blame them.

Halstead found the man he assumed was the bouncer at the end of the bar talking to the bartender. He was pretty much what Halstead had expected. Big all over with a neck almost as thick as Col's. The dull look in his eyes made him well-suited for the job of bouncer. He would not be bargained with or pled with. If Greenly or the bartender told him to pitch someone out on their ear, he would do it without hesitation. If they pulled a gun, he would shoot them. And if someone was called a cheat, he would scare the accused into either admitting his guilt or proving his innocence.

The bartender eased away as Halstead approached the bouncer. The big man looked Halstead up and down real slow, first focusing on the silver handle poking out from beneath his coat before seeing the federal star on his lapel. "That thing real?"

"As real as it gets," Halstead told him. "What's your name?"

"Brad," the big man said. "Bradford, if this is an official call. It's my last name. My first name—"

Halstead did not care what his first name was. "You working here last night, Brad?"

"Yes, sir," he pointed to the lookout chair at the opposite end of the bar. It was a tall chair set on a platform that gave whoever sat there a clear view of the saloon. "I was perched up there the whole night with my shotgun across my lap. From there, I can keep an eye on the tables and an ear on what's going on in the rooms upstairs. If any of the ladies gets in trouble, they just call out and I'm in there in no time flat. Even got an axe to break down the door if a man is foolish enough to block the door. That's the way Mr. Greenly likes it."

Brad may not have realized it, but he had already answered several of Halstead's questions. Now it was time to see if he was telling the truth. "You remember any strangers come in here last night? Any new faces who might stick out in your mind?"

The bouncer did not even pause to think it over. "Can't say as I can. It was just a regular old night in here, except for the fact that Cassie got killed the next morning. That was a real shame. Everyone liked Cassie."

Halstead was more interested in the man Cy had described, but he could not forget there was also the young girl's murder to solve. "Anyone like her in particular last night?"

"No more than usual," Brad said. "She had her regulars." He checked the door before asking, "Is the sheriff with you?"

"He's outside talking to someone else," Halstead lied. "Why?"

"It's just that he's one of her more regular clients and he doesn't like to think anyone else has a go with her. I imagine he's feeling bad about what happened to her, and I didn't want to say anything that would make him feel worse. Boddington's a bad man to anger."

Since it was clear Brad didn't know anything about Cassie's murder, Halstead decided to ask him about Ace. "You sure you didn't see anyone in here lugging a saddle or some saddlebags with him last night? Might've played a game of cards with a drunk named Cy?"

Brad laughed. "Cy tell you that? That he was playing cards?"

Halstead did not laugh. "Why?"

"Because old Cy's never had enough money to get in on a game. Likes to watch though. Sometimes, when things are slow, thc boys will take pity on him and let him in on a game. Throw a few hands to send a little money his way. But his word don't count for much. He's liable to see lots of things, including an old ghost or two. Why, I doubt that fool has drawn a sober breath in ten years. Usually doesn't come in here until much later, though, when the bar crowd is looser with their money and more apt to buy him a drink. He's more than happy to accept their sympathy. He's harmless, so we let him get away with it."

Brad even tried a smile. "I can let him know you're looking for him if he comes in here later."

"I already talked to him," Halstead said as he looked the place over. The lookout chair was certainly in the center of things and afforded him a clear view of the tables and the bar. Just about the only place he could not see was the back room where Halstead could see men playing cards now. He pointed in that direction and said, "What's going on back there?"

Brad looked around as if he had no idea of what

Halstead was talking about, then said, "Oh that's the place Mr. Greenly reserves for high-stakes gambling. Not just anyone can go back there, least of all Cy. They have to be invited. By Mr. Greenly personally."

"That so?" Halstead kept looking at the room. "There happen to be any strangers back there right now? Maybe a fella with a fancy moustache?"

"Can't rightly say," Brad told him. "I just got here myself and haven't been back there yet. I never go back there unless Mr. Greenly tells me to." He held up a big hand. "And before you ask, I won't go see who's back there and neither will you."

Halstead grew very still. "That so?"

Brad slowly pushed himself off the bar and stood to his full height. Halstead figured he was about a head shorter than the bouncer. He was not threatening, just showing Halstead what he was up against. "Afraid so. The rules of the house go for everyone, even if they have a star on their shirt."

Halstead did not flinch when he heard a heavy hand slap on the bar next to Brad. The bartender said, "And a good afternoon to you, Deputy Halstead. Please allow me to bid you a proper welcome to the world-famous Green Tree Saloon of Silver Cloud, Montana. Mister John Greenly himself, proprietor, and I am your humble barman Todd Robinson. I'll be your escort through this Garden of Eden this evening. You name your poison and I'll serve it right up for you. We've got everything from panther piss to Billy goat spit and anything in between, except for laudanum and opium. Our beloved benefactor, Mister Emmett Ryan himself, forbids it, you see, and we're all the better for it. But you can cry in your beer for no extra charge, and the bad advice I give you is on the house."

Neither Halstead nor Brad broke off their look.

Robinson gave Brad's shoulder a good shove. "Come on, big fella. On your way. Can't you see you're impeding commerce? The good deputy here is a thirsty man. Why, it's written all over his face. What would Mr. Greenly say if he saw you standing between a man and his whiskey. Fly away to your big chair, big turkey, and let me help the deputy commence with the serious prospect of good drink."

Reluctantly, Brad turned and slowly walked the length of the bar toward the lookout chair at the opposite end.

Halstead looked at the bartender. His bald head gleamed in the weak light of the saloon and his long beard was a tangle of iron gray hair. But the eyes behind his spectacles gleamed.

"Hope you don't expect me to thank you for breaking that up," Halstead told him. "It would've ended worse for him than you think."

"I don't get paid to think, deputy. I get paid to serve the public, just like you. Now, what'll it be?" He placed a surprisingly massive hand on a barrel right behind him. "I've got a new beer with the tap just hammered in by my own two hands not fifteen minutes ago."

"That's some set of paws you've got there," Halstead remarked.

Robinson looked at them and laughed at himself. "The result of decades of hard work and dedication. Clumsy at all things except for pouring any number of spirits for your choosing. Now, what'll it be."

Halstead went back to looking down toward the back room. "No thanks. I'm not here to drink."

"That's a shame," Robinson observed. "I was kind of hoping you would. It'd give me the chance to undo some of that fiction Brad was pouring in your ear just now." The bartender shrugged. "But like I said, I don't get paid to think."

Halstead caught the man's meaning and suddenly found himself thirsty. He fished a coin out of his pocket and placed it on the bar. "Make it a beer. Why so helpful?"

Robinson spoke as he found a glass and worked the tap. "Might be because Cassie was a friend of mine and I don't like the idea of the man who killed her running around while she's in a box up at Doc Mortimer's place. Might also be because I saw the man I heard you talking about come in here last night and play a couple of hands with Cy over his shoulder, just like you said."

Halstead had always been suspicious of kindnesses, especially sudden kindnesses from strangers. "Then why did Brad lie to me?"

"Because he was paid to," Robinson said, "by the same man you're looking for."

Now Halstead knew why Robinson was being helpful. "Let me guess. He didn't pay you."

The bartender grinned as he placed a frothy glass in front of Halstead. "You're a mighty perceptive man, deputy. The territory needs perceptive lawmen like you, especially with statehood being right around the corner."

Halstead ignored the flattery. "You happen to know where this fancy man spent the night?"

"Upstairs with Petunia," Robinson told him. "Mr. Greenly likes his girls to be named after flowers. Daisy, Petunia, and the like. It goes with the garden idea he likes for the place.

I'd stay away from Rose, if I were you. She's thorny and not just by disposition. She's also got a case of the clap."

"I'll keep it in mind. Know where the fancy man is now?"

"He goes by the name of Ace," Robinson told him, "and he's in that back room you keep looking at." He produced a bar towel and began to wipe a spot on the bar. "But you'd do well to mind Brad. I have no doubt you could probably take him, but a man with a shotgun is still a man with a shotgun."

"Thanks." He tossed another coin on the bar. "Keep my beer warm for me, will you?"

"I'll watch it as if it was my own sister's virtue."

Halstead stepped outside and found Boddington was trying to tamp down the bandage on his broken nose. "If you're done trying to beautify yourself, you'd best come in."

"You found him." The sheriff immediately followed him inside and walked beside him as they walked the length of the bar. "Where is he?"

"In the back room playing cards."

"Good." The sheriff pulled his Colt from the holster on his hip and kept it against his leg. "Big Brad up there won't like it, but we'll brace him together."

"No," Halstead told him. "You watch the boy in the lookout chair. I'll handle Ace. You're too likely to shoot him."

Boddington cursed, but did not argue with him. When they got closer to the lookout chair, Brad was already looking down at them. The shotgun was across his lap.

"Sheriff," Brad said to Boddington. "You know the rules. Like I told your friend here, no one's allowed . . ."

The bouncer stopped talking when Boddington laughed

and patted the bouncer's knee as he slipped the Colt between the bouncer's legs. "Those rules are a courtesy I allow Greenly to enjoy when it suits me. Now, just sit right there and keep looking at me. No reason for anyone to get hurt, now is there? Tell me, how's your ma and pa? Heard the good woman's rheumatism is kicking up again."

Halstead continued walking under the stairs and entered the back room. Five men were seated around a card table and judging by the number of coins and paper in the center, it looked like they had quite a game going.

He focused on the man sitting with his back to the wall facing him. His black hair was well-oiled and combed straight back. His moustache sported a nice curl at each end, which Halstead figured was due to a healthy amount of wax.

The rest of the men gradually looked up at him from their cards. Ace looked at him last.

The man closest to him had a close-cropped gray beard and sported a pearl gray hat that matched his suit. Judging by his clothes, he was no drover. "Evening, marshal. Or should I say, deputy marshal? How may we help you?"

"You can't." Halstead was looking at Ace. "But he can. The rest of you can leave. Keep your cards and your money on the table. They'll be here when you get back."

The man with the gray beard got up slowly and stood next to Ace as he gestured for the other gamblers to leave. "Come, gentlemen. The sooner they finish their business, the sooner we can all return to our game."

As the gamblers left, the man with the gray beard mouthed something to Halstead silently. "Twenty-two. Right sleeve."

The man tipped his hat and followed the others out

into the saloon. Halstead heard them stop at the lookout chair and say hello to Boddington.

Ace slowly placed his cards face down on the table and folded his hands on top of them. His left sleeve was buttoned. His right sleeve was not.

"You sure you're looking for me, marshal? I can't see why. I haven't donc anything wrong since I came to town."

"That remains to be seen." Halstead had no doubt he was one of the men he had seen from the Hudson Gang. He may not have gotten a good look at his face through his field glasses, but he would recognize that moustache anywhere.

Halstead knew he had every reason in the world to arrest him right then and there but decided to let things play out first. Cassie's death had changed things and not for the better.

"Why'd you tell Cy you saw me kill Cassie?"

"Cassie?" The gambler furrowed his brow. "Who the hell is Cassie? Oh, you mean that whore they found dead in the alley out back?" He tried a smile. "I didn't know that was her name."

"But you knew enough to tell Cy I'd killed her, didn't you? And pay him to tell Boddington I did it."

"Cy?" he repeated. "Can't say as I know any Cy?" He shrugged. "I'd really like to help you, deputy, but you keep asking me about all these people I've never even met."

"You were hoping the sheriff would lose his temper and come gunning for me, weren't you?"

Ace cocked his head to one side. "Now why in the world would I want to do something like that? I don't even know you."

"Because your kind always likes to get someone else

to do their killing for them," Halstead said. "Would've been a good plan had it worked. Then you and your boys could bust your boss out of jail, turn tail, and head back to Rock Creek. Go back to scaring the hell out of some poor townsfolk."

Ace slowly shook his head but never took his eyes off Halstead. "Mister, I think you've been sampling too much of that rot gut Greenly passes off for bottled and bonded in this place. Seems to have scrambled your eggs a little." He raised his left hand and tapped his temple. "Up here."

"Maybe," Halstead allowed. "You've got another bottle of that Texas Lightning you gave Cy?"

Ace shook his head. "I already told you I don't know any Cy. And I'm getting really tired of repeating myself."

Halstead's eyes narrowed. "Come to think of it, I think I've seen you somewhere before. You look awfully familiar. Just can't place it."

Ace slapped his hands on the table. "Well there's your answer for you, deputy. I hear that all the time. People tell me that very same thing wherever I go." He cocked his head to the other side. "Guess I've got that kind of face."

"It's not like that," Halstead went on. "I've seen you before." He snapped his fingers as he kept his hand beside his hip holster. "Maybe at the end of my field glasses. Just outside of Rock Creek yesterday."

"Rock Creek?" the gambler repeated. "I'm afraid that's just flat out impossible, deputy. I was in the complete other side of the territory in Helena. Say, that's where you marshal boys are based out of, aren't you?"

Halstead ignored the question. "Though, come to think of it, maybe I didn't see you through my field glasses."

Ace smiled. "I like the way you think, deputy. A man who listens to reason is my kind of man."

"After all," Halstead went on, "you were too busy running the other way once the shooting started."

Ace's smile faded.

Halstead said, "Guess I'd have to ask you to stand up and turn around so I could be sure, since all I saw was your back."

Ace slowly shook his head. "That's not a nice thing to say, deputy. But I think we've gotten off on the wrong foot. What do you say you take a seat so we can talk about this like a couple of civilized men? Maybe have a drink so we can get this sorted out proper like."

Ace kicked an empty chair at him while his right hand shot out.

Halstead cleared leather and shot him in the head before the chair reached him or the derringer reached Ace's hand.

The gambler's head snapped back and struck the wall before falling forward and hitting the table.

"You still there, sheriff?" Halstead called back to Boddington.

"Yeah," the sheriff called back. "What happened?"

Halstead opened the cylinder, removed the spent bullet, and dropped it on the table before replacing it with a fresh one from his belt. "We came to an understanding." He snapped the cylinder shut and replaced it in the holster on his hip.

He reached over the table and pulled the derringer from Ace's dead hand. It was a twenty-two. Just like the gun that had killed Cassie. He placed it in his pocket for later.

Before he left, he decided to sneak a peek at Ace's

cards and was surprised by what he saw. A full house. "Should've stuck to cards, Ace."

He plopped the cards on the table and walked out into the saloon.

Boddington had stepped away from Brad. He was holding the bouncer's shotgun at his side. "You went and killed him?"

"Seems that way," Halstead said. "But go check if it'll make you feel any better."

Boddington pushed past him as Greenly came rushing out from the other side of the stairs. He had a pistol in his hand.

He looked up at Brad. "What the hell is going on out here?"

Halstead slapped the gun out of his hand and snatched Greenly by the throat as he proceeded to drag him out of the place backward. "John Greenly, I'm placing you under arrest as an accomplice in the attempted murder of a peace officer."

The pimp struggled to keep his feet under him as he back peddled toward the front door of his own saloon.

Halstead offered the bartender a subtle nod as he passed. He also noticed that his beer was still there, just like Robinson had promised.

At least one man in The Green Tree was a man of his word.

Chapter 15

The townspeople on the streets of Silver Cloud that early evening stopped and stared as Halstead dragged Greenly across the thoroughfare to the jail. Trailing Col behind him, the mustang stepped high in the hard mud of Main Street while the prisoner struggled to keep his balance. Halstead's tight grip on his throat served as an incentive to keep up the pace.

Upon reaching the jail, Halstead wrapped Col's reins around the hitching rail and hauled the prisoner up the stairs backward and into the jail.

Tim and Dan Upman got to their feet as they watched Halstead pull the owner of The Green Tree into jail by his neck.

"Damn it," Greenly protested as Halstead paused just long enough to fish the iron ring of keys from his coat pocket and open the door to the cells. "You've got no call to treat me like this, Halstead. I didn't do anything to you."

"You knew Ace was staying with one of your girls," he said as he found the right key and opened the door. "You were in the alley when Cy told Boddington I'd murdered Cassie and you said nothing. You knew we were looking for Ace and you kept your mouth shut."

He pulled the door open and dragged him into the cells. "Ace tried to kill me, so that makes you an accomplice before the fact."

Greenly gagged when Halstead held on to his neck until he threw him into the cell across from Hudson and locked the door.

"A judge will see it different, Halstead!" Greenly yelled back.

"I know the judge," Halstead told him. "You don't. He'll see it my way, and he doesn't like accomplices. If you know anything about what happened to Cassie, you'd better start talking. Boddington was awfully fond of that girl and he's not in a forgiving mood."

He was about to close the door to the cells when he heard Boddington call out to him from the street. "Don't shut that door just yet, Halstead."

He and the two Upman boys watched the sheriff lead Brad the bouncer into the jail with the double-barreled shotgun at his back. "Keep moving into the cells, big fella. The one next to your boss ought to suit you just fine."

Halstead knew Brad was going to throw a left hand his way before the big man knew it himself. So when the punch was thrown, Halstead ducked it easily and buried a left hook into the bouncer's stomach and finished it with a hard right hand to the kidney.

The blows brought the big man to his knees and a boot to the rear from Boddington. "Get up, pansy. You'll have plenty of time to rest later on."

Brad struggled to his feet as the sheriff corralled him into the cell next to Greenly and slammed the door shut. He told Halstead to toss him the keys, which he did, then locked the cell door.

Boddington stepped back into the office with the shotgun in hand, shut the door to the cells, and locked it. He noticed his two deputies gawking at him and Halstead with their mouths open.

"Shut your gobs," Boddington said as he tossed the keys on his desk. "You'll let the flies in."

"What happened?" Tim asked, cradling his arm in its sling.

"You arrested Brad?" Dan asked. Halstead noticed he had taken off his head bandage, revealing the nasty cut above his right eye. "Why'd you do that?"

Tim added, "Brad's a good man. He's our friend."

"Brad's an accomplice." Boddington went to the stove to pour himself a cup of coffee. He seemed to remember it was the same cup that Halstead had been using. He looked at the deputy before pouring his coffee into it. "You got anything that's catching."

"No."

"Stupid question." Boddington laughed to himself as he poured the coffee. "The plague is probably afraid of catching *you*. Anything that goes against you doesn't live too long, not even a cold." His mug filled, he looked at his deputies. "You should've seen this man work, boys. Cleared leather faster than any man I've ever seen and hit that slick bastard straight between the eyes."

He sipped the coffee before allowing himself to drop into the chair behind his desk. "Where'd you learn to shoot like that, boy?"

Halstead did not see the reason for Boddington's amazement. "It was point-blank range, sheriff. I couldn't have missed if I'd wanted to."

"You were more than ten feet away from the man,"

Boddington reminded him, "and I've seen men miss a lot closer than that, especially when the other fella's going for his gun." He toasted him with his mug. "And my compliments on avoiding my question about how you learned to shoot like that."

"Practice," Halstead told him. "A whole lot of practice." He did not like to talk about such things with men he did not know and trust. He was getting a sense of the kind of man Boddington was and was beginning to like what he saw. But they still were not at the point where he trusted him. In fact, there were only two men in the world he really trusted, and it was time for him to tell them what had happened here today.

"I've got to get to the telegraph office and let Mackey know what's happened. I'll let you know if I get a response." Another thought came to him. "You need me to make a statement to Doc Mortimer about what happened here, him being the town coroner and all?"

"Good thinking," Boddington agreed. "You want me to wait until you get back here before I start to work on Greenly or do you want me and my boys to handle that?"

Halstead headed for the door. "I've already had my fun. Don't let me stop you."

The sky was already beginning to darken as he rode Col along Main Street to the telegraph office. Another night was coming to Silver Cloud, which was one more than he had counted on seeing when he had brought Hudson there. He hoped his new message to Mackey would cause his boss to pull him out of there and bring Hudson back to Helena immediately.

By sending Ace into town, Zimmerman had decided to try to free Hudson. That meant the remaining seven members of the gang were still out there and intent on coming for their boss. He was not particularly worried. He had managed to hold ten of them at bay easily enough. Seven were much more comfortable odds.

Hc ignored the looks he drew from clusters of townsfolk who had stopped each other in the street, no doubt trading lies and rumors about what had just happened in The Green Tree. By the end of the night, after the story was retold in front parlors and saloons all over town, greased by liquor and broadened by exaggeration, he figured his killing of Ace would be blown up into a tale of epic proportions.

There would be no shortage of witnesses who would claim to have seen the men square off from opposite ends of the bar, with Halstead having been faster on the draw, only to blow Ace away with both pistols blazing hot lead. Those who liked law and order would claim Ace had it coming, while the others would say Halstead cheated.

He did not care what they said, so long as they did not try to talk to him about it. He took the fear in their eyes as they glanced at him as a good sign. Mackey always said a lawman should avoid getting too friendly with the people he protected. Familiarity bred contempt, and there were already plenty of people who had contempt for the law, such as it was in the Montana Territory.

He steered Col past a wagon, stepped down from the saddle, and hitched her to the railing post in front of the telegraph office.

There was a line of five men and women waiting to hand their telegram slips to the clerk. But when they saw

Halstead had entered the office, they promptly left without saying a word.

Halstead found the clerk gaping at him just as the Upman boys had done back at the jail. "Looks like I'm not too good for business."

"They'll come back," the clerk said. "How can I help you, deputy?"

He took the telegraph pad that a customer had been writing on when he had walked in, flipped to a clean page, and began writing. "I want you to send this to Marshal Mackey in Helena and request a prompt response just like last night."

He kept the message brief.

DEAD WHORE N TOWN. ACE INVOLVED,
NOW DEAD. HUDSON GANG NEAR.
REQUEST IMMEDIATE RETURN TO HELENA
WITH HUDSON.

He handed the pad to the clerk. "When you get it, you can find me down at the jail."

"Sure thing." The clerk took the pad but did not look at it right away. "Say, deputy. Did you really kill that gambler like they're saying you done?" He looked at the Colt handle on Halstead's belly. "Was it really like they say? Both them fine pistols blazing away?"

Halstead looked around the office as if he was concerned someone might be listening, then leaned on the counter secretively and said, "Swords."

The clerk's mouth dropped open again. "What was that?"

"We used swords," Halstead told him. "Went at it like a couple of English knights. Stabbed him right through the heart, too."

The clerk frowned when he realized he was being put on and returned his attention to the pad. "I'll bring any response to the jail as soon as I get it."

Halstead grinned, enjoying the little man's disappointment. "I'll be waiting."

He left the telegraph office and found the customers who had been waiting inside had gathered on the boardwalk like pigeons around stale bread. They quickly moved past him and back into the office when they saw him.

"I do admire human nature," a man on a gray gelding said. "If one were to be kind enough to call it nature."

Halstead recognized the man as the old gambler who had been playing cards with Ace. The man who had warned him about the twenty-two in Ace's sleeve.

Halstead saw the man was not carrying a gun and figured he meant him no harm. He unwrapped Col's reins from the rail and climbed up into the saddle. "I don't call it anything. People do what they do. It's not up to me to try to figure it out. Just clean up after them once they've done it."

The gambler smiled. "Then I admire you, sir. I wish I had the luxury of taking people as they were. Alas, I make my trade as a gambler, so reading people is part and parcel of my profession."

"Still got to play the man sitting across from you," Halstead told him. "Can't always pick who you're playing against. Sometimes, you just have to follow their lead."

"Not when I can help it." The gambler extended a gloved hand to him. "Lance McAlister, at your service, sir."

Halstead shook the man's hand. "Jeremiah Halstead. Deputy U.S. Marshal. But something tells me you already knew that."

"Wouldn't be much of a gambler if I didn't keep track of such things. I always try to know who comes and goes in this town. To see if they matter to me or not." He gestured toward the jail. "Do you mind if I ride with you?"

Halstead did not see a reason why he should mind, and the two men began riding together in that direction at an easy pace. "I wasn't expecting a handshake. I figured you'd be cross with me for interrupting your game like I did."

"Nonsense," McAlister said. "I was losing anyway. Your dead friend was quite the card sharp. I suppose they didn't call him 'Ace' for nothing."

"He wasn't my friend," Halstead told him. "And he was holding a royal flush. You would've lost even more. Guess I did you a favor by killing him."

"You did the world a favor, sir," McAlister said. "He was a man of low breeding and a nasty disposition. He was given to treating the rare flowers of The Green Tree rather harshly."

Halstead caught that. "Sounds like you knew him pretty well."

"Only in passing," McAlister told him. "He came to town about four times a year or so. I always made it a point to play with him when he was here. He was a shrewd gambler. The first couple of nights in town, he'd always lose. Then, when he had us hooked, he'd buy his way into a big game of the men who'd played with him in the previous days and drain us dry. I always thought he cheated, but for the life of me, I could never prove it."

"If you knew his game, why'd you play with him after you beat him the first time?" Halstead asked. "Why not just quit while you were ahead?"

"Because I'm a gambler, sir," McAlister explained. "Always wanted to be able to say I'd beaten the devil at his own game. Must sound foolish to a man like you, I know, as I take it you're not much of a gambler."

"Nope," Halstead allowed. "Not with cards, anyway."

"Count yourself lucky, then. It's not a life I'd wish on my worst enemy, but yet, it's the only occupation I've ever been good at." He paused as a new thought appeared to come to him, though Halstead figured he had been working up to whatever would come next since he had been waiting for him at the telegraph office. "Halstead. I know that name. You wouldn't happen to be related to Sim Halstead, would you?"

And there it was, right on time. "He happens to be my father."

McAlister slapped his leg as if recalling a fond memory. "Of course. I should've known and not just from your last name. You have the look of him, you know. Complexion aside, of course, there's no doubting you're his son."

Unlike Wheeler at the livery, Halstead wondered if he actually knew his father. "Most people see my color and take me for a half-blooded Indian."

"Not me," McAlister said. "I'm a student of humanity, sir, and I see beyond mere appearances. You're his son, all right. The eyes and nose give it away immediately."

He figured the old codger was working up to something, but he was still the first man beside Aaron and Billy who had noted the resemblance. "That's good of you to say."

"Ah, I remember him fondly," McAlister went on. "He wasn't a gambling man, of course, but I suppose that's why we were friendly. Opposites attracting and all that. Many was the night the two of us spent in the Tin Horn back at Dover Station, exploring the mysteries of life over a bottle of whiskey."

Halstead nodded. "Couldn't have been much of a conversation. My dad was a mute for the last ten years of his life."

McAlister recovered nicely. "The conversations were a bit one-sided, of course, but men of the world such as we have a language all our own. A language that does not require words."

"He didn't drink either," Halstead lied. His father only drank around Aaron and Billy and Pappy once a year on the Fourth of July. At least that was what he had told him in their letters. "Why'd you lie to me, McAlister. What's your real game here?"

The gambler shrugged. "It wasn't a total lie, deputy. I did know your father, or at least of him. He was always very quiet and very staid. Reserved. Liked to keep to himself. I was in the Tin Horn one night when Mackey and that colored deputy of his put down some ruffians who set to raising Cain in the place. Mackey was the sheriff at that time and made us all give statements to what we had seen. Mackey was in the right of course, and I was proud to have said so officially. I remember the deputy asked the questions and your father wrote down what we said. He had a most elegant penmanship."

Halstead figured McAlister knew at least that much, which meant he was not a total liar. "He did at that. Sounds like that might have been before Darabont and his bunch attacked the town."

"I left before that happened," McAlister said. "Heard

about it afterward, of course. Heard about what happened to your daddy in the hunt for those monsters. Despite my earlier exaggerations about knowing your father, I hope you'll accept my belated condolences on his passing. I saw him help Mackey cut down those men at the Tin Horn that night. He was very brave."

Halstead felt his throat begin to tighten the way it always did whenever he thought about his father. It was as if all the pain Sim had felt during that time of his life came back to visit him. "Thanks, but you still haven't answered my question. Tell me why you're really here or go away."

McAlister ducked his head a bit as they continued riding beside each other. "I suppose it *is* a game, isn't it, deputy? Everything's a game to an old gambler like me. You've been more than fair with me, despite my fiction about your father, so I'll be more than fair with you. There's a good bit of money beginning to be placed on a wager in town. The biggest pot of money I've seen in the year since I've been here. And it has to do with you, Jeremiah Halstead. Most pointedly about how long you'll stay alive."

Halstead may not have been expecting it, but he was not entirely surprised by it. Some men would bet on anything, including when one would die. "That so? What are the odds?"

"I won't bore you with the details, but let's just say they are overwhelmingly against you, even after what you did to Ace just now. The reason is simple and it's why I wanted to talk to you now. It seems Ace was not riding alone."

"I already know that," Halstead said. "He ran with the Hudson Gang and they're coming here to try to free John

Hudson from my custody." He looked at McAlister. "That the big surprise you wanted to tell me?"

"I wish it was," McAlister said. "They sent Ace ahead of them to get the lay of the land before the rest of them rode in here. He wore out a horse getting here so fast and had to make part of the journey on foot."

"I knew that, too. Boddington and me found the horse earlier today and followed his tracks to the saloon right before I killed him."

"I figured as much," the gambler admitted. "But what you don't know, what you couldn't possibly know, is that Ace didn't get here early just to keep an eye on you. He came here to hire on some men who might be willing to fight against you. Had quite a bit of money to help him do it, too. More than he had won at cards."

That *was* news to Halstead. "How many did he get to join him?"

"I don't know," McAlister said, "and if I did, I'd tell you. If I find out, I'll let you know. But I can tell you he spent a good part of the day hitting up most of the saloons in town asking for men to help him gun you down. Boddington, too. None of the men have anything against you personally, but there's no shortage of men in this town who hate Boddington and the Upman boys. They're meaner than they need to be and tend to take the money off the drunks they roust for wandering the streets. If they can't pay the fine, Boddington makes them sign over whatever they've got instead. Horses, land, you name it. Most of the mines are controlled by Emmett Ryan, and since the sheriff and his men are beholden to Ryan, he leaves the miners alone. But everyone else is fair game to Boddington. That's why I doubt Ace had any trouble finding men to join his cause. Not against you, but against Boddington. They plan on using the presence of the Hudson Gang as their chance to exact revenge. A revenge, I might add, that is not without merit."

"Going against Boddington's the same as going against me," Halstead told him. "At least for now."

By then they had reached the jail. Halstead drew Col to a halt, and McAlister did the same. "You got any other cheerful thoughts for me, McAlister, or are you done spreading cheer?"

The gambler laughed. "I should hear more tonight about the men Ace hired. I'll stop by here tomorrow and let you know how many he signed on. I'll let you know if I hear about the rest of the gang coming to town, too. Ace was awfully vague on the subject."

Halstead would have expected that. The Hudson Gang had not remained on the loose for so long by being careless. "He didn't strike me as a fool. But I appreciate the warning just the same. And the warning about the hideout gun in Ace's sleeve."

McAlister smiled. "I realize now you didn't need the help, but I prefer to see a fair fight when I can." He held out his hand again to Halstead. "No hard feelings about my tall tale about your father?"

Halstead normally would have held on to some resentment, but he found it hard to hold a grudge against the gambler. He supposed that was why he was good at what he did. "None at all."

The two men shook hands, and McAlister backed his horse away as Halstead climbed down from his saddle. "Now I've got a piece of advice for you, McAlister."

The gambler turned his horse to face him. "And what might that be, sir?"

"Don't bet against me."

The gambler grinned. "I wouldn't dream of it." He touched the brim of his hat before riding away. "Be seeing you, deputy."

Halstead wrapped Col's reins around the hitching post and walked up the steps to the jail. He looked through the window and saw Boddington looming over Greenly, who was cringing in a chair. The sheriff was sticking his finger in Greenly's face as he bore down hard on the pimp.

Halstead decided his talk with McAlister had been time well spent. He wondered if Greenly was one of the men who had hired on with Ace to go against him and the sheriff. It certainly looked like there was no love lost between the two men. An understanding between Greenly and Ace would certainly go a long way to explain why he had kept his mouth shut about the outlaw spending the night in his place. He had to figure Brad the bouncer was in on it, too. Both would be locked up for the foreseeable future, so they were out of the fight no matter what happened next. But if either of them would crack about what they knew, his money was on Brad being the one to spill. In his experience, a big man broke easier than a smaller, scrappier one.

Halstead placed his hand on the door, but stopped before going in. The cool air of the coming night moved across his neck and he suddenly felt tired. Not tired in the way sleep could cure, but tired in the way his soul felt when he had done too much. Seen too much.

It was a feeling he used to have in prison down in El Paso, back when the screaming and the crying and the endless rattle of chains and curses felt like it had scarred his mind. When he was too sick to leave his cell. When even the threats and beatings of the guards were not enough to rouse him.

He knew he should go inside and help Boddington question Greenly. His mere presence might be enough to put the pimp off balance.

But at that moment, it was Jeremiah Halstead who was off balance.

He killed easily and killed well, but it always took a toll on him. It was a problem he had written to his father about many times over the years they had spent apart and each time, his father's response had been the same.

"Taking a man's life is supposed to cost you something, son. It shows you still have a soul. And a soul comes in handy if you're going to wear a star. It gives you something to pin it to besides your shirt."

He had killed three men in the past two days. All three had deserved it, but three men were still dead because of him.

His hand trembled as he pulled it away from the jailhouse door. He sat on the bench on the boardwalk, alone, and allowed another cool wind to blow across him like a comforting hand.

He ignored the tear that fell from his eye as he looked up to the darkening sky to the place where he liked to think his father was. "I sure could use you now, Pop. I really could."

He looked across the thoroughfare when he saw a stocky man step out of The Green Tree holding a pail and begin to make his way toward him. He recognized the man as Robinson, the bartender.

It was already dark enough on the unlit boardwalk to hide his face, so Halstead did not bother to wipe the tears from his eyes. He allowed them to dry there as a reminder that he still had a soul or something like it. They would be gone by the time the lamplighter reached this part of town and he doubted Robinson would notice his reddened eyes.

Robinson climbed up the steps and sat next to Halstead on the bench, setting the pail between them with a formal finality.

"I brought you something I figured you'd be needing right about now," the bartender said as he removed the lid and revealed a bucket full of beer with a glass floating atop it. "You never did get the chance to finish the beer you paid for. I brought some extra for you and Boddington. God knows you boys earned it today."

Halstead had never been much of a beer drinker, but the smell made him consider it. Whiskey would dull his senses too much, but beer might just take enough of the edge off.

But Halstead hesitated. It all seemed a bit too good to be true. "You brought us beer even after we arrested your boss?"

"I brought it *because* you arrested him." Robinson pulled the glass from the pail, filled it up, and wiped the glass clean with his apron. "I'll take a swig of it first, just so you don't think I spiked it with anything." He drank deeply from the glass, filled it up, and wiped it down again before handing to Halstead. "See? As pure as mother's milk."

The deputy took the glass and held it without drinking

from it. "Well, you did what you said you would. You kept my beer warm for me."

"Told you I'd guard it as if it were my sister's virtue," the bartender reminded him. "Unfortunately, Rose is my sister. The girl I told you about who has the clap, remember? So you can take my guarding skills with a grain of salt."

Halstead laughed despite his dark mood. "She really your sister?"

"I wish it were otherwise," Robinson admitted, "but alas, it's true."

Halstead looked at the glass of beer. "She didn't drink from this, did she?"

Robinson shook his head. "She's always been more of a port girl. Whiskey when the customers are buying. She considers beer too common for her."

Halstead decided it was worth the risk and downed a couple of deep swallows of beer. He set the glass down next to the pail lest he be tempted to finish the whole thing.

"Mind if I ask you a question?" Robinson asked.

Like McAlister before him, Halstead figured the bartender had come to him with more than simple conversation on his mind. But he had brought a pail of beer with him, which granted him certain rights as far as Halstead was concerned. "Go ahead."

"You've got all of these people out for your blood right now. Why are you sitting out in the open like this?"

It was a fair question, and Halstead had one of his own. "McAlister told me there's a good amount of money going around about how long I'll live."

Robinson jerked his head toward The Green Tree Saloon.

"Those degenerates will bet on anything. But that's not why I'm asking. I'm genuinely curious is all."

Halstead did not dare tell him why he had sat on the bench in the first place. He saw a chance to heighten his reputation in town and took it. "I like it here. It's peaceful in this part of town at this time of night. Besides, it'll give people a chance to take a shot at me if they want. And give me the chance to narrow the odds even more in my favor."

The thought made him want another swig of beer. He dunked his glass in the pail and let it drip freely without bothering to wipe it. "I hear Ace was recruiting men to line up against me. Any idea how many he got?"

"I was going to get to that," Robinson said. "Sounds like McAlister beat me to it. He's getting awfully chatty in his old age. Last number I heard was at least fifteen."

Halstead hesitated for a moment before bringing the beer to his lips. With the seven remaining Hudson Gang members on the way, that meant he could be up against as many as twenty-two men. Before he drank, he said, "Surprised it's not thirty."

"Some say it is," Robinson allowed. "But that's just saloon talk. Beer-hall bravery as my dearly departed old man used to call it. I'd say the number is much lower than that, and after what you've done to Ace, I doubt it'll be that many. Even if they took his money, these boys won't hold allegiance to a dead man, especially one you killed. And since Ace didn't strike me as the kind who kept a list, his friends won't know who to hold to account once they get here. But even if it's just the seven of them, you won't have it easy. The Hudson Gang is a rough bunch."

Halstead finished his beer and set his glass down next

to the pail. Robinson went to refill it, but Halstead stopped him. "Not yet."

Robinson kept the lid on the pail and sat back. Halstead hoped he might take that as the cue to leave, but the bartender seemed in no hurry to go back behind the bar. Halstead asked him, "How about the rest of the town? You think they'll stick up for me and Boddington if the time comes? I hear there's no shortage of people who hate Boddington's guts."

"That's an understatement," Robinson said a little too quickly for Halstead's taste. "They won't lift a hand to save Boddington or his men. Too many have been burned by him over the years, but I'm sure McAlister told you all that. That's not to say the good people of Silver Cloud are a bunch of mice, either. If trouble breaks out between you and the Hudson boys, the shopkeepers will keep it contained to wherever it happens. They're liable to shoot at anyone who threatens their businesses or homes. But they'll shoot Boddington just as fast as they'll shoot any outsiders who break their windows or shoot in their direction and claim it was done in the confusion of the moment." He looked at Halstead. "I know that's not a particularly comforting thought, but it's the way it is."

Halstead figured that was something he could count on, even if it was not much. "If that's the case, I'd say you're taking a hell of a chance being seen out here with me. I don't want anyone getting the wrong idea about you being a friend of mine."

"I'm fine," Robinson assured him. "With Greenly locked up, I'm the only one who can run The Green Tree. Mr. Ryan still runs this town, and he makes good money off his take of the place. He has an instant hatred for anyone who gets between him and his money. Anyone touches me, they'll have to contend with him. Besides, I'm here for myself."

Halstead looked at him. "Meaning?"

"Meaning The Green Tree used to belong to my father until Greenly came along and swindled him out of it. It flat out killed the old man. He died of a broken heart. I've been saving up a good long while to be able to buy Greenly's share of the place from him, but he refuses to sell. But if he goes to prison, I'm pretty sure Mr. Ryan will let me buy out Greenly's share so the place keeps running normally. Like I said, Ryan likes his money."

Halstead had heard about Emmett Ryan a few times since coming to town but had not seen him yet. "This Mr. Ryan ever come to town? Maybe I could talk him into putting out a good word for us with the citizenry?"

"Not a chance." Robinson pointed behind them. "He's got a place here, sure, but he's too busy keeping an eye on his mines up in the hills. He doesn't much care about what happens down here. He leaves the town to Boddington's care. Though he usually sends his foreman, Earl Perkins, into town once a week to carry messages and report on what he sees. He's kind of like an archangel in that regard, bringing tidings down from on high. But Mr. Ryan won't care about what happens with you and the Hudson Gang until the dust settles and he sees who's left standing."

Halstead let out a heavy breath. He'd had his fill of rich men trying to keep a town under their thumb. It was a nice change to see one who did not really care about the town he owned, even if it left Halstead at a disadvantage. "Guess not having to worry about him getting in the way is something."

That was when he remembered about Cassie. Even after everything that had happened with Ace, they still had a dead woman's murder to solve. "Over at the saloon, you said Cassie was a friend of yours."

Even in the darkening light, he saw Robinson grin. "Yeah. She was a special one, that girl. Had big dreams of making more of herself in this world. I can't tell you how many girls in her line of work have told me the same thing over and over again. But I think Cassie could've actually pulled it off. She wasn't just cunning, but smart, too."

Halstead did not let that go. "I found some books in her room that were pretty heavy reading. Not the kind of stuff you'd expect a girl like her to enjoy."

Robinson fished out a cigarette he had already rolled from his pocket, stuck it in his mouth, and thumbed a match alive. Halstead noticed, his hand trembled just a bit before he waved the match dead and tossed it into the thoroughfare. "Where were they?"

"Under the bed. Why?"

"No reason," he said. "Just thought she'd given them back is all. Sounds like she didn't."

Now Halstead knew he was truly onto something. "Who do they belong to?"

The bartender took a deep drag before taking the cigarette from his mouth. "No. No way. Cassie was a friend and I liked her, but I've got no intention of seeing her again any time soon if you get my meaning."

Based on what little he knew about Silver Cloud, he figured Robinson's sudden bout of caution could only mean one thing. "Mr. Ryan gave her those books, didn't he?"

"I didn't say that." Robinson looked at him. "Listen, Mr. Halstead. I like you. I'm rooting for you and yes, I've got some pretty selfish reasons for doing so. But whatever brought you here is going to be over soon. When it's over, you'll either be dead or climb up on this fine mustang here and head back to Helena. I'm going to have to keep on living in this town. My life is here, and as it happens, my saloon, too. I'm not going to throw all that away by biting the hand that feeds me. Now, I'll help you as much as I can with the Hudson Gang. I'll be happy to tell you everything I hear, but Cassie's a different matter entirely. I hate to disappoint you, but that's how it is. You want to know more, lean on Greenly. He can tell you everything you want to know."

Halstead did not like it, but he had to accept it. Robinson had already helped him out quite a bit and not just by bringing over a pail of beer. He did not expect the bartender to pick up a rifle and stand beside him, but there were other ways a man like him could help with the coming fight. "Any other ideas you've got for me?"

"Yeah," Robinson said as he finished his cigarette and flicked it into the thoroughfare. "That jail is awfully crowded, and I wouldn't recommend sleeping in there tonight. I'd move into the Hotel Montana if I were you. The place is clean, and it's run by the Reyes family, which is good for you."

Halstead had seen the hotel as he had ridden through town. It was near the telegraph office and the bank in the center of town. But he had not heard of the Reyes family. "Why's that good for me?"

"Because they lock the doors at night and have an armed man who keeps an eye on the place until sunup. Got their own livery in the back, too, just for their guests. And since I figure there's a good chance you probably speak Spanish, it might be good to be able to converse with someone in something other than English, especially if any strangers come lurking around."

Halstead had to admit he liked the way Robinson thought. "For a bartender, you're pretty smart."

"Guess that's why Cassie and I got along so well," he said as he stood up. "We both fooled ourselves into thinking we were destined for better things."

Halstead remained sitting alone on the bench with the pail of beer at his feet as he watched Robinson cross the thoroughfare and head back to The Green Tree.

Night had finally settled in over the town and he looked to his left to see if he could spot the lamplighter going about his duties. Like the clockwork on the bank tower, he saw the old man was already going about his appointed rounds.

The streets were populated with couples on a stroll and men on their way to get something to eat or drink. A tinny piano had started up from one of the saloons along Main Street, and he knew bawdy singing would soon follow.

Two people had died in town that day and perhaps more would join them before the clock struck midnight, but life went on.

Here in Silver Cloud and down in El Paso. In Helena and every other city in the world.

Tomorrow, the Hudson Gang might come to town. He might find himself dead by this same time tomorrow night. Maybe the seven of them would be dead.

But none of that would change the fact that a young woman had been killed by someone in this town. It may have had something to do with Halstead. It might not.

Either way, he was determined to find out why before any bullet from a Hudson man found him.

And the man who could tell him why was just on the other side of the wall from where he sat now.

He had some work to do.

Halstead picked up the pail of beer as he stood up and stroked Col's muzzle. "I haven't forgotten about you, old girl. Stand easy. I might be needing you before this night is through."

He went into the jail and brought the beer with him.

CHAPTER 16

Boddington backhanded Greenly hard enough to almost knock him out of the chair.

"The next words out of your mouth better be the truth," the sheriff yelled, "or I'll set my boys to work on you."

Greenly spat out a tooth as he shook off the impact of the blow. The blood on his lips only made his sneer look more sinister. "A fat man with a busted arm and a shrimp who can hardly stand up straight? I'll take my chances."

Boddington brought back his fist this time when Halstead slammed the jailhouse door. The four men looked at him.

The sneer on Greenly's face faded.

Halstead set the pail of beer on the desk. "Brought some refreshments for you boys. Beer courtesy of our friends over at The Green Tree."

The Upman deputies licked their chops like coyotes who had come upon a fresh kill.

Boddington slowly lowered his fist. "Get anything out of him yet?"

Halstead shook his head. "Get anything out of him yet?"

"Just a lot of sass." Boddington brought his hand back

as if he was about to belt Greenly again, which made the pimp flinch. "Nothing useful."

"And you won't get anything out of me, either," Greenly said. "None of you, not even that federal bastard you brought in here with you." He looked Halstead up and down. "I was talking to Mr. Hudson while you had me locked up back there. He told me all about the great Jeremiah Halstead. His boys are going to carve you up like a Christmas goose when they get here. Them fancy guns of yours won't do much against the likes of them."

Halstead picked up one of the chairs against the wall and carried it as he slowly walked over to Greenly. Boddington moved out of the way, and the prisoner sat back as far as he could go in his chair but did not dare to try to get up.

Halstead set the chair down only a few inches in front of him and sat down. He leaned forward, making sure the brim of his black hat was as close to Greenly's as possible without touching him.

Halstead sat that way, motionless and quiet, peering into Greenly's eyes. The only sound in the office was the Regulator clock on the wall ticking off the seemingly endless silence that hung between them.

The longer the quiet held, the more Greenly began to try to shift himself in his seat under Halstead's glare. But Halstead had positioned himself too close to the man for him to be able to get comfortable, which had been his intent.

Greenly clearly did not like being stared at quietly. Few people in Halstead's experience did. But when yelling and beatings failed to generate a result, Halstead found uneasy quiet often did the trick.

After the clock had ticked sixty times—and Halstead

had been counting—he said, "I know what you're thinking, Greenly."

The prisoner's lips moved, but no sound came out.

"You're looking at this nice, shiny pistol sticking out right above my belly," Halstead went on. "It's just sitting there, winking at you, almost daring you to make a play for it. Go ahead. Give it a try. Maybe you'll get it before I break your arm. Maybe you can even use it before Boddington guns you down. You might as well go for it, Greenly. I know I would if I was in that chair. Because no matter what happens to me, you're never getting out of here alive. No one's coming to save you. No one gives a damn about you. If I get killed, someone else will come from Helena to get you. They'll see to it that you swing for what you did. Swing for the murder of Cassie."

Greenly's chair creaked as he pushed himself as far away from Halstead as he could. But as he was already against the wall, there was nowhere for him to go. "I . . . I didn't kill anyone. I didn't kill Cassie."

Halstead remained still. "I say different. I say the two of you had yourselves an argument. I say you lost your temper and killed her with the same derringer you knew she kept hidden in her room to protect her from men like you. A girl in her line of work has to be careful and a derringer comes in handy, doesn't it? Small, compact. Not too much gun for a woman her size to handle, especially if she knows how. And Cassie knew how, didn't she, Greenly? She knew how you used to look at her. Different from the way you looked at the other girls. Different because she was different, wasn't she? Forbidden fruit from that dump you call a Garden of Eden across the street."

"No," Greenly sweated. "It wasn't like that. You don't know what you're talking about."

Halstead did not relent. "You could've ordered her to allow you in her bed, but you didn't, did you? You wanted her to ask you in, but she never did. She never thought you were good enough, did she? And that made you mad."

Greenly looked at the Upman boys, then at Boddington as if one of them might help him. Might say something to call this man off. None of them said a word, and Halstead did not move.

"I didn't want anything to do with her," Greenly sputtered, "and that's the truth."

"Because you knew she'd never take you willingly," Halstead pushed. "You can admit it now. She's dead. You won."

"I didn't win anything!" Greenly screamed. "You think I wanted her dead? She was my best earner. Her getting herself killed caused me more grief than her living ever did."

"Sure you say that now," Halstead said, "but when it happened, in that split second when she pushed you too far, things were different. The whole world was different."

Halstead edged closer. The brim of his hat almost touched Greenly's needle nose. "What did she do? What was it that finally broke it for you? Did she laugh at you?" Halstead nodded. "Yeah, that was it, wasn't it? She laughed in your face at your weak attempt to get in her room. A man like you doesn't like to be laughed at, do you?"

The pimp's face trembled as he tried to return Halstead's glare. "She never laughed at me. She wouldn't dare."

"She must've done something to set you off," Halstead kept on. "What was it?" He reached into his pocket and pulled out the derringer he had taken from Ace's dead hand and pressed it against Greenly's heart. "What was it that made you take this gun and end her life?"

"Nothing!" Greenly shrieked. "I told you I didn't kill her."

Halstead did not think he did, but he knew who might. "Best tell me now so this can go a lot easier on you with the judge. Tell me the truth, and I might be able to save you from swinging but only if you confess now. You shot her with this gun, didn't you? Then, in your panic, gave it to Ace to hold on to, didn't you? Figured a guy like him could always use a hide-out gun. You give it to him to hold on to for you and you're in the clear." He pushed the tiny gun hard against his breastbone. "Didn't you?"

"I didn't kill her!" Greenly said just before the sobs came. "I didn't. You can tell me I did a thousand times, and the answer's still going to be the same. I found her in the alley just like I told you I did."

Halstead withdrew the derringer and handed it back to Boddington, who took it. "You've seen your share of bullet holes, haven't you, sheriff?"

"I believe I have," Boddington replied.

"And you'll be willing to swear in a court of law that the bullet we found on Cassie's body came from a small gun like that, wouldn't you?"

"With pleasure."

"And I'd wager Doc Mortimer will say the same thing," Halstead said.

"He already has," Boddington said. "I've got it right here in his official report. Turned my stomach to read it."

Halstead inched even closer to Greenly who was sobbing heavily now. "Sounds like bad news for you, Greenly. Who do you think the judge is going to believe? The word of a pimp or the expert testimony of two lawmen and a town doctor?"

"I didn't kill her, damn you!" Greenly shrieked. "I told you that."

"Quit telling us and prove it to us." Halstead remained still and kept his voice calm. "You say you didn't kill Cassie? Then tell us who did. I've already got you dead bang for conspiring to kill me. Unless you start talking, you'll swing for Cassie, too." He poked him in the breastbone with his finger. "Come on, Greenly. Do yourself some good. Confess and we'll make sure the knot breaks your neck on the drop."

Greenly's face was soaked with tears and spit as he screamed, "I didn't touch her because she wasn't mine! She belonged to someone else."

Halstead felt Boddington close in and held his right arm back to keep him away. He did not dare let up now. "Who did she belong to, Greenly? Who were you afraid of? Boddington? Is that it? Did he kill her? Don't be afraid. I won't let him hurt you."

"Not him." Greenly's voice broke as he looked at Halstead as if they were the only two men in the room. Halstead had seen men fold like this before. Everything else had faded away and the only hope he had was the man in black glaring at him now. "She belonged to Mr. Ryan."

Halstead felt whatever wall Greenly had built in his mind crumble as the tears flowed freely now.

He also heard Boddington back away and sag against his desk.

Halstead inched away from Greenly. A reward for finally giving something up. "She was Mr. Ryan's girl."

"Yeah," Greenly sobbed. "Mr. Emmett Ryan himself. He

didn't like anyone to know about it. He didn't want anyone to think he was just as human as everyone else. He makes everyone think he's just this humble rich man who lets the rest of us fools work and slave for him like those idiots in his mines. He doesn't let anyone see him drink. He doesn't let anyone see him smoke and he doesn't want anyone to know he had a thing for the pretty blond whore in a two-bit saloon, even if he owns the place and everyone who works in it. He needed someone who would keep their mouth shut and his secret a secret and that man was me."

He used the extra room Halstead had given him to finally wipe a sleeve across his eyes and clean himself up a bit. Halstead let him.

"Why'd he come to town to see her?" Halstead pushed. "Why not bring her up to his place after dark?"

"Because someone would've known," Greenly sobbed. "He doesn't even trust Perkins enough to keep his mouth shut. He has to look like he's pure, even to him. And he wouldn't bring her to his place here in town because she wasn't good enough for him. Besides, someone might see her coming or going. That's why she had a room across the alley above the dress shop. If I'd have said anything or let anyone else say anything, he would've had Perkins cut my head off and put it on a spike."

Halstead looked back at Boddington, but the sheriff was in no condition to answer. He had lost all of the color in his face and looked almost as bad as Greenly did.

He looked at Tim Upman and said, "Earl Perkins is Ryan's messenger boy, isn't he?"

"He's his foreman up in the mines," Upman confirmed. "He also sends him into town to handle things for him from time to time. Go to the bank. Deliver letters to people. Things like that."

Dan Upman added, "Can't remember the last time I saw him come into town himself."

Halstead turned his attention back to Greenly. "Did you see him last night? Mr. Ryan. Was he in town last night when Cassie got killed?"

"I don't know," Greenly wept. "I never knew when he was around. That was the point of the separate room for her."

A new thought came to Halstead. "Is that why she came to me? To get me to say something she could bring back to him later when she saw him?"

"I said I don't know!" Greenly screamed. "I never knew when he was there. All I know is he used to come way after dark and go up the back way to see her. She never told me when he was there, and I never dared to ask. The less I knew about it, the better, believe me."

Halstead sat farther back in his chair and allowed everything Greenly had just said to settle in. "Why didn't you just say all that in the beginning?"

"To who?" Greenly pointed at Boddington. "To him? He thought him and Cassie were practically married. If I'd have told him about Ryan, he would've beaten mc worse than he already has." The pimp laughed at the sheriff through his tears. "You big, stupid bastard. I kind of liked seeing you fool yourself into thinking she cared about you. The way we used to laugh together about all the things you said to her. All the promises you made to her. About your ranch in . . ."

Halstead heard Boddington move and bolted from his chair to keep the sheriff off him. He pushed Boddington back behind his desk and struggled to keep him pinned there while he told the deputies, "Get Greenly back in his cell. Now!"

Halstead kept his shoulder against Boddington until the deputies carried the hysterical prisoner back to his cell. He held the sheriff there, quietly, until Boddington calmed down.

"I'm fine, Halstead."

"You sure? You don't look fine."

"Yeah," Boddington panted. "I'm fine."

Halstead slowly eased away from him but kept himself between Boddington and the door to the cells until the deputies returned and were about to lock the door. "Don't lock it. You two get over here and keep an eye on your boss. I need to go back there and talk to Hudson."

Before he moved away from Boddington, he placed a hand on his shoulder. "He's not going anywhere, Barry. I promise you that. Now, take a seat and relax."

Halstead turned to the two deputies. "Get him a mug of beer from the pail. Only one. Take some for yourselves, too."

He did not bother to tell them to avoid getting drunk, as there was not enough left in the pail to do the job.

Halstead left the three men in the office and walked back to the cells. Brad got to his feet and glared at him as he passed. Greenly was curled up in a ball on his cot, sobbing into his pillow.

John Hudson looked like a man who didn't have a care in the world. His large frame barely fit on the cot he lounged on with one leg on the floor to balance him. His thinning dark hair had not seen a comb in days and his beard was getting more wiry than normal. One of the Upman boys had removed the shackles from his wrists.

He made a mental note to tell them to put them back on later.

Halstead did not like the way the prisoner was laughing at him when he stopped in front of his cell. He gave Hudson the same treatment he had given Greenly. He stood in front of him in silence and watched the outlaw laugh.

"What's the matter, Halstead?" Hudson taunted him. "Come to gloat about what you did to Greenly? Want me to beg you not to do it to me? Hell will freeze over before I beg you or any other man for anything. And if you came to pull me out of here and beat me up like you did Greenly, go ahead. I'd welcome it because you'll have to kill me if you do. I'm no pimp, Halstead. I won't break so easy."

Halstead waited until he had run out of words before telling him, "I killed Ace today."

He watched his expression of defiance mix with surprise.

Halstead went on. "I had him cornered and gave him every chance to go for his gun. All that big talk about him being as good with a Colt as he was with cards didn't really mean much at the end. He was just stupid and slow, and I shot him." Halstead pointed to the center of his forehead. "One shot right here. Ended the whole thing. Died with a whimper, too."

Hudson gritted his teeth as he grabbed the metal bedframe. "It couldn't have happened like that. You must've back shot him to get the drop on him like that. No way you could've killed him in a straight up fight."

"Don't take my word for it," Halstead told him. "Ask the big fella in the cell next to Greenly. He saw the whole thing, didn't you, Brad?"

"I wish he'd killed you, mister," the bouncer said.

"What do you care? You took his money, didn't you? Now you don't have to worry about doing anything to earn it. Keep behaving yourself, and I'll tell the judge you were a good boy. You'll probably only get five years."

Halstead did not flinch when Hudson came off his cot and lunged at him through the bars. He did not need to move because he had already judged the distance and knew he was just out of reach of the outlaw's clawing fingers.

"You're a dead man, Halstead!" Hudson yelled. "Do you hear me? My men are coming for me and when they do, they're going to get me out of here. But not before they burn you alive. Do you understand me? They'll hurt you in ways you never thought you could hurt."

"No, they won't," Halstead told him. "Ace was said to be your best man with a gun. He's dead. Your brother is dead. Weasel is dead. And soon, you'll be dead. Either by my hand or the hangman's rope, the end will be the same."

Hudson strained against the bars with everything he had to grab hold of Halstead, but his arms simply were not long enough to reach him. "Do it now, then, damn you. Let me out of this cage and let's get this over with. Just you and me."

"No need," Halstead told him. "You're the bait now, Hudson. If your men come to town, and it looks like I can't take them, I'll kill you before they can spring you out of here. But I wouldn't count on that happening, even if they do show up." He decided to twist the knife a little deeper before he left. "Ed Zimmerman's running the show now, and with Harry and Ace and Weasel dead, there's a good chance the rest might decide to cut their losses and let you swing. They don't need you anymore, John. They might figure going up against me and Boddington and his men just isn't worth the bother."

"They'll come," Hudson said defiantly. "They'll come because they're my men and because I'm the only one who knows where the money is buried."

Halstead grinned. "Keep telling yourself that."

Halstead ignored Hudson's threats as he shut the door behind him.

He found Boddington at his desk, slumped over the mug of beer his men had poured for him while they scooped beer out of the pail with their coffee mugs.

Halstead had to admit that the sheriff was a sorry sight. The bandage over his broken nose was filthy. His eyes were ringed with black. The eyes themselves were red as they stared at something far beyond the walls of the jail. He was probably looking back on his memories of the dead woman he had loved, trying to understand how he had been so wrong about her.

Halstead had never been one to pity a grown man, no matter his troubles, and he did not pity Barry Boddington now.

That did not mean he liked seeing the man like this. "I'm sorry you had to hear all that, sheriff. I know what it's like to be disappointed in people. I know what it's like to feel like they've made a fool out of you. No one'll think less of you for being hurt, least of all me."

Boddington's vacant expression did not change. "You know my real name is Bartholomew? Bartholomew Boddington, Junior. Growing up, everyone called me Little Bart or Bart Junior or just plain old Junior. But my old man was a mean, nasty old drunk who only cared about his mine. His claim. He used to bore me and my sisters to death about how rich we were all going to be one day. Any money he ever managed to get went to keeping food on the table. The rest was spent on whiskey. When he wasn't drunk or working, he'd beat the hell out of us, saying we didn't appreciate all he did for us."

He looked up at Halstead. "Want to know how he died?"

"If you want to tell me."

"In his sleep." Boddington shook his head. "All those years of torment and hell he caused his family and he just didn't wake up one day. Got drunk, passed out, and never woke up again. From that day on, I'd beat any man who ever dared to call me Junior. I made them call me Barry instead. I swore I'd never become like him, but after what that pimp told us just now, I see that I have. I'm just like him. A fool who pinned his dreams on a future that would never pan out. He had his copper mine. I had Cassie." He took a swig of beer and set the mug down on the desk. "Guess we can't get around what we really are, no matter how much we try to tell ourselves otherwise."

Halstead had never been much for giving advice. He had already made too many mistakes in his young life to be able to tell anyone how they should live theirs. But he could not just leave the sheriff to wallow in pity and regret. He would most likely need him in the coming days, and his deputies would not be enough to cover for him.

"Just because you're in the habit of making mistakes doesn't mean you have to keep on making them. Change or don't change. Either way it's up to you. But there's no sense in kicking yourself over things that have already happened. Best to just figure out what you're going to do today. Figure out how we're going to go about asking Ryan about Cassie."

Boddington looked down into his mug of ale. "Easier said than done. On all counts."

Halstead figured he had dispensed all the comfort he could for the man and decided he ought to get going. "The cells are too crowded for me to sleep in, so I'll be taking a room at the Hotel Montana. I can come back here later after I'm settled in if you want."

Boddington shook his head. "Me and the boys will keep an eye on things here. It's our job. We'll do it. We'll come fetch you if we need you."

Halstead saw the Upman boys were enjoying their beer and decided he should probably come back to check on things after he got something to eat. He would not trust those two to keep the beer warm, much less help Boddington watch the prisoners.

He tucked one of the Winchesters under his arm, opened the jailhouse door, and slid his rifles into the scabbards on Col's saddle. He left the front door of the jail open. The place could use a little air.

Chapter 17

From a hill on the outskirts of town, Ed Zimmerman looked over Silver Cloud through the same field glasses he had taken off a dead cavalry officer the gang had ambushed about a year before. John Hudson had let the remaining soldiers in his patrol go, unarmed of course, in the hopes that their story of the Hudson Gang would carry through their ranks. Zimmerman knew the story would draw the ire of the blue coats but adding to their legend had always been of greater concern to John.

Since all of the lamps along the boardwalks of the main thoroughfare were now lit, Zimmerman could get a good idea of the layout of the town. Buildings of various sizes were huddled together along a single, long main street. A clock tower dominated the sky above the town. It would come in handy if they decided to ride in.

Given the hour, he judged the lights he saw from certain buildings must have been saloons. He wondered which one of them was The Green Tree. Before Zimmerman had sent him ahead, Ace had told him he would set up shop there while he hired on men to back them against Halstead.

"Don't know what you hope to see," Cliff said. "It's pitch black out there."

It was not totally black. There was a half-moon shining in the clear night sky. Zimmerman kept looking anyway. "So says the one-eyed man."

"Don't need two eyes to have enough sense to know there's nothing you can see from this far away," the black outlaw said.

"Common sense means you don't ride into a place afore you look it over," Mick told him. "They got lights burning down there enough for Ed to see plenty."

"I don't feel like ridin' into no trap," Bug added. "If it takes looking through them glasses to make us safer before we go in, I'm all for it."

Cree said, "Ace not coming out to see us is a bad sign, boys. Mighty bad. He should've been here an hour ago by my reckoning."

"Your reckoning ain't worth spit." Bandit pulled his coat closer at the neck. "That randy bastard is probably gettin' himself ridden by one of them sportin' ladies while we're freezing our asses off up here on this damned hill. You know how you can't count on him for nothin' except whorin' and gamblin', Ed. Should've sent me in there like I asked."

"You're a worse heathen than Ace ever was," Bug said. "You'd be doing all the things you're saying he's doing and worse if you were down there instead of him."

Zimmerman enjoyed listening to the banter of his men as he looked over the town. And they *were* his men now. The more they argued amongst themselves, the less likely they were to unite against him when things got thick. And things would get awfully thick awfully fast. He had no doubt about that.

He decided to stir the pot a little. "What about you, Pole? Any complaints about my administration so far?"

"Nope," Pole answered. "I ain't here to think."

"Good man." Zimmerman lowered his field glasses and tucked them back into his saddlebag. He had seen enough to make his decision, but Cliff had been right in his own way. There was only so much he could see from this distance.

"You up for taking a ride, Bandit?"

"Sure am," he said.

"Good. I want you to ride down there and find a saloon called The Green Tree. Once you find it, ride past it and look the town over. I want to know where the sheriff or town marshal's office is. The bank and the general store, too. Then double back and go into The Green Tree. Ask one of the gamblers if they've seen Ace. Don't ask the bartender."

He looked at Bandit despite the darkness. "I repeat. Don't ask the bartender. Bartenders are a chatty bunch who remember people, and I don't want you being remembered. Not just yet. You can have one drink to blend in but make it a beer. No whiskey."

"I've got it." Bandit sulked. "No whiskey. Just beer."

Zimmerman wanted to make sure he understood. "If I smell whiskey on your breath when you come back here, I'll kill you. If you're not back here in an hour, I'll kill you. That clear enough?"

"I said I got it," Bandit answered. "But don't worry. I know what you need me to do."

Zimmerman knew he did. Like Ace, Bandit could

always be relied upon to do what he was told. That was why he was fairly certain Ace was dead, but he needed to be sure before he decided how to approach the town. "The rest of you men should set to building a fire. No reason for us to freeze up here while we're waiting. Get some coffee and biscuits going. If we go into town, we won't have time for supper."

The men laughed as they dismounted and went about carrying out his orders.

Bandit edged his horse next to Zimmerman's and said, "You want me to ask about Halstead while I'm at it?"

"No," Zimmerman told him. But then another thought came to him. "Don't ask about Ace right away, either. Hang around for a bit after you order your beer. Listen to what the men are talking about. You might not have to ask about Ace or Halstead at all. In fact, it would be better if you didn't. Just listen to what they say. And remember what I told you about the whiskey. Be back in an hour. Don't forget."

"I won't forget," Bandit said as he put the spurs to his horse and rode down toward the town.

Zimmerman watched him ride away beneath the light of a half-moon and thought back to another hillside atop another Montana town not so long ago. He had been a follower then, a Darabont man through and through. The Devil's Cut to the bone.

But Darabont was dead and now he was the man in charge of a group of his own. Zimmerman vowed he would not make the same mistakes his mentor had made. He would not leave his enemy alive to live to fight another day. He would not find himself handed over to Blackfoot

Indians, who buried him up to his neck while red ants ate him alive.

Jeremiah Halstead was one of Aaron Mackey's men. Darabont had underestimated the drive and commitment of a man he wrote off as a small-town sheriff. A wise man never turned his back on a fighter like Mackey. A wise man used such men to test his own mettle.

Zimmerman would do so in the case of Jeremiah Halstead. If the young deputy killed him, so be it. But if Zimmerman killed him, he would use that death to build upon what Darabont had started long ago. A band of outlaws that would hold the territory in terror until it extracted everything they wanted.

He closed his eyes as he smelled the fire the men had built and wished he had been the one to have burned Dover Station down. He had missed his chance then. He would not repeat the mistake here at Silver Cloud.

He climbed down from his horse and led it to the campfire. "Get it moving, men. I'm dying for some coffee."

Bandit rode through town at an easy gait.

He knew he only had an hour before he had to get back to Zimmerman and the boys, but being on time would not count for much if he had an incomplete report. Zimmerman was a hard one for details and Bandit did not aim to disappoint him. John Hudson had let things slide when this had still been his gang, but Zimmerman had always been a different sort. He wondered if that difference might be the reason why one Hudson brother was in jail, the other was dead, and Zimmerman was now running things.

Bandit kept such thoughts to himself, as opinions tended

to only confuse things. He found it best to keep a clear head and a focused mind, which he did now as he rode along the thoroughfare.

He was glad the jail was the first building he spotted on Main Street. It happened to be across the street from The Green Tree Saloon, which seemed to be doing a bustling business. There would certainly be plenty of chatty types in there. More than half his work was already done. Now all he had to do was find the general store and the bank and he could hit up The Green Tree for some information and a beer. Maybe two if he was quick enough about it. He doubted even Zimmerman could tell if he'd had more than one.

He slowed his horse a bit as he took a closer look at the jail on the other side of the street, hoping he might catch sight of Halstead in there. Instead, all he saw was a stocky man behind a desk and two other men. One was fat and the other skinny. They looked like the number ten standing next to each other as they were. There was no sign of Halstead.

He kept his slow pace as he kept riding up the street. There was certainly more to the town than he had first thought. It might not have been as spread out as other towns like Rock Creek was, but they had managed to pack in a whole lot of town into a much longer space.

Other stores and shops and saloons were mixed together. Couples strolled and barflies flitted from one saloon to the other. He did not bother to remember the names of the saloons as he imagined each one was just as good as the next. Only The Green Tree mattered, and he had already found that.

He caught sight of the large clock tower that was part

of the bank. He made special note of where it was, just like Ed had told him to.

Across the street was the telegraph office, which was closed now, and the Silver Cloud General Store was right next to it. This was all good news for Bandit. Ed would be pleased that all the places he was interested in were bunched together throughout the town. It would make it especially easy for Bandit to remember.

Bandit had fallen into a bit of a lull as he took in the town. His horse had lapsed into an easy lope as if he, too, was enjoying the ride.

Bandit pulled on the reins a bit when he saw a man dressed in all black riding just ahead of him. It was too dark by then to see his features, but the mustang he rode looked awfully familiar. He and the others had spent most of the previous day seeing the same view as they chased down Halstead and John Hudson.

He practically pulled his horse to a full stop when he saw the man climb down from the saddle in front of a large building. The sign in front of it read the Hotel Montana.

The lamps on the boardwalk were not particularly bright, but bright enough to show the tan, smooth face of the man they had been chasing. The same man who had killed Weasel and Harry.

Jeremiah Halstead in the flesh.

Ed had told him to find out what he could about Ace and Halstead. He had not told him what to do if he actually saw Halstead.

But Bandit did not need anyone to tell him to do the obvious. He knew Zimmerman wanted Halstead dead. And he aimed to give the new boss exactly what he wanted.

He pulled his Colt from his hip and drew a careful aim

at Halstead just as the lawman reached the front door of the hotel. Bandit's horse shied away as he snapped off three quick shots at him.

Through the gun smoke, he could see Halstead had fallen but could not tell if he had hit him.

He snapped the reins to get closer to the boardwalk, his gun aimed at where he knew Halstead had fallen.

Bandit had only noticed the deputy had dropped to a knee just before a bullet ripped the hat clean off his head. A second shot slammed into his right shoulder and a third hit him in his right side.

Instinct overcame thought and Bandit spurred his horse away from the man as fast as it could move. More shots rang out at him as he raced along Main Street. He thought about turning to return fire, but realized his right arm was flapping against his side and his gun was gone.

He rounded the corner when he reached the end of Main Street and jerked his horse to the left. He rounded what looked like a feed store and spurred his horse to take another left down the back of the buildings along Main Street.

Bandit's bare head sent a shock of cold through his body as he sped through the night wind. His right arm was numb, and he could feel the warmth of his own blood spilling across his belly. He kept his left hand cracking the reins and did not dare feel for blood. He could not risk falling. He had to get back to Zimmerman as soon as he could and tell him what had happened.

It was too dark for him to see how far he had left until he reached the end of town, but the light spilling out from an upcoming alley told him he was heading in the right direction.

He had just about reached the alley when, out of the corner of his eye, he saw Halstead charging out of the alley on his mustang. Horse and rider crashed into him at full speed, sending Bandit and his horse tumbling aside and off balance.

His horse screamed as its legs failed, and momentum from the impact sent it and Bandit falling to the right. Something in the back of Bandit's mind told him to jump off, but there had been no time. He screamed as his right leg was crushed beneath the weight of his horse. A lightning flash of pain coursed through his body as the horse rolled off him, got to its feet, and galloped back the same way Bandit had been riding.

Good, Bandit thought as he heard his horse run into the night. *At least Zimmerman will know what happened. I told him what he needed to know after all.*

He rested his head on the ground and looked up at the half-moon shining high above him. Although the horse had run off, he still felt pinned to the ground. He had seen enough men in his condition to know he was done for. His right arm was numb. He was bleeding from the side and his right leg was crushed.

But he had seen his shot and taken it. He had known the consequences and had no regrets save for one. He would not be able to spit in Halstead's face. He would not live long enough to see that bastard die.

He could feel his pain begin to ease a little and a kind of lightness come to him. He knew this was it. The end was rushing toward him. And he imagined there were worse ways to go than to do so while looking at the moon.

But his view of the moon was blocked by the dark outlinc of a man. A man blacker than the night that surrounded him. To Bandit's dying eyes, he seemed to absorb the darkness around him and make it even darker. The only brightness he saw was the glint of moonlight caught by the barrel of the pistol this figure now aimed down at him.

His voice sounded like the darkness itself. "Zimmerman send you?"

Bandit coughed and felt the warmth of his own blood fill his mouth. "Yeah. And you'll be seeing him. Real soon."

"Maybe. But you won't."

Bandit tried to curse when he saw the barrel flash but did not hear the bang.

Chapter 18

Boddington ran out onto the boardwalk as soon as he heard the shots. He had not had the time to grab his Winchester and did not think to go back for it now.

He knew the shots had come from the direction of the Hotel Montana, the same place where Halstead had said he was going. He knew the man was in trouble.

He ducked his head back into the jail and yelled to his deputies, "You boys get your rifles and stand guard here."

Boddington drew his Colt and began running along the boardwalk. He had been fast as a younger man, but now in his early forties, found he did not have the same wind he had once enjoyed.

He ran as fast as he could, ignoring the pain each step caused in his broken nose. He dodged the curious townspeople who had begun to gather on the boardwalk now that the shooting had stopped. He raced in between couples without apology. He pushed tipsy men aside as he looked for some clue as to what was happening up the street.

Everyone was looking in the direction of the Hotel Montana, but while he could see the front door of the place was open, no one was gathered there. He figured that whatever had happened there had since moved elsewhere. The single shot he heard ring out from behind Main Street told him it was over, which only served to make him run faster.

He was forced to skid to a halt when a crowd clustered at the mouth of the alley that ran between the land office and the barbershop was too thick for him to get through. He jumped down into the thoroughfare and made his way around them.

He saw Bob Willbury standing at the front of the crowd, holding an old mining lantern aloft.

"You see what happened?" Boddington asked the old miner as he peered into the alley.

"Saw that new marshal of yours go charging along here like a bat out of hell," Willbury told him. "Afraid my lamp can't cast a light that far."

Boddington peered into the darkness and raised his pistol as he called out. "That you, Halstead?"

"Come along," the deputy answered. "It's over."

Boddington took Willbury's lantern from him and ordered the crowd to stay where it was. No one looked like they were anxious to defy him.

His Colt leading the way, Boddington walked gingerly in the darkness, unsure of what the lamp might reveal at the end of the alley.

When he reached the end, he lifted his lantern and found Jeremiah Halstead standing over a man splayed flat on the ground. The lawman was dumping his spent cartridges on the corpse and filling the cylinder with fresh bullets from those on his belt. His mustang was calmly standing off to the side, untethered and unbothered.

"Take it easy, Boddington," Halstead said without bothering to look up. "He's as dead as he's liable to get."

The sheriff lowered his Colt as he approached the dead body. The lantern cast light on an ungodly sight. The man's right leg was at an ugly angle and flatter than it ought to be. The belly of the man's shirt and coat was splattered with blood. and his right arm had clearly been bleeding.

The hole in his forehead was still smoking. The vapor, he supposed, escaping a warm body on a cold night.

"Bring the light closer," Halstead told him as he fed the last of the fresh bullets into his pistol and flicked the cylinder shut. "I need to see his face."

Boddington did as he was told. "You mean you killed him without getting a good look at him?"

"Didn't need to, seeing as how he shot at me first."

They both took a knee as Boddington held the lamp close to the dead man's head. His vacant eyes were a mix of anger and surprise. "Who was he?"

"One of Zimmerman's men," Halstead confirmed. "I figured it was, but now I'm sure. Saw him through my field glasses when I turned to face them yesterday. Don't know his name, not that it matters now."

Boddington noted how Halstead had said it. Another man might have said he was one of the bunch who had been chasing him since Rock Creek. But not Jeremiah Halstead. No one chased him. He had turned to face them.

"Seems to me like you're getting pretty good at killing these Hudson boys," Boddington said. "By what you told me, this one makes four, don't it?"

"Still six of them out there," Halstead said, "and one of me."

"Six against four," Boddington corrected him. "Me and my boys will be with you. Some of the others in town, too. They'll find Silver Cloud ain't no field of daisies. This town's got grit." He looked down at the dead man on the ground. "When word about this starts to spread, we'll have no trouble getting volunteers."

"Volunteers to help us or to protect Emmett Ryan's interests?"

Boddington could not see the difference. "In this instance, it just so happens that they're both on the same page of the ledger."

"And what happens when they're not?" Halstead asked. "What happens if I have to go up against Ryan? What then?"

Boddington did not like the question and was glad he did not have to worry over an answer because Doc Mortimer and a couple of men he had drafted to assist him ran into the alley. The doctor's oil lamp leading their way.

Mortimer ran his light over the dead man and glared up at Halstead while his two assistants turned away and gagged. "What in God's name did you do to this man?"

"His horse faltered and rolled on him," Halstead reported. "That's why his right leg is like that. Crushed the middle of him, too, near as I can see."

Mortimer pointed at the hole in the man's forehead. "The horse do that, too?"

"No. That was me. You'll find two more like it in his right shoulder and his right side. I think the belly wound would've killed him even if the horse hadn't rolled on him, but you can be the judge of that."

Mortimer shook his head as he took a closer look at the dead man on the ground. "We had an outbreak of Yellow

Fever a few years back. Lost about one person a day to it for a couple of weeks." He looked up at Halstead. "Congratulations, Mr. Halstead. You're the deadliest thing to hit this town since."

"Lucky me." Halstead holstered his Colt on his hip. "I've got to check into the hotel. I'll be there the rest of the night if you need me."

Boddington said, "I'll walk with you if you don't mind."

But Halstead surprised him by saying, "It just so happens that I do. Mind, that is."

Boddington thought he was joking at first, but quickly saw he was not. "What's gotten into you?"

"Back there in the jail just now," Halstead explained, "I saw the look on your face when Greenly told us Cassie was Ryan's woman."

Boddington was glad that was all this was. "He mocked me, Halstead. He threw things in my face, only things she could've told him. Private things I'd hoped would stay private. I lost my temper and went after him. You can't hold that against me."

"I'm talking about before that," Halstead explained. "When he first mentioned Ryan favored her. You didn't look surprised or even angry. I almost thought it might've been jealousy, but that's not possible, given the kind of work she did. You looked like you had just lost your best friend. You didn't know about her and Ryan, did you?"

Boddington felt sweat break out on his upper lip and knew how Greenly must have felt when Halstead went to work on him. "No, I didn't."

"And since Ryan's your boss, you figured he'd respect you enough to leave Cassie alone. He knew you had feelings for her, didn't he?"

"Ryan's not my boss," Boddington tried. "I'm elected by the people, just like the mayor."

Halstead pulled one of the sheriff's fancy dark cigars from the inside pocket of his coat. "And where did these come from? You can't afford these on your salary. I'd bet the mayor's got a box just like these on his desk, too. Maybe with an envelope full of money as a reminder of who you really work for."

Halstead put the cigar back in his pocket. "No need to deny it, sheriff. It's the same in every town I've ever been in. I'm not blaming you for it. I'm just telling you I know where your loyalty will be if it comes down to it. Which is why I need you to keep your distance until we have a chance to talk to Ryan about all this."

Boddington had figured Halstead would want to talk to Mr. Ryan when that idiot Greenly mentioned his name. "I'll send word to him first thing tomorrow morning. See if he can't see us in the next day or so."

He could not tell if Halstead believed him or not. The deputy marshal was an awfully hard man to read, even harder in the darkness. "I'll be at the Hotel Montana if you need me for anything else tonight. I'll be by the jail first thing tomorrow." He looked back at the dead man at the end of the alley. "I think we've all had enough excitement for one day."

Boddington stood in the center of the alley and watched Halstead walk back to his horse and climb into the saddle. The crowd that had spilled out in between the boardwalk parted as he rode the mustang past them and toward the Hotel Montana.

When he was out of sight, Boddington walked back to

Doctor Mortimer as he examined the man Halstead had just killed.

The doctor was hastily jotting something down in his notebook by the light of his lamp. “That man can’t leave town fast enough for my tastes. I can’t complain about the business he sends my way, but death seems to follow him wherever he goes.”

Death, Boddington thought, *and destruction.*

Chapter 19

For the second time that evening, Halstead wrapped Col's reins around the hitching post outside the Hotel Montana. He patted the mustang's neck as he said, "Let's hope no one takes a shot at us this time, old girl."

The small group of townspeople who had gathered in front of the hotel scattered when Halstead walked up the steps onto the boardwalk.

Only two people remained in front of the open door of the hotel. A short, well-dressed man with dark features, a square jaw, and a pin in his paisley ascot. A shorter woman whose thick black hair was pulled back into a tight bun stood next to him. Her dark red dress was plain, but Halstead could tell the material was expensive.

The man cocked an eyebrow as he looked up at Halstead. "May I help you?" His English was accented, but his voice deep and clear.

"My name is Jeremiah Halstead and I'd like a room for the night," he said in Spanish. "Maybe two nights if it's available."

The woman looked at him in disbelief at hearing her

native tongue coming from this man. "Your Spanish is flawless, sir," she responded in kind.

"It should be," Halstead told her. "It's my native language."

The man's cold demeaner melted a bit as he extended a hand to their new guest. "Forgive me, sir. We had been told you were a half-blooded Indian."

Halstead smiled as he shook the hotelier's hand. "Don't believe everything you hear. My father was white, and my mother was from Nogales."

The couple smiled widely then. "I am Antonio Reyes, and this is my wife, Maria."

He exchanged pleasantries with the couple who beckoned him to come inside. "Please, allow us to make you comfortable. Would you like us to place your horse in our private stable in the back? I assure you it's quite safe."

"That's one of the reasons why I'm here," Halstead told them as he went inside. "You come highly recommended by the bartender down at The Green Tree."

"Todd has been a good friend to us over the years," Maria said as she hurried behind the front desk.

A young man of about eighteen who looked like a younger, taller version of Antonio entered the lobby from a back room. Antonio told him to take Halstead's horse to the stable and tend to it carefully. The boy did it without question.

"That is my son, Miguel," Antonio said proudly. "Everyone who works at the Hotel Montana is family. You may rest easy while you stay with us."

"Nogales," Maria sang as she turned the hotel register for Halstead to begin filling out. "My father was from

Nogales, but I was born in Arizona. Antonio and I both were."

"So was I," Halstead told them as he signed the register. "But when my mother died, my father sent me to live at a mission in El Paso." He saw the disappointment on their faces and quickly added. "He was a sergeant in the cavalry and couldn't raise a young boy on his own. The nuns at the mission took very good care of me."

Antonio looked at the pistol handle jutting out above his stomach. "From what we have heard, sir, you can take care of yourself these days."

The new rig he wore was getting an awful lot of attention. He was beginning to wonder if he should try something more subtle, but he was growing awfully used to having both guns readily at hand. Now he knew why Mackey always wore a belly holster instead of a gun on his hip.

He finished filling out the register and flipped the heavy book around so Maria could add whatever she needed to add. He gestured toward the front door and the bullet holes in it. "Hope nobody got hurt when that idiot opened fire on me just now."

"The only casualty," Antonio said, "was a picture I have never liked in the first place."

Maria tapped her husband in the chest. "That was a picture of my mother, God rest her soul."

Antonio was wise enough to change the subject. "You said you may be here for a day or two?"

Halstead did not like sharing his plans with anyone, but he felt he could trust the Reyes family. By staying there, he already was. "It could be longer or shorter, depending on what orders I receive from Helena. Count on one day at least for certain. You can send a telegram to my boss in Helena and he will confirm payment."

"We have plenty of time for that," Maria said. "First we must give you our best room. And don't worry about the hole in the door. We will leave it there with pride, showing the world that the great Jeremiah Halstead chose our hotel to stay."

Halstead felt himself blush. "Just about the only great thing about me is all the trouble I seem to be causing around here."

"Have all of the men you have killed in Silver Cloud tried to kill you first?" Antonio asked.

"Yes, they have."

"Then this is not trouble, sir, but justice," Antonio told him. "You will be safe here. The front door is locked every evening at nine o'clock sharp and my brother Ignacio keeps watch over the place until we open again at dawn."

Halstead was glad the place was as safe as Robinson had claimed it would be. "Why?"

"We have many saloons in Silver Cloud," Maria explained. "Many drunken people who forget where they are supposed to be staying. Some of them have less honorable intentions in mind. We live here, too, and sleep better knowing a guardian is watching over us. Ignacio is a quiet man but has the ears and eyes of an owl. That is why we call him *El Buho*."

Halstead smiled. "There are worse things a man could be called. Believe me. I've been called just about all of them."

Maria came around from the other side of the desk and linked her arm with his. "And now, you are called a guest of the Hotel Montana, and we are proud to have you. Come, let me show you to your room."

Ed Zimmerman was the first man to his feet when he heard a horse rapidly approaching the camp in the darkness.

The others quickly got to their feet and moved away from the fire. The sounds of hammers being thumbed back on pistols reminded him of crickets in springtime.

Zimmerman left his pistol holstered, knowing there was a time to act and a time to listen.

But there was no doubt that the sound of the approaching horse was a bad omen. It was heading fast for the camp with no sign of slowing down. Bandit had not called out, either, though he must have seen the small cook fire by now. He was smart enough to know better than to ride into a camp of armed men unannounced, even if the men were his friends.

Zimmerman's concerns proved valid when the horse broke from the darkness and charged straight for the fire. The outlaw sidestepped the frightened animal and grabbed hold of its reins, putting tenderness in his voice as he called for it to be calm as he pulled it into submission. He had always had a way with horses and had not lost his touch.

"That's Bandit's horse," Cliff said as he and the others thumbed down the hammers of their pistols. "Where the hell is he?"

The others joined him in asking questions to which Zimmerman was trying to answer by looking the horse over. The entire right side of the horse was filthy and caked in drying mud, but its left side was relatively clean.

He ran his hand over the animal's right side, but the horse shied away from his touch. Zimmerman persisted and touched the animal's front leg, which caused it to almost buck. He stopped his examination and loosened his hold on the reins, allowing the horse to have some freedom to move on its own. It was clear to see that it favored its right legs, its foreleg in particular.

He checked the saddle next and saw that Bandit's Winchester was still in its scabbard on the right side, though the wooden butt stock was now cracked. Bandit was a man of many flaws, but he had always kept his weapons in pristine condition and admonished the other members of the gang when he felt they did not do the same.

Even before he noticed the blood on the saddle horn, the evidence forced Zimmerman to draw only one conclusion.

"Bandit is dead," he told the group.

None of the men said a word. None of them questioned him or gasped in surprise. He was only confirming what they had already known when the horse returned without its rider.

"That bastard Halstead," Cree said, breaking the silence. "That no good, son of a—"

"Knock it off," Zimmerman yelled. "Getting angry won't bring Bandit back. Neither will curses or threats." He let go of the reins and allowed the horse to join the others picketed close by. He faced the men, who had all stepped into the fire light. "And we're not going to ride into town with guns blazing if that's what you're thinking. We're going to take our time. We're going to plan this out and we're going to do it together. Sneaking around to try to get a handle on Halstead hasn't worked too well for us."

"As I recall," Bug said, "it was your idea to send Ace running here hell bent for leather to try to hire on men for us."

"And to send Harry out to talk to Halstead while Weasel snuck into that stand of pines to get him," Mick added.

"Now there's four of us dead," Cliff added. "All thanks to that big brain of yours. Never placed as much stock in it as John did. And look at where it got him."

Zimmerman smiled. The men were not just standing near the fire. They were standing in a line against him. And every one of them still had their pistols in their hands, though they weren't pointing them at him. Yet.

Only one man had kept his mouth shut. "What about you, Pole? You got anything you'd like to add?"

"Nope," Pole said. "Like I already told you, thinking ain't my best quality."

"I'm afraid I'll have to insist on an answer this time," Zimmerman told him. "It's four against one at this point. I'm not John Hudson. Every man has an equal say in this bunch, including you."

Pole shrugged. "I follow whoever's in charge. Right now, you're in charge so I reckon I'll still follow you. We're all still alive, which says something about you knowing what you're doing. And since we didn't see how Ace or Bandit got killed, who's to say they didn't do something that got themselves that way. I doubt Halstead got a good enough look at all of us to know who we were just by sight. Ace had a big mouth. Probably drew attention to himself. And Bandit was awfully sore about Ace probably getting killed. Most likely saw Halstead and tried to take him on by himself. Yeah, they're probably both dead. They might be in jail, too, which is about the same for all the good they can do to us there. Can't say that's your fault or not, so my money's still on you."

Pole looked at the remaining members of the Hudson Gang. "But if you boys decide to pick a new leader to head this bunch, I'll go along with whoever you say. You'll get no trouble from me. I'm keeping my powder dry for that Halstead devil. I think we all should."

Zimmerman watched Mick, Bug, and Cree, as each looked at Cliff. The black man was the biggest in the group and the oldest. Zimmerman knew if anyone was to replace him, Cliff was the likeliest choice.

Ed Zimmerman remembered what Alexander Darabont had done on those many occasions when he was faced with a similar situation. He did not bristle when the rabble he led challenged his authority. He simply stood before them, heard their complaints, and used the power of suggestion to get the horde to follow him wherever he went. He had a gift for being able to make men believe his decisions were actually their idea.

Zimmerman's nature being what it was, his first inclination was to gun down Cliff as an example and force the others into submission. But he decided to give Darabont's way a try first.

"I'm glad you men felt free enough to speak your mind," Zimmerman said. "But I want to remind you of a couple of things. Confronting Halstead in the pines was not my idea. A couple of you suggested that and, when Harry asked my opinion, I said Weasel's idea sounded best. All of us agreed Harry should be the one to try to distract Halstead while Weasel snuck around the back, including

Harry. Halstead proved to be more capable than we, all of us, thought."

He looked at each man in turn to watch his statement settle in with them before continuing. "I didn't take control of this group. You men chose me, remember? And we all agreed that Ace's horse was in the best condition to make a dash to Silver Cloud. As a matter of fact, I recall Cliff was the one who looked over the horses and told us that very thing. Didn't you, Cliff?"

The big man said nothing. He simply glared at Zimmerman with his remaining eye.

Zimmerman went on. "Sending Ace also made sense because he said he had friends in town he could hire to join us in freeing John. I don't remember any of you having any objection at the time. Not even Ace. I certainly don't remember any of you volunteering to go. I know I didn't."

Zimmerman could sense their resolve weakening, though Cliff kept staring at him. *Two points down. One to go.*

"Now, I'll admit that sending Bandit into town was my choice," Zimmerman went on, "though he volunteered to go. I didn't order him to do it, but I did order him to keep a low profile when he did so. I even warned him not to drink, didn't I, Mick? You were closest. You heard me, didn't you?"

Mick toed the dirt with his boot. "Yeah. I heard you tell him that. Told him just to listen and find out what he could pick up about John and Ace and Halstead."

Zimmerman kept himself from smiling. Any hint of arrogance could turn the tide against him and force him to kill Cliff. He did not want to shoot Cliff. He had no idea if Ace had hired on any men in Silver Cloud and would prefer to ride against Halstead with six guns instead of five.

"Given the condition his horse is in, it looks like Bandit was discovered. Either that or, as Pole said, he saw a chance to kill Halstead and, against my orders, tried to gun him down." He nodded toward Bandit's horse, which was nosing the grass with the other horses along the picket rope. "You could say that animal is an example of what happens when people don't follow my strict orders, couldn't you?"

Cliff took a long step toward him, then stopped. "That sounds an awful lot like a threat, Zimmerman."

Zimmerman had hoped to have been more subtle than that, but he remembered Cliff was a blunt man. "Of course not. I've ridden with you boys long enough for you to know me pretty well. I never threatened a single man in this outfit, and I never will. I'm also not the enemy, fellas. I'm just one of you, trying to figure out how to spring John from jail and, the way I see it, the best way to do that is to kill Halstead. Anyone think any different?"

None of the men responded. Cliff continued to glare at him.

"I'll take that as a yes," Zimmerman concluded. "So, the only question is how we go about doing that. I had been hoping Bandit would've returned with some details about the layout of the town and other details, but since that's not going to happen, we're going to need a new plan."

"And just what might that be?" Cree asked.

"I'd kind of like to hear that myself," Mick added. "Might help me decide whether or not you're still the one to run this outfit."

Zimmerman knew he had turned them. All of them except Cliff, who only continued to stare at him in silence.

Zimmerman asked them, "I take it we all still want to free John?"

All of the men nodded. Even Cliff.

"Good. And since sending in men one by one doesn't seem to be working very well, I say we should ride in as a group. This very night."

"And tomorrow?" Cliff asked.

"We strike. And if you'll give me a few moments, I'll tell you exactly how we're going to do it."

Chapter 20

Jeremiah Halstead had almost forgotten how good a thorough washing could feel. A quick shave had scraped away the stubble and made him feel even better.

As he toweled away the shaving soap from his face, he looked around the room. Maria Reyes had not been exaggerating when she had told him it was the finest room in the Hotel Montana. The bed was just about the biggest and softest he had ever seen. There was even an outdoor balcony that gave him a decent view of Main Street, not that there was much to see at that time of night.

As he finished wiping the shaving soap away from his face, he saw a much older man than his twenty-four years looking back at him. The soft brown eyes his mother had once loved had turned harder since coming to Montana. Maybe prison had done that to him. The lines around them were deeper. His skin was still light brown but had grown paler without exposure to the bright Texas sun.

His face had grown gaunt and his shirt collar hung loose around his neck. This was due to his three years in prison and the winding road he had taken since his release. The road that had led him north to Dover Station and the grave of his father.

His life had been a much longer road than he had ever expected it to be, but he had no complaints. He could blame others for some of the suffering he had endured along the way, but not for the path he had chosen. He had decided to become a lawman because he sought a profession that would have made his father proud. Decisions had consequences, and those of Jeremiah Halstead had been no exception. Not even the betrayal that had sent him to jail had been enough to make him regret his decision.

Whenever his confidence began to waver, which happened more often than he cared to admit, he looked at the silver star Mackey had pinned to his coat and remembered that this was the man he was. The man he had become.

He finished toweling off and began getting dressed. He had brought another change of clothes in his saddlebags, which Maria had been kind enough to iron for him. As he dressed, he wondered what Mackey would say about what he had done from Rock Creek until now. Would he approve? Would he be angry? Was there something he could have done better. Was there something he should not have done at all?

Halstead figured he should start putting together his report to Mackey, at least in his mind, but decided it might be bad luck to do so. There had already been enough attacks on his life in the past couple of days to remind him how dangerous this assignment was. He did not want to tempt fate by beginning a report he might not live to finish.

Now fully dressed, he knew he should be hungry, but was not. He was too anxious to eat and too tired to even think about food. He had never known a weariness like this. He was too tired to even sleep. He had heard of other people having that problem, but he had never experienced it until that evening. He needed sleep, but the run-in with the Hudson man earlier that night made sleep impossible. He felt like an overwound clock and wondered if some night air on the balcony might do him some good.

But going out there unarmed might get him killed. He looked at his pistol rig hanging on the headboard but did not have the energy to put it on. He grabbed his Winchester repeater instead and stepped out onto the balcony.

The balcony was large enough to span the width of the front of the hotel. He walked to the railing and set his rifle against it as he took in Silver Cloud at night.

It gave him a view of the town that was much better than what he could see from the ground. He saw the rectangular light on the boardwalk cast by the sheriff's office at the end of Main Street. He still did not understand why a jail would have such a big window and had wanted to ask Boddington about it, but events had prevented him from bringing it up. He thought they should at least board it up while they were holding Hudson, Greenly, and Brad. All that glass just tempted fate even in the best of times. He made a mental note to take up the notion with Boddington when he saw him in the morning.

He remembered the telegram the clerk had delivered to him just after he had gotten settled in his room. Antonio had insisted the clerk give it to him instead of allowing him up to the room. He did not want anyone to know exactly where the deputy was staying.

Antonio apologized to Halstead for the inconvenience, but Halstead told him there was no need to apologize. He knew the hotelier took the security of his guests seriously and he was grateful for it. The hotel was the first truly civilized place he had been since leaving the comforts of Helena. He would make it a point to stay here whenever he had call to be in town in the future. Even if Mackey balked at the cost, he would gladly pay for it out of his own pocket.

Transporting prisoners was tough enough in the elements, so when he had a chance to enjoy a bit of comfort, he would take it.

If I live long enough, he reminded himself.

He unfolded the telegram and read it. The light that spilled out from his hotel room allowed him to do so without bothering to light the lamps on the porch. It was a terse message typical of Mackey.

> GOOD NEWS ABOUT HUDSONS. REMAIN IN TOWN UNTIL FURTHER NOTICE. STAY ALIVE.

He had hoped a second reading of the telegram might help him understand it better, but it had not. He put the telegram back in his pocket and leaned on the railing. Why was Mackey ordering him to stay in Silver Cloud? His mustangs were hearty and well rested. He could make the trip back to Helena in a day of hard riding. The land between here and the capital was relatively flat, and he might make it in better time than that.

There were only six Hudson men left, and he was confident he could outrun them. Their horses had recovered from the chase from Rock Creek, but they were still out of shape and overweight.

The Hudson Gang was already on the outskirts of town. The man he had killed proved that. They would be in town by morning if they were not already here. He figured Zimmerman must be in charge of them by now and probably had been since Halstead had killed Harry Hudson.

Sending Ace ahead of them, even if it had cost him a horse, was a smart move. Sending the second man into town as a scout had been smart, too, though the man he had sent in had been dumb enough to try to kill him. Halstead figured the man must have recognized him and, with his back turned, decided to take a chance on killing him.

The dead man's horse had probably run back to the camp, which meant Zimmerman already knew his man was dead. He may have only known Zimmerman by reputation, but from what he had heard of the man, he doubted he would make the same mistake twice. The gang would come in force now. All six of them together. And they would bring trouble with them when they did.

Halstead knew he should not feel alone, but he did. Boddington was a bully; the kind of man Katherine Mackey might call a bore. But he was tough and knew how to handle himself. He could count on him to fight if things got thick. But his deputies, even without the injuries Halstead had inflicted on him, were a different story. He sensed no grit in them and knew they followed Boddington's lead. There was no way of telling how a man might act once the bullets started flying. He doubted they would run, but if they got rattled, all they would do is waste valuable ammunition. The best he could hope for from them is to draw fire and stop bullets intended for Boddington or him.

He felt himself getting wound up again at the thought of what was to come and forced himself to take in a deep breath of cool night air and hold it. All of this was out of his control. The time for making a run for Helena was long past. The Hudsons were on even ground with him now. All he could do was make the best fight of it he could and hope the townspeople were as tough as Boddington had boasted.

He slowly released the breath he had been holding and focused on the town instead. He admitted it was a pretty place by lamplight. He could hear the music echoing along the deserted streets, but it was kept to a dull roar. He saw men staggering from one saloon to another, but nothing that drew his attention.

The thoroughfare was deserted save for a single man riding at an easy pace toward his hotel. The jangle from his gear mixed in with the saloon sounds that reached the balcony.

The dappled gray he rode looked familiar, even though he could not see much in the weak lamplight along the boardwalk. The rider managed to keep the horse within the thin band of shadows that ran along the middle of Main Street. The outline of the rider looked like he was wearing a rumbled hat and coat, but Halstead could not see enough to be sure.

But the closer the man got to the hotel, the more every instinct in Halstead's body told him this man was Ed Zimmerman. He remembered the way he had seen him sit on his horse outside the stand of pines near Rock Creek. He only wished he could see the scalps hanging from his saddle horn so that he could be absolutely sure it was him.

But even if he'd had his field glasses in hand right now, he doubted he would be able to see that much detail in the darkness. It was tough to get a fix on a man who rode the shadows as well as this man did.

He could see the rider look up at him as he approached the hotel. Halstead took his Winchester in hand and held it on his hip. He knew he was silhouetted by the light from his room, which made him an easy target. He needed the rider to see his rifle. He needed the rider to know that he had been seen.

The man and his dappled gray continued their easy lope past the hotel and kept riding along Main Street, remaining in the shadows until he rode into the darkness at the end of the thoroughfare.

Halstead kept his rifle on his hip for a while longer and wondered if he had made a mistake. The Jeremiah Halstead of El Paso would have plugged the man on general principles. If he'd found he had shot the wrong man, the people would have understood. So would the judge. An innocent mistake in a lawman's quest to save his life. Jeremiah could have even lived with the mistake, something he had learned from his time in Texas.

But Montana was a long way from Texas, and Aaron Mackey would not accept one of his men killing a man simply on a feeling. Halstead knew Mackey had never been the kind of man to hesitate to kill, but only when he knew who he was killing.

He sat down in one of the chairs on the porch and kept the rifle across his lap. The cool air helped dull the growing ache in his head. If trouble came for him, he would hear it. He would be ready.

* * *

Halstead jumped out of his chair when he felt a gentle hand on his shoulder. He whirled around with his rifle, ready to blast whoever his attacker might be, when he saw it was only Antonio Reyes. The hotelier stood calm and erect, with his hand on the chair where Halstead had slept in.

It was only then that Halstead realized it was morning. He had spent the entire night out on the balcony. That beautiful bed had gone to waste.

"Good morning," Antonio said in Spanish. "I hoped you had spent a comfortable evening last night. Was the bed not to your liking?"

Halstead stood up from his crouch and immediately regretted it. His back and legs hurt, and his head ached even worse. His arms were stiff, and his feet felt overstuffed in his boots.

"Looks like I fell asleep out here," he admitted. "Never had a chance to try out that nice bed in there." He looked longingly at it and cursed himself for sitting down in the first place.

"I wish I could advise you to sleep in it now," Antonio said, "but I'm afraid you have visitors. I will tell them to leave if you wish."

He slowly forced himself to stand up straight and stretch out the kinks. "Who is it?"

"Sheriff Boddington and Earl Perkins. They said they bring a message from Mr. Emmett Ryan. They say he wishes to see you."

It was only then that Halstead realized Antonio was wearing a gun on his right hip. It was an intricate leather holster, and the pistol it held caught the early morning light. The hotel man obviously kept his weapon in good condition and did not wear it just for show. "You're armed."

"I'm cautious. As I told you, the Hotel Montana always protects its guests." He gestured inside the room. "I took the liberty of bringing you some coffee and tortillas and cheese for your breakfast. I suggest you eat them before you go downstairs, as I believe you may have a very long day ahead of you."

Halstead rolled his shoulders and stamped his feet to get the blood flowing in his body again before he went back into his room. "Thank you, Don Antonio, but it sounds like I won't have much time for breakfast."

Antonio followed him into the room and said, "If you'll permit me to offer a suggestion, I recommend you enjoy your breakfast and make them wait."

Halstead had not been expecting advice. "Why?"

Antonio clasped his arms behind him. "You are a young man, and I am older than you. I have seen more of life than even you have seen in all of your travels. You are Jeremiah Halstead, a deputy United States Marshal. You have made a name for yourself here in Silver Cloud, and I am confident you soon will continue to do so elsewhere. Beside this, you are also a representative of the federal government in Washington. People must learn that such a man cannot be treated like a dog who comes immediately when he is summoned. You must take your time and enjoy your nourishment at a pace of your own choosing."

Halstead appreciated the flattery but pulled on his gun rig anyway. "That's real nice of you to say, but don't believe everything you've heard about me. I'm just running a prisoner from one place to another so a judge can hang him for what he's done. The rest of it just got in the way of me bringing a man to his death. That's all."

"Forgive me, sir, but you are much more than that," Antonio persisted. "You are building your reputation whether you like it or not. Every man does this whether he carries a gun or runs a hotel or farms the land for his living. People will not treat you with the respect you deserve. They will treat you with the respect you demand of them. By taking a few moments to drink your coffee and enjoy your breakfast, you will teach them how to treat you. You will show them who and what you are. Not just a man with a gun. Not just a man of the law. But a man who demands respect in all ways. For the star on his chest. For the man he is."

Halstead smiled. "Even when a man like Mr. Ryan summons him?"

Antonio's eyes flashed. "Especially then."

Halstead finished putting on his rig while the older man's words sank in. He supposed the man had a point. He had never really thought of it that way. "If I stay here too long, you're going to make me pretty cocky."

"Only fools are arrogant, my friend, and you are no fool. A man like you will never be arrogant as long as you remember who and what you are. That is the only way others will know it, too." He gestured to the tray of coffee and tortillas and cheese on the table. The silver coffeepot and the smell of warm tortillas reminded him of his childhood in El Paso. And his stomach reminded him of how hungry he was.

"Take fifteen minutes to refresh yourself," Antonio encouraged him. "Fifteen minutes isn't a very long time here. Mr. Ryan is a busy man. He can afford to wait for you. But you cannot afford to be weak when facing your enemies."

Halstead decided Don Antonio had a point and went over to the table and sat down. Don Antonio smiled as he poured him a cup of coffee from the silver pot.

"You think Mr. Ryan is my enemy?"

"I don't know." Antonio finished pouring the coffee and wiped the spout with a napkin before placing it on the table. "And neither do you. You must treat every man you meet for the rest of your stay in Silver Cloud as if he is your enemy until he proves he is not."

Unable to resist the smell of the tortillas and cheese any longer, Halstead began to fix himself breakfast. "Thank you for the advice, Don Antonio. Tell them I'll be down in a bit."

Antonio bowed as he walked away. "It is I who should thank you. Maria said you are too skinny and must eat. If I were to bring your tray back to her untouched, she would be very angry with me. My wife is a wonderful woman, but her temper frightful."

Halstead laughed, truly laughed, for the first time since he had left Helena. "Looks like we've both got our challenges, doesn't it?"

"Every man does," Don Antonio said as he left. "It's how he faces them that counts. Your horse will be saddled and ready for you immediately."

Chapter 21

As he descended the stairs with his Winchester, Halstead enjoyed the angry glares he drew from Boddington and the man with him he figured to be Perkins. The stranger looked like a miner. He may have been average height, but he had broad shoulders and a thick neck and arms that he must have earned from a lifetime of working in the mines.

Antonio's son, Miguel, came to him and offered to place the rifle on his horse, which was waiting out front. Halstead handed it to him and thanked him for the offer.

The stranger interrupted Boddington's attempt at an introduction. "You finish taking your bath, sweetie?"

Halstead nailed him with a right cross to the jaw he never saw coming. The miner dropped like a sack of wheat to the lobby floor.

Boddington looked down at the fallen man. "I warned you to be nice, Earl. The good deputy here doesn't take kindly to sass." He winked at Halstead as he flattened the bandage on his nose. "I learned that the hard way."

The man uneasily got to his feet as Halstead said, "I'm Jeremiah Halstead, Deputy United States Marshal of the Montana Territory. You'll call me deputy or Mr. Halstead.

Not Jeremiah, not Jerry, and sure as hell not sweetie. Do it again and Ryan's going to have to find himself another lap dog."

Perkins shook his head to clear it and made a move toward Halstead. Boddington easily stepped in front of him to block him. "Mr. Ryan wants to see us at our earliest convenience. I've known Mr. Ryan long enough to know that means right now. I imagine he doesn't hold much weight as far as you're concerned, but he's a mighty powerful man around here. Best to leave as soon as possible."

Halstead did not care about what Ryan wanted. "How far is his place from here. I think I saw one of the Hudson men in town last night, but I couldn't be sure. Even if I'm wrong, they're definitely close if they're not in town already. We'll need to keep an eye on the jail in case they try to spring them."

"Already thought of that," Boddington told him. "Tim and Dan have the jail locked up tight and are loaded for bear. No one will get in the place while we're gone. I can promise you that."

"And what about that pretty window you boys have?" Halstead told him. "One chair through that thing and Hudson's boys will crack that place wide open."

"Don't be so sure," Boddington said. "That glass is a lot thicker than it looks. It's stopped many a bullet in its day. It's the same type of glass Mr. Ryan installed on the windows at the bank. The last bunch that tried to break it got cut to ribbons without even making a scratch. As it just so happens, Mr. Ryan's place is only a short walk from here."

Perkins smirked. "Sounds like you're all out of excuses, *Mister* Halstead."

Halstead did not like it, but he imagined Boddington knew what he was doing. He'd had his reservations about Perkins before he had met him. Now he was sure of them. "Are you going to take us there or does Boddington have to show you the way?"

"I know it well enough," Perkins sneered at him. "Follow me."

The home Emmett Ryan kept in town was not what Halstead had been expecting from a man of such wealth. The inside of the place was narrow, almost cramped. The furnishings were comfortable, but simple and looked like they may have come from a catalog from one of the stores back east.

The only expensive-looking part of the place was the large shelves crammed with books in the front room. They all looked well-worn and were not just for decoration. Reading had never been Halstead's strong suit, and books had never held much interest for him, so he was not surprised that none of them looked familiar. Some of them were not even in English.

Boddington sat at the edge of his upholstered chair as if he was afraid he might break it.

"Sit back," Halstead told him as he crossed his legs. "You look like a schoolboy."

"Mr. Ryan prefers a certain formality from his guests," Boddington told him.

"Sounds like you know him pretty well," Halstead observed.

"I should. I was a foreman in his mines for ten years."

Halstead had not known that. He was about to ask him

more when the side door opened and Emmett Ryan walked in wearing a wide smile. Perkins entered behind him and remained in the doorway.

"Forgive me for making you gentlemen wait so long," Ryan said, "but it couldn't be avoided."

Halstead stood and shook the hand he offered. "Jeremiah Halstead, Deputy U.S. Marshal."

"I've heard." Ryan grinned at him. "Your reputation precedes you, deputy."

Halstead was not sure if that was a good thing. He did not care, either.

The mine owner turned his attention to Boddington. "Barry, my old friend." The two men surprised Halstead by embracing each other as if they were brothers. "It's been too long. I take it the jail is treating you better than the mines ever did."

"Different type of toil, Mr. Ryan," Boddington said, "though it's nice to enjoy the daylight now and then."

"Good man," he said as he leaned against his desk and gestured for the men to sit back down. "I understand you two have quite a lot to handle these days since you've brought that Hudson fellow into town." Halstead heard a hint of a brogue as Ryan spoke. Not as thick as Pappy's had been, but enough to notice.

"As for you, deputy, you've made quite an impression since coming to our humble hamlet in the hills."

"Just doing my job," Halstead said. "A job we're anxious to get back to, so I'd appreciate it if you could tell us why we're here."

"It's how you do your job which is the reason why I wanted to see you, deputy." He gestured toward the bandage on Boddington's broken nose. "The way you go about your job is a tad too forceful, don't you think?"

Boddington tried to play it down. "That's all water under the bridge, Mr. Ryan. A misunderstanding is all. We're both well past it, aren't we, deputy?"

Halstead looked at Ryan. "What's it to you?"

"What's it to me, he asks." Ryan's gray eyebrows rose as he looked back at Perkins by the door. "Did I hear him right, Earl?"

Perkins dead-eyed Halstead as he nodded.

"It means quite a bit to me, deputy," Ryan told him. "I know you're new here and have been too busy since your arrival to know we do things a certain way in this town."

"Your way," Halstead said.

"And why not?" Ryan asked. "After all, Silver Cloud is my town. Always has been. Always will be. It was nothing but a jumped-up mining camp at the base of the hill when I came here. Now look at it. A thriving concern that not only provides services and comfort to my workers, but a way of life for the people who call this place home. Everything that happens here is my business. All those who live here my family, the only family I have in the world. And all those who pass through here are my guests." He leaned a bit at the waist. "That makes you my guest, deputy. And while we try to be as hospitable as possible to outsiders, we also require them to be polite while they're under our roof."

He pointed at Boddington's nose. "That was most impolite, deputy. So was the vicious assault you inflicted on his deputies. A broken arm on one and a busted head on the other. Most impolite indeed."

Halstead was beginning to see where this was headed

and crossed his arms. "I get it. I broke something of yours and you're mad about it."

"Mad?" Ryan shook his head. "Nae. Incensed is more like it. Barry Boddington has been with me for a lot of years. First as a foreman and now as the man who keeps order in town. My town."

"Your town," Halstead said. "Your man."

"That's right." Ryan grinned. "You're a quick one, aren't you?"

"A quick what?"

Ryan leaned forward and spoke clearly. "A quick half-breed. Or at least that's what I've been told you are. In my experience, the native savages of these parts have always been an ignorant bunch of heathens at best, but you're a different sort. From Texas, I hear. That would make you, what? Apache? Comanche?"

"American," Halstead said. "For what it's worth, my father was white, and my mother was Mexican."

"Still a breed as far as I'm concerned," Ryan went on, "though I've no quarrel with the Mexican people. Always found them to be hard working folks. Especially the whores."

Halstead fought the urge to backhand him for the implication. He touched his own ear instead. "Your accent is different. I'd bet you're from Ireland, aren't you? I hear a bit of a brogue in your voice."

Ryan looked genuinely surprised. "I certainly am. You've got quite a pair of ears on you, boy. I thought I'd lost my brogue a long time ago, but a bit of the old country seems to follow me no matter how far I roam from it. I'm surprised you could hear it."

"Some of the nuns that raised me were from Ireland,"

Halstead said. "I got pretty good at picking up what part they were from by hearing them talk, but I can't place yours."

"Wexford," Ryan said. "Southern part of the island. I doubt you've heard of it."

Halstead smiled and looked away.

Ryan's smile faded. "What's so funny?"

"Nothing. Just remembered something my friend's father used to say. Something about the best thing to come out of Wexford was the road to Dublin." In fact, Pappy had said the same things about most counties in Ireland, except for his beloved Longford.

Ryan's eyes narrowed. "And the best road for you to take, Deputy Halstead, is the one that takes you back to Helena. You and your prisoner. The sooner the better. For your sake."

Halstead was glad he had found a way to get to the man. Even from the grave, Brendan Mackey's tongue was as sharp as ever. "Why the rush to get rid of me so soon? I'm curious."

"Because you're trouble, that's why. The people of this town haven't known a moment's peace since you arrived. First you assault Barry and his deputies, and we've already established they're my men. Then you killed not one, but two men yesterday. One in The Green Tree Saloon and the other in an alley off North Street."

"Don't forget about Cassie," Halstead reminded him. "Cassandra Browne. She died while I was here, too. You going to blame me for her death, too? You can if you want, but somebody already tried that once. Didn't end too well for them."

Mr. Ryan feigned astonishment. "Why, Deputy Halstead.

If I were a less-confident man, I could take that as a threat."

"Take it any way you like." Halstead glanced at Perkins by the door. The man had taken a step forward but had not reached for the gun on his hip. "But I'm not threatening you, Ryan. I'm asking a question. Somebody killed her. Who do you think did it?"

"I haven't the slightest idea," Ryan said. "Why would I?"

"You just told me this is your town and that you know everything that happens in it. Also said you're responsible for everything that happens here, too. What about Cassie, Ryan? You responsible for killing her too?"

"Halstead," Boddington whispered. "Careful."

But Halstead was beyond being careful. "What about it, Ryan? I asked you a question."

"Cassie Browne," Ryan repeated as if trying to recall something. "You mean the whore who was found dead in the alley? What possible reason in the world would I have to kill her?"

Halstead had to admit he was awfully convincing. "Someone sent her to see me when I first got into town. I figured it was you."

Ryan laughed. "I only rely on whores for certain things at certain times, deputy. Information is not one of them."

Halstead sensed the tension grow in Boddington beside him but stayed with Ryan. "I hear different. I hear Cassie was a favorite of yours."

Ryan was no longer laughing. "You hear wrong, Halstead."

"Not this time. Greenly told us everything."

Ryan snapped a look at Boddington. "Is that true? Why

is this the first I'm hearing of this? Barry? Answer me, damn you."

But Boddington only looked down at his boots as he dug his fingers into the arms of the chair.

"Don't get mad at him, Ryan," Halstead continued. "We've both been kept pretty busy since Greenly told us everything. Too busy to clean up your messes for once."

Perkins took one step too close. Halstead got to his feet as he pulled his Colt from his belly holster, freezing Perkins in place. "Unbuckle your belt, let it fall to the floor, and put your hands on the bookcase."

But Perkins did not comply. "Just give me the word, Mr. Ryan, and this breed will find himself in the bottom of Old Mary in no time."

Ryan pushed himself off the desk and held out his hands. This time, his shock was real. "What's the meaning of all this? Deputy, put your gun down. Perkins, do as he says before he kills you."

"Best listen to the man." Halstead thumbed back the hammer of his Colt. "I won't tell you again."

Perkins cursed as he undid his gunbelt and let it fall to the floor. He faced the bookcase and put his hands against it.

Halstead kept his gun on Perkins as he said to Ryan, "You'd best get over there next to him. I'm placing you under arrest for the murder of Cassie Browne."

Ryan's eyes darted from Halstead to Boddington and back again. "Has everyone in this town lost their damned mind? Why in God's name would I want to kill a whore? Yes, I slept with her from time to time. Yes, I wanted to keep it quiet because I didn't want her throwing my name around hoping it would get her special treatment. That doesn't mean I killed her."

Halstead was more than happy to tell him. "That special treatment include you giving her fancy books to read? Books like the ones in that case Perkins is holding up for you now?"

"Books?" Ryan asked. "What books are you talking about? I wouldn't waste a handbill on her much less a book."

Halstead scrambled to try to remember the titles. "*The Prince* and *Leviathan* and *The Communist Manifesto* sound familiar?"

"This is absurd." Ryan seemed to forget all else and went to check his bookshelves. "I'd no sooner give those books to her than I'd give an alley cat a steak. It's too much meat for her, and she'd never be able to finish it."

Boddington gripped the armrests tighter as everything unfolded around him.

Halstead watched Ryan check his shelves and watched him grow frustrated when he could not find the books in question.

"They aren't there, are they?" Halstead told him. "Because they're locked away in the sheriff's desk at the jail. Seems like she was a lot more to you than just a working girl. You don't give a woman like that those kinds of books if you don't think much of her."

Ryan ignored him as he took out one book and placed it on another shelf. Halstead tracked his movements while he kept his gun on Perkins in case he had a gun stashed among the books. "These are all out of order. I never put them back like this." He stepped away from the case and ran his hands over his hair. "It just doesn't make any sense."

Boddington spoke through gritted teeth with his head down. "Maybe Cassie took them when she was here last."

"Don't be stupid, Barry," Ryan chided him as he kept examining his collection. "I never let that yellow-haired cur anywhere near my home."

Boddington slowly raised his head. And when he did, he was looking at Perkins. "Maybe he stole them and gave them to her. Maybe he's the one she laughed at instead of Greenly."

Ryan's mouth opened as he looked at Perkins.

Halstead realized that fit and he gripped his pistol tighter. "What about it, Perkins? Were you in town the other night running an errand for Ryan here? You send her to me for information so you could make yourself look good in front of your boss? What happened? Did you push her too far? Did she laugh at you? Was that it?"

Ryan began to approach his foreman like a man slowly waking from a dream. "Earl. I know you were in town that night but tell them they're wrong. I don't care about the books, but by God, tell them you didn't—"

Perkins turned from the bookcase. A small .22 pistol in his left hand.

Halstead and Boddington fired at the same time, both shots hitting him in the center of the chest.

The derringer went off as he fell back against the shelves and began to slowly slide to the floor.

Ryan cried out as he fell, and Boddington rushed to his side.

Halstead kept his gun aimed at Perkins as he walked

over to him, stepped on his hand, and scraped the tiny pistol away from it with the side of his boot.

The foreman looked up at Halstead as he gasped for breath. The red bubbles rising from the holes in his chest meant Perkins was not long for this world. Halstead still needed some answers from him.

"That was Cassie's gun, wasn't it? The one you took from her and killed her with. Why?"

"She wanted to be better," he gasped. His breathing became more labored. "I wanted to be better. I told her we were supposed to be together, but she laughed . . ."

His body went slack. His breathing stopped, and his chin sagged against his chest. His eyes took on that vacant look that Halstead had seen countless times before. A gaze that saw nothing in particular, but possibly everything a man could hope for.

Halstead opened the cylinder of his Colt, removed the spent cartridge, and let it drop onto Perkins before replacing it with another from his belt. "He's dead," he announced as he snapped the cylinder shut and tucked the Colt back into the holster on his belly. "How's Ryan?"

"Shot in the leg," Boddington said. "Went straight through but not before hitting the bone."

"Sounds bad," Halstead said flatly. "You'd best fetch Doc Mortimer. We wouldn't want our owner to die on us, now, would we?"

Boddington got back to his feet and ran from the room as fast as he could manage.

Ryan had propped himself against the bookcase and undid his ascot. "I can't believe it. I can't believe Earl would kill her over that. Over nothing. She was just a whore." He looked over at Perkins's corpse. "All of this bother over a lousy, yellow-haired whore."

Cassie's words came back to him like a whisper on the wind. "We're all whores, Ryan. In one way or another."

Halstead turned and left the wounded man alone and prone on the floor with the body of the monster he had paid to protect him.

Ryan called after him, "Don't you think this is the end of it, half-breed. You've made an enemy here today. An enemy the likes of which you've never seen before. You'll pay for what you've done here today. You'll pay, by God, if it's the last thing I do."

Halstead did not bother to answer him. There was no point.

It was not until he reached the front door of Ryan's house that he heard a blast that shook the ground. He ran outside and looked down Main Street and saw smoke and flame billowing from the jail.

The Hudson Gang had come to Silver Cloud.

Chapter 22

Halstead unwrapped Col's reins from the hitching rail, jumped in the saddle, and raced toward the Hotel Montana at a dead run.

Don Antonio was in the doorway, with Miguel and Ignacio close behind. "What do you want us to do?"

"I'm headed to the jail," he told them. "Stay here and stay sharp."

He steered his horse around the panicked townspeople who were running away from the blast, shot down a side alley next to the hotel, and rode down South Street. The thick smoke billowing out of the jail could lead him into riding into a gun barrel. Riding blind was riding reckless, and he could not afford to make a single mistake where the Hudson Gang was concerned.

He took a right at the end of the alley and rode down South Street, where there were fewer people to get in his way and he was less likely to be seen.

A shot rang out high and to his right and he felt the heat of a bullet pass near his head. Halstead sat lower in the saddle and rode as close to the mustang's neck as he could. He did not bother to turn to see where the shot had come from. He knew it had come from the clock tower of the bank. He could not do much about that now. He needed to get to the jail and fast before they freed John Hudson.

He rounded the corner at the back of The Green Tree and jumped down from the saddle, flipping Col's reins around the railing of the saloon's back porch.

He drew his Colt from his belly holster and ran to the corner of the saloon so he could get a better look at what was happening across the street in the jail.

The smoke was too thick to see much at first, but as the wind changed and began blowing east, he saw the entire front of the jail had been blown apart. The front window Boddington had boasted about earlier had been shattered. Its thick glass shards littered the boardwalk and thoroughfare among the broken, smoldering planks of wood that had once been Boddington's office. The smoke was still too thick for him to see if the rest of the jail still stood, but there was no doubt that the front of the building was in ruin.

The amount of glass that far into the street meant the blast had come from inside the jail. How had they gotten dynamite inside the jail? The Upman boys were not much, but he doubted they were foolish enough to leave the jail unguarded.

"That's far enough, Halstead," a man called out from the edge of the smoke.

Halstead's eyes watered as he peered into the smoke looking for the man. A woman screamed. He used his pistol to track the sound of crunching glass as it moved to his left.

The wind shifted again, blowing the smoke northward. That was when he saw Greenly; his skinny arm wrapped tightly around a woman's neck. He recognized her as the same woman who had cradled Cassie's head in her arms the previous morning. The soiled dove they called Daisy.

Greenly sneered at Halstead's pistol from behind Daisy's head. She was much shorter than the lanky pimp who lifted her off the ground as they moved away. Greenly was trying to keep her head close to his own.

"Please!" Daisy pleaded to Halstead. "Please don't let him kill me."

"Shut your mouth," Greenly yelled at her before turning his attention back to Halstead. "Thought you had me dead to rights back there in that cell, didn't you? Thought I'd just wallow around back there, waiting around until you were good and ready to take me up to Helena."

Daisy screamed again as he lifted and pulled her farther away from the smoke.

Halstead's pistol tracked them the entire way.

"You thought old Greenly was just some pimp you could push around?" Greenly laughed. "Come any closer and I'll break her neck."

Halstead remained still. "Don't move."

"You don't give me orders anymore," Greenly bellowed. "You hear?"

"I wasn't talking to you." Halstead fired and the bullet struck Greenly on the top of the head.

As his grip faltered, Daisy broke free and ran past Halstead toward The Green Tree.

Halstead kept his gun trained on Greenly as the man staggered back a couple of steps before dropping to his knees and sagging backward. He remained in that position, looking up at the sky before falling over on his right side.

Halstead crouched when pistol fire from the jail began to ring out and bullets filled the air around him. He made it to the cover of the side wall of The Green Tree Saloon before bullets found his position and tore large chunks from the wall, forcing Halstead farther back than he would have liked.

He heard a voice from behind him mixed in with the gunfire. "It's Todd, Jeremiah. Come in the saloon the back way. There's better cover in here."

Halstead turned and saw it was, indeed, the bartender, and he followed him around to the back door of the saloon. He was glad Col was still where he had left her.

"What the hell happened?" Halstead asked when they were finally far enough away from the gun shots to talk.

Robinson led him through the back door. "I was cleaning the bar when I happened to look up and see a rider throw a stick of dynamite through the open jail door. It sure didn't blow like a full stick would, so I have a feeling they only used half of one."

Halstead cursed the Upman boys. "Why was the door open in the first place?"

"Daisy must've forgotten to close it when she delivered food to the prisoners from Maddie's. Cassie used to do it to pick up extra money, but Daisy started doing it today."

Half a stick of dynamite sounded just about right to Halstead. He had seen some of the inside of the jail through the smoke. A full stick would have blown the entire place into toothpicks.

"How many Hudson men are in the jail?" Halstead asked

as he made his way into the saloon. The few customers that still remained were hidden behind their chairs.

"Sorry, Jeremiah," Robinson said. "I was too busy keeping my head down when the blast hit. It busted in our front window and put one hell of a crack in the mirror behind the bar."

None of that information helped Halstead any. He holstered his pistol, motioned for Robinson to grab hold of one end of a card table while he grabbed the other. They carried it to the closed front door, which had been shredded by the explosion, and set the table down on its side. It would not provide him with much cover, but it was better than standing plastered against the side of the building like he had been.

The pistol fire stopped, and Halstead told Robinson to get the rest of the customers out of the saloon by the back door. As soon as they were clear, he decided to see how closely the Hudson Gang was watching him. He drew his Colt from his belly holster and used the barrel to push the remnant of the front door outward as he ducked out of the way.

More pistol fire rang out again, with some of the rounds easily punching through the table he had just set in the doorway as cover.

Halstead took off his hat and poked his head over the saloon's shattered window to try to get a better look at the condition of the jail.

A good wind had picked up, carrying the thinning smoke up Main Street and giving him his first clear view of the entire jail. He had already seen that the entire office part of the building was a shredded mess. Pieces of the roof had been blown atop other buildings on either side of it and out onto Main Street. Only a few remnants of the walls on either side were standing.

The wall that led back to the cells was still there, though the door to the cells was gone. The back wall did not look like it had given way and he knew there was no back door to the jail. That was good news. The only way in or out was still through the front and, for now, Halstead had that part covered.

He saw the remains of Boddington's desk had been overturned and he saw there were about three men taking cover behind it. The cell doors were all open, but he could not tell if any of the prisoners were still inside.

"Jeremiah Halstead!" a lone voice called out. He did not recognize it. "You still alive?"

"Depends on whose asking," he answered back.

"You are a hard man to kill, Jeremiah Halstead," the voice came back. "Just so happens that so am I."

Halstead figured this was the new leader of the Hudson Gang speaking. The one he had heard was called Ed Zimmerman. "How about you step out into the street and let's find out?"

The man laughed. "You first, deputy. I'll follow your lead."

"Fill me full of lead is more like it," Halstead yelled back.

"Guess that's why you're so hard to kill. Good man. The name's Ed Zimmerman. You might not know me except through your field glasses, but I'm in charge of this bunch now."

"That so?" Halstead yelled back. "I thought John Hudson was still in charge."

"So did I," Zimmerman admitted, "but it looks like ol' John got his bell rung during the explosion. We think he'll be fine, but until then, I'm running things."

Halstead doubted his next tactic would work, but he had to give it a try anyway. "Send him out so the doctor can take a look at him. I promise I won't shoot."

"If I was that stupid," Zimmerman responded, "you and me wouldn't still be having this conversation. But, to show you I've got some human feeling left in me, I'll agree to hand over the deputies to you. On the house. You've just got to decide if you want them all at once or if we should just chuck the pieces out to you as we find them."

Halstead shut his eyes as a great round of laughter kicked up from the jail, echoing across the street. The Upman boys had served their purpose early in this affair.

"Can't guarantee we'll get all the parts in the right places," Zimmerman went on, "but we'll do our best."

Another louder round of laughter came from the jail. Halstead listened hard to try to discern how many men Zimmerman had with him, but it was tough to tell.

Robinson crouched beside Halstead. "Those bastards killed the Upman boys."

Halstead did not have time to entertain the bartender's anger. He called out to Zimmerman instead. "How about you leave those boys where they are while all of you come out with your hands up and empty. I promise you won't get killed, and you'll get a fair hearing in Helena. Come out now and I might be able to keep the judge from hanging you."

That brought the most amount of laughter from the jail. A particularly high-pitched cackle grated Halstead's nerves.

As the laughter continued, Halstead whispered to Robinson. "Go out to my horse and bring me the two rifles I've got there. You have a gun behind the bar?"

"Boddington brought back Brad's shotgun yesterday."

"Good. After you bring me my rifles, I need you to set up back there and keep it trained on the front door. This bunch is liable to make a run at us, and I want to be ready when they do."

Robinson moved away at a crouch as the laughter from the jail died down.

Zimmerman began speaking over the laughter. "That's a nice offer, Mr. Halstead, and we thank you for the laugh. Things have been pretty tense for us for the past two days. Haven't had much to laugh about on account of you."

Halstead decided there was no reason to respond.

"And you being the hot-headed, heroic type," Zimmerman went on, "I think it's only fair that we get a few things straight. You're cornered and alone in a saloon and being surrounded by all those liquor bottles, you might be tempted to stick an old rag in one, light it, and throw it our way. Don't do that. It'll only get a lot of innocent people killed. Not here, mind, but in other places around town."

Halstead did not like the sound of that.

"See, I've done this more than you have, so I know better than to have all my men bunched up in one place. Got 'em spread all over town. Got themselves a fair number of hostages, too. I figure you're pretty good at math and know you've got the Hudson Gang whittled down to about six. You'd be right. But Ace managed to hire on a few more boys before you shot him in the back, and they've decided to honor their commitment to our cause. Seems their hatred of Boddington overcame their fear of you. Any firebombs you chuck this way will only get some good people killed. You don't want that, now do you, Mr. Halstead?"

Halstead doubted Zimmerman was bluffing. He had hit the jail and already gotten what he wanted. But Hudson must have been too hurt to move or they already would have been miles out of town by now.

Zimmerman was in the same fix Halstead was. He was stalling for time until he and his men could make a break for it. He would probably try to hold out until dark when it would be safer to go for their horses. Halstead had not seen them on the street, so he figured they must be somewhere close by. Maybe behind the jail on North Street.

Halstead decided to keep Zimmerman talking. "I didn't shoot Ace in the back. I shot him the same way I'm going to shoot you. Right between the eyes."

He ducked back behind the wall as more pistol shots rang out from the jail. Most of the bullets sailed harmlessly high above him into the bar without coming close to striking him.

Good. Keep wasting bullets.

The last of the gunshots had died away when he heard something rumbling toward him. He shifted his Colt into his left hand and drew the gun on his hip just as the remnants of the front door of the saloon and the table he had placed there were crushed beneath the hooves of a horse. The rider and been crouched low over the saddle as the frightened animal leapt into the building and panicked. Its eyes were wide and wild as it looked for a way out again.

The man began firing wildly in every direction except where Halstead was.

Halstead flipped onto his back and opened up with both guns blazing up at the rider. Two of his bullets missed him and slammed into the ceiling. The other three hit the man in the chin and chest and sent him tumbling from the saddle, crashing down into one of the few card tables the horse had not destroyed.

Fearing the frightened animal might stomp him to death, Halstead holstered one Colt on his hip and grabbed hold of the reins with his left hand. The ceiling of the saloon was not high enough for the horse to raise too much on its hind legs, but it still kicked out wildly while Halstead soothed it down.

"Easy, baby," he cooed as he stroked the horse's neck with his gun still in his hand. "Easy. It's all over now. Calm, baby. Calm."

The horse was hardly at ease, but at least Halstead had it under control. He took the reins and wrapped them around a chair, hoping the feeling might give the animal a sense of calm for the next few moments.

The rider he had shot was still alive, pawing at the bleeding wound under his chin. Halstead could tell he did not have long to live, not that he cared. He did not recognize this man from the stand of pines outside of Rock Creek, and he figured this must be one of the men who Ace had hired in town.

He undid the man's gunbelt and threw it over to the corner that had become his safe haven. He was glad to see the man's slugs matched his own as he was beginning to run low on bullets. He removed the man's regular belt, too, and slung it over his shoulder. He would be putting that to good use very soon.

He pulled a Winchester free from the saddle scabbard and skidded it along the floor toward where he was planning to make his stand. He pulled down the saddlebags, too, and let them hit the floor with a thud. He hoped the outlaw had stowed some bullets in there because he was going to need every round he could get his hands on.

"You in the saloon," Zimmerman called out. "How'd you like the present we sent you?"

The men laughed as Halstead got the dying man to his feet. He had just enough life left in him to stand somewhat on his own as Halstead hauled him up and draped him over the saddle. He used the belt of the dying man to quickly cinch his hands through the stirrup.

He unwrapped the reins from the chair and pushed the horse toward the ruined front door of the saloon. It slipped and skidded on the broken wood before finding its feet. Carrying the dying man across its saddle, it ran into the daylight and toward the jail before taking a hard left and bolting out of town.

"Afraid I didn't like it much," Halstead called out as he dove back to his corner. "Figured I'd send it back. Hope there's no hard feelings."

He was glad to hear more bullets pepper the boardwalk and the walls of The Green Tree. It meant he was starting to get to them. *Good.*

He kept his head low as he took stock of what he had. The outlaw's pistol was empty, so he tossed it aside. He dumped out the contents of the saddlebags onto the floor and a couple of boxes of bullets spilled out. He gladly used them to replace the spent bullets in his revolvers.

He slid some of the other rounds into the empty loops on his belt and kept the rest on the side. He was glad for the ammunition, but pistols would not help him much at this distance. Only his Winchesters would give him a chance to hold Zimmerman and his bunch at bay.

The best he could hope for was to keep the men pinned down in the jail for as long as he could until they decided to make a break for it with John Hudson.

Until that happened, he had no idea what Zimmerman and his bunch might try to do. He could not control it either, so he did not make it worse by anticipating anything. All he could do was hold his ground and make sure he was as ready as possible for anything.

The gunfire stopped again, and he was just about to begin going through what was left in the saddlebags when Robinson returned in a crouch holding both Winchesters. He had also managed to carry Halstead's saddlebags over his shoulder until he reached the deputy.

Halstead could not remember a time when he was as glad to see someone.

He slid the Colt into his belly holster and took hold of the rifles, placing them against the wall beside him. "How are things out back?"

"Your horse is still there," Robinson reported. "But people are hiding back there like a bunch of scared rabbits. They were too far away for me to talk to without shouting, and I didn't want to call attention to us. They seem safe where they are."

Halstead saw there was nothing in the outlaw's saddlebags that could help him, so he tossed the entire mess aside to give himself more room. "What about the rest of town?"

Robinson frowned. "I heard what that fella said, but I

couldn't see much from the back of the saloon, just what was on South Street."

Halstead had to go on the assumption that Zimmerman was telling the truth. He could end this with a couple of flaming bottles of whiskey chucked into the jail, but that would result in a lot of dead civilians. Halstead did not dare risk it.

He spoke more to himself than to Robinson as he said, "He's got a man up in the clock tower. He shot at me as I rode here down South Street. That gives him a fine view of the town and everything in it. And if he had thought to put a man up there, he probably had them in other places, too."

"The general store would probably be doing a good business this time of day," Robinson told him. "And I can think of half a dozen other places he could be, too."

Smart, Halstead thought. *Damned smart.*

Robinson nudged Halstead's shoulder. "Tell me what you want me to do and it's done."

Halstead was glad to have the help, but the bartender was still a civilian and this was not his fight. He needed to keep him safe.

Maybe there was a way he could help and keep the rest of the civilians safe, too. Leaving him in charge of watching the jail was too much to ask, but he thought of another way.

He handed Robinson the Winchester he had taken off the dead man. "Take this and round up the civilians you saw. Bring them to the back door of the Hotel Montana. The Reyes family will make sure they're safe. Stay with them and help Don Antonio any way you can."

But Robinson would not take the rifle. "Never was good with them. My fingers were always too big."

Halstead could not force him to take it. "Fine but get the others to safety and stay with them."

"Like hell I will. This saloon's mine now that you plugged Greenly. I'm not going to let this bunch ride in here and raise hell just because they feel like it."

Halstead was about to argue with him when Robinson pointed to the lookout chair that was now riddled with bullets. "I spent five years bouncing here before I got my turn behind the bar. And I didn't have any shotgun on my lap when I did it. I earned that spot my own way." He held up his pair of large hands and thick forearms. "With these. Give me something else to do, damn it, or I'll find something."

Halstead could tell Robinson was resolved to help in one way or another, so there was no use in trying to stop him. If he was going to help, he might as well do it Halstead's way.

"Fine but getting the civilians to the Hotel Montana still goes. Keep them moving as close to the backs of the buildings as possible. I don't think the shooter in the tower will be able to hit you that way. The angle's too steep."

"I'll remember," Robinson promised. "What then?"

"Once they're safe, see if you can find out if they're holding hostages anywhere else." He held a finger up to him. "Don't go looking around for yourself. Just ask if anyone saw some men entering other buildings. Don't go trying to rescue them." He tried to hand him the Winchester again. "At least not unless you take this with you. I've also got a pistol if you need it."

But Robinson left the firearms alone. "Don't worry

about me. I've got an old friend of mine hanging on the wall in the back who'll help me out. I'll be more useful with something I know."

Halstead held his hand out to him, and they shook. "I don't know whether you're brave or crazy but thank you."

"No braver or crazier than you are," the bartender told him. "I'll let you know what I find out."

Halstead watched Robinson run at a crouch to the back of the saloon, where he paused by the lookout chair, took down a large axe from a pcg on the wall, and headed out the back.

He felt a small amount of pity for Zimmerman's men. Robinson looked mighty comfortable with that axe and probably knew how to use it.

Chapter 23

"We can't just sit here like mice," Miguel Reyes told his father in Spanish. His Winchester was in his hand. "Mr. Halstead is in trouble. We have to help him."

Don Antonio admired his son's bravery but not his stupidity. "We don't know where he is, Miguel, and this is no time to run around town to find out."

"He's in the saloon, papa," his son pleaded. "You saw them shooting at him there just like we all did."

Antonio had seen men from the jail shooting into the saloon. He also knew the boy got his stubborn streak from him. "Yes, I saw it, but we don't know if he's even still alive. He may be dead or dying. I don't want the same thing happening to you. Your place is here with us, keeping your family safe."

Miguel was growing impatient with his father. "If he was dead, they would be riding out of town by now. Mr. Halstead is still alive, and he's all alone down there."

Antonio lost his temper. "And he'll be just as alone if you are with him! I may have taught you how to shoot a gun, but it is different when men are shooting back at you." He looked at his brother for help. "Tell him, Ignacio. You have seen war."

His brother was keeping an eye on the street from the front parlor. He did not speak often, so when he did, young Miguel usually listened. "Halstead knows what he's doing. You don't. If you go there, you may get him killed protecting you. You may get yourself killed, too. Obey your father or I'll take that rifle from you and send you into the kitchen with your mother and aunt."

Antonio was glad Ignacio's words were enough to take some of the fire out of the boy. He remembered the fire he had once had in his belly when he was Miguel's age. And despite all of the years that had passed since, he had no idea why young men were so eager to be reckless with their lives. Perhaps it was because they did not yet know what life really was.

As Miguel sat in one of the chairs by the door, Antonio joined his brother at the window. "How bad is it?"

Ignacio continued to look out the window. "There is a man in the bank tower with a rifle. He can kill anyone on Main Street from there. I saw a woman try to run from the general store, but a large black man grabbed her and bring her back inside. There are many people in there. They must be holding them against their will."

Antonio cursed to himself. "There are likely others elsewhere in town."

Ignacio nodded. "But not here. If they come here, we will kill them."

Antonio rubbed his palm on the pistol at his hip. "Yes, we will, brother. Like before."

"Like many times before." Ignacio let the curtain fall back into place. "I'll go upstairs to Halstead's balcony when it is darker. I doubt anything will happen before then. Trapped men get bolder in the dark, especially when they have nothing to lose."

Both men turned when they heard Maria call out to Antonio from the back of the hotel. Antonio told his brother to keep watch in the parlor as he ran back to check on his wife. Miguel was already ahead of him.

He found Maria and her sister, Mercedes, crouching in the kitchen, pointing toward the back door. "Someone is pounding," she whispered as another series of heavy knocks sounded.

Miguel began to raise his rifle, but Antonio pushed it down and gestured for him to block the way into the kitchen. Antonio pulled his pistol and moved to the pantry at the opposite side of the door.

Through the back door, he heard a man say, "It's Todd Robinson. I've got some people with me who need help. It's safe, I promise you."

Miguel went to open the door, but Antonio stopped him. "If something happens to me, kill anyone who comes through that door."

The boy nodded his agreement to what his father had ordered, and Antonio called out in English, "Is that really you, Todd?"

"Sure is," the bartender answered. "And I've got about ten women and children with me who are scared silly."

Finally recognizing his old friend's voice, he lifted the heavy bar from the back door and opened it. He saw Robinson on the back porch, ushering in the women and children he had brought to the hotel. Maria led them into the hotel's main dining room as Miguel stayed behind.

Robinson stepped in, set the axe he was holding aside, and helped Antonio replace the bar across the back door.

"Forgive me for being cautious, my friend," Antonio said, "but things being as they are, one can't be too careful."

"Don't blame you a bit." The bartender watched Antonio slide the pistol back in its holster and saw Miguel holding his rifle. "I figured you'd be ready, which is why I brought these folks here. Found them huddled behind the church like a bunch of cats looking to get in out of the rain."

Miguel annoyed his father by interrupting them. "How is Deputy Halstead?"

"Full of spit and hellfire." Robinson grinned. "I don't know if they've got him pinned down in the saloon or if he's got them pinned down in the jail. If there's any quit in that man, I ain't seen it yet."

"I should go help him," the young man said.

Robinson set a beefy hand on his shoulder. "The best way to help him is to stay out of his way. If we see anyone closing in on him, we can try to do what we can, but we're more of a help to him from here."

Antonio was grateful his old friend had set his boy straight. Sometimes a son would listen to reason from someone other than his father. "What's happening down there anyway?"

"Looks like Hudson's friends tried to blow up the jail to spring their boss free," Robinson told him. "Killed the Upman boys for certain, but they only destroyed the front part of the jail. The part where the cells are is still standing, but the cells are open. I figure they've got about five men in there, hunkered down behind good cover. They said they've got men all over town with guns on people in case anyone makes a move on the jail, but I don't know that for certain."

"My brother said there is a man in the bank tower and some men in the general store," Antonio told him. "There are likely men elsewhere, but we don't know where."

Robinson had clearly not known this. "Sounds like we're up against a pretty smart bunch. Think I'll take a look around so I can tell Halstead where we stand."

Antonio knew he could not talk Robinson out of it. His friend had always been a brave, if stubborn, man. "You can't go with just an axe. Take my rifle with you. Or my pistol."

Robinson waved him off. "Best if you keep them. You're liable to be needing them before all of this is over. Besides, I've always been better with my hands anyway."

"Let me go with you," Miguel said. "I can shoot pretty well. My father and uncle taught me."

Antonio bristled at his son's arrogance. "Forgive my son's poor manners, my friend. His mother and I indulge him too much."

Todd inclined his head toward the hallway and Antonio figured he wanted to speak in private. Antonio told Miguel, "Stay here and listen at the back door. Others seeking shelter may come. Do not open the door. Just come get me if they do."

Miguel did not look happy about being excluded but did not dare defy his father further.

When they reached the front desk, Antonio told Robinson, "My son is a handful."

"Can he ride?" Robinson asked in a hush tone.

"Like the wind," Antonio said proudly. "With or without a saddle. Why?"

"Because I've got a feeling that just might be the best way he can help us," Robinson said. "He's anxious and excited and we both know he'll only get underfoot if he stays around here. I say we put that energy to good use. If you think he's up for it, I think we should send him to Helena for help."

Antonio did not like the idea. "Can we send a telegram instead?"

"I can't be certain," Robinson admitted, "but I'm pretty sure this bunch is smart enough to have already cut the telegraph lines between here and Helena. Riding there would be the only way we could get word to them."

Antonio thought it over. He had made the trek to the capital many times and knew the trail well. It was reasonably flat terrain and the path easy to follow. On a good horse, the boy could make it in under a day, but it was already well past noon, and he would not be able to make it before nightfall.

"He would have to ride in the dark if he left now," Antonio said. "I don't know if he is ready for that."

"He might not be, but his horse sure would," Robinson pointed out. "Halstead rode into town with two mustangs. One is still tied up behind the saloon, but the other is stashed in the livery. All your boy would have to do is point himself toward Helena and the horse will help guide the way back to its home, even in dark."

Antonio had not thought much about Robinson's plan before but decided it just might work. It also might help save the town if the Hudson men did not leave later that night.

"His mother won't like it," Antonio said, "but we must try something." His mind was made up. Miguel would ride to Helena. "I only ask that you escort him to the livery first. The man in the bank tower has a rifle and may shoot at him. I would feel better about it if he had someone to watch over him between here and the livery."

"Consider it done," Robinson said.

"Antonio!" Ignacio called out from the front parlor. "Something is happening. Come quick."

Antonio and Robinson joined him at the window and looked in the direction where Ignacio was pointing.

They watched Sheriff Boddington pushing a man in a wooden wheelchair along the boardwalk on the opposite side of the thoroughfare. Doc Mortimer trailed behind them carrying a medical bag. They were headed in the direction of the jail.

Antonio had to squint to see the man in the wheelchair was Emmett Ryan. His leg was propped up and stuck out before him like a battering ram.

"What the hell are they up to?" Robinson asked aloud.

"I don't know," Antonio admitted, "but I think we're about to find out." And it just might be the distraction they needed.

He pulled Robinson away from the window. "Come. We haven't a moment to lose."

Chapter 24

Boddington carefully eyed the street as he pushed Ryan and the heavy chair along the boardwalk. The wheels of the chair squeaked something awful, and he knew they had probably drawn every rifle in town. At least it drowned out the pounding of his own heart in his ears.

"I still think this is a bad idea, sir," Boddington told Ryan. "Things are pretty hot down at that part of town."

"This is still my town, Barry, and I don't want them getting any hotter," Ryan said. "Hence our journey into the mouth of the beast."

If we make it that far, Boddington thought.

"At least let me go down there and take a look around first," Boddington asked. "Make sure it's safe."

Ryan laughed despite the circumstances. "And risk you joining forces with Halstead against them? Or worse, getting yourself killed by avenging the attack on your jail?" The rich man shook his head. "Not a chance. Besides, you wouldn't want to leave me and the good doctor exposed on the street without protection, would you?"

Boddington cursed himself for thinking he could outsmart Emmett Ryan. The man was always one step ahead of everyone, especially him. He supposed that was why he ran things and Boddington just did whatever he was told to do.

"I've been shot at before," Doc Mortimer said. "I know how to handle myself."

"No need with the good sheriff here to watch over us," Ryan said.

The sheriff and the doctor strained to carry Ryan and his chair across the mouth of the alley to the other side before they continued the slow trek down to the jail. The amount of debris from the jail in the thoroughfare surprised him. And the likelihood that both of his deputies were dead finally struck him. They might not have been much, but they had been his, and he felt a certain amount of responsibility for their deaths.

"Miserable bastards," Boddington said aloud. "Must've used a whole bunch of dynamite to crack my jail."

"Half a stick at most," Ryan observed. "Maybe even a quarter stick. A whole stick would have destroyed the place and killed everyone in it. I know my explosives, Barry, and so did you once upon a time. All this town living has made you soft."

But Boddington's blood was up. "Had I been there instead of stuck in that house with you—"

"You'd be dead," Ryan finished the thought for him. "I already lost one good man today because of Halstead. I'd hate to have lost you, too."

When they reached the ruined jail, Boddington was surprised to see the entire front part of the building had been obliterated in the explosion. The roof was gone and only a few planks of the walls remained standing. The back where the cells were located seemed to be in decent condition. The smoke drifting from the place burned his eyes.

"Hello in the jail," Ryan called out. "This is Emmett Ryan. That name mean anything to you?"

"Mr. Ryan," came an immediate reply. "Sure, I've heard of you. Don't think there's a man in the territory who hasn't."

"Good. Then you know I mean you no harm. I am in a wheelchair and we are unarmed, save for the sheriff who only has a pistol. Who am I talking to?"

"Ed Zimmerman," the man said. "Sorry for all the trouble, but it couldn't be avoided. What's on your mind?"

"We mean you no harm," Ryan said once more. "We're just here to talk."

Boddington tried to see where Zimmerman was, but all he could see from that angle was the edge of his overturned desk in the middle of the rubble. The man must be talking from the cells.

"Glad to hear it," Zimmerman answered, "not that there's any harm you could do to us even if you were of a mind to. I've got men all over town who'll put a bullet in your brain if you move funny and don't forget it."

"I won't forget," Ryan assured him. "I've brought the doctor with me to tend to any of your men who might be injured."

"No need for a doctor," Zimmerman said. "Undertaker might come in handy, though. Got a couple of dead men on the street. A couple in here, too. Look like they were deputies. I can toss out their pieces to you if you want. Halstead didn't want them, but maybe you will."

Boddington gripped the handles on Ryan's chair until

they cracked. Doc Mortimer grabbed his arm to steady him down.

Boddington looked over at the saloon while Ryan talked to the man who had destroyed his jail. The front of the place was riddled with bullet holes. Every window was shattered. He spotted a dead man lying in the middle of the thoroughfare and realized it was Greenly. He figured that was probably Halstead's doing. He imagined the deputy was holed up somewhere in the saloon and probably had him in his sights right now. He would not blame the man if he shot them down just for speaking with Zimmerman.

Ryan said, "Since we can't offer you any medical help, I was hoping we could come to something of an understanding."

"Depends on your idea of an understanding, Mr. Ryan."

"Silver Cloud's my town and these people are under my protection," Ryan said. "What's happened already can't be helped. I'm not here to talk about that. I'm talking about what happens next."

"And I've been thinking of nothing else," Zimmerman answered. "What do you propose?"

"That you and your men ride out of here right now without harming anyone else. The damage has been limited to the jail and the saloon at this end of town and I want to keep it that way. So, if you boys agree to ride out of here now, take whoever you came here to take with you, I can guarantee you safe passage."

"And how does an old man with a busted leg in a wheelchair propose to do that?" Zimmerman asked.

"By remaining here with you while you mount up and leave here in peace. Sheriff Boddington will see to it that

Halstead doesn't bother you while you climb on your horses and go. I'll also be glad to put myself in harm's way to prevent anything from getting out of hand."

The laughter that came from the ruined jail cut through Boddington like a knife.

No one had laughed at him in years.

Zimmerman spoke over the laughter. "That's a mighty kind offer, Mr. Ryan, but it sounds to me like you're offering me a bill of goods I already own. I won't fight your claim on the town, but for the time being, it's mine. I've got men all over the place who'll take care of anyone who tries to take it from us until we're good and ready to leave. And if your sheriff is anything like his deputies, I doubt he'll be much help to us against Halstead. But I like the way you think, so I'm willing to make a deal with you."

"I'm listening," Ryan told him.

"If you can convince Halstead to lay down his weapons and come out of the saloon with his hands up, I'll not only promise not to kill him, but me and my men will withdraw immediately. Hand your town back to you lock, stock, and barrel with nary another drop of blood being spilt."

Ryan seemed encouraged. "Is that all?"

"There's a condition," Zimmerman called back.

"I figured. What is it?"

"That Halstead agrees to stay here until sunup tomorrow. After that, he's free and clear to come after us if he wants." Zimmerman paused for a moment to let the offer sink in. "That's more than fair, don't you think?"

Boddington knew Halstead would never go for it, and it was a waste of breath discussing it. But he also knew Ryan was his own man and would do whatever he wanted.

The mine owner looked toward the saloon. "Halstead. You been listening to all of this?"

"Sure have," the deputy called back.

"I won't ask you to come out with your hands up, but can you at least agree to allow them to ride out of town on their own without shooting them?"

Boddington flinched when a loud boom came from the saloon and he saw the top of his overturned desk crater inward. One of the men using it for shelter was thrown backward. His rifle skittered through the debris. He did not have to see the fallen man to know he was dead by the twitching of his boots.

The remaining men in the jail began firing at the saloon until Zimmerman yelled for them to save their ammunition.

When the shooting stopped, Zimmerman said, "Guess you've got your answer, Mr. Ryan. I don't hold it against old Halstead, though. I'd do the same in his shoes. Still doesn't do much for you, I'm afraid. But my offer still stands if you can get Halstead to go along. If not, well, I guess we're going to be stuck here a while until we can reach some kind of understanding."

Ryan pounded the arms of his chair and muttered, "This is unacceptable."

Zimmerman added, "I also know a man like you doesn't like taking no for an answer. You're probably ready to boil over right now, and you're thinking about making some kind of threat. I'd suggest you hold your tongue as you're in no position to do much of anything. I told you I've got men all over town and I meant it. I told Halstead that a lot of good people will get killed if he tries anything and the same goes for you. I know you've got men up in the hills working your mines and I know what a rough bunch miners can be. If you care about them, you'll leave them where they are. Their dynamite, too. I plan on leaving here when I choose to, and you don't want me coming back here when I'm done. Now, tell me you understand that and be on your way."

Boddington watched Ryan's jaw set on edge and knew the man was steaming. But he knew Zimmerman was right. They were out in the open here on the boardwalk with no telling how many rifles aimed in their direction. They were in no position to make any threats. Ryan's foolishness had put them in a bad way. He only hoped his mouth did not get them killed.

Zimmerman called out, "Cree, you know how much I hate waiting on an answer."

A rifle shot rang out from the clock tower and split the air between Boddington and Ryan.

"Next one goes through your head," Zimmerman said. "Now, by God, I'll hear you agree to my terms."

"I agree, damn you," Ryan spat. "I agree."

Zimmerman laughed. "Good boy. Off with you then. You've got five minutes to get off the street or my men will kill you."

Boddington turned the chair and quickly began wheeling him away before the miner's pride got the better of him. Doc Mortimer led the way, walking much quicker than he had on the way to the jail.

"Don't forget to work on Halstead," Zimmerman called after him. "He's the fly in the ointment here, not me, and don't you forget it."

Chapter 25

Zimmerman took off his hat and plopped down on the cot that had once been used by Halstead. John Hudson was still in the same cell they had found him in, even though the door was still open. The narrow doorway provided them some measure of cover from Halstead's bullets.

"Well," Zimmerman said as he crossed his legs on the cot. "That sure was eventful."

Hudson clearly did not appreciate the humor. "I've had enough of eventful to last me a lifetime, Ed. I still want to know how the hell you plan on getting us out of this."

"Can't say as I have much of a plan," Zimmerman admitted. "I figured we'd blow the jail, get you out of here, and be on our way. Most of these places have a back door of some kind, but this place doesn't. I also wasn't planning on Halstead still being alive, much less having us pinned down like this. I thought sending that boy to charge the saloon might've put a dent in Halstead's defenses. At least wounded him some. But it looks like that failed, too."

"You and your damned theatrics," Hudson spat. "If you'd

just gunned down those deputies instead of blowing the place up, we would've been clear of this place by now."

"Maybe," Zimmerman allowed, "but Halstead would've been right on our trail. He would've picked us off one by one as we made our getaway. You've spent more time with him than we have, John. You know how tough he is. Facing him in open country, especially with him behind us ain't likely odds." Zimmerman took a quick look out the door at the gory sight of the hired man Halstead had shot through the desk. Half of his head was gone. "That boy can *shoot*."

"He killed my brother," Hudson said. "I'm the one he ought to be worried about, not you."

Zimmerman thought about that. Hudson's criticism about his theatrics was certainly understandable. Perhaps the dynamite had been too much. Reports he had received of Halstead being in the jail had proven wrong. If he had known there were only two deputies in the jail, he would have handled things differently.

But there was no use in worrying about what had already passed. They were in the thick of it now, and there was nothing to be done about it except see it through. There would be plenty of time for regret later, but for now, he needed a plan.

He decided to dump it back into Hudson's lap. "You've always been the brains of the outfit, John. What do you think we ought to do?"

Hudson did not hesitate. "How many men have we got left?"

"Fifteen." Then he remembered the man Halstead had just killed. "Fourteen, assuming none of the others got killed. The main core of us is still intact. Cree's up in the clock tower of the bank. Cliff has some men with him holding down the general store, which was full of customers. Bug's out front there and Mick and Pole are out back tending the horses and minding North Street. I figure we wait until night before you and me get out of here and send one of the new men we hired to spread the word to the others to clear out. Tell them to meet us back at Rock Creek so we can get our money and leave the territory for a while. Maybe head to California."

"None of that helps us right now, does it?" Hudson growled. "We can't do anything until we clear Halstead out of that saloon."

"He won't be able to hit what he can't see," Zimmerman reminded him. "Waiting him out until dark is still the best plan."

Hudson did not give up. "What about the dynamite you used to blow this place? Got any of it left?"

Zimmerman was glad he had already thought of that. "No. One of the men we hired had stolen it from Ryan's mines. We asked him for a box, but he was only able to scrounge up one measly stick. And we only used a bit of it here."

Hudson pounded the wall and began pacing around his cell. He kicked the door open. "Damned thing might as still be locked for all the good it does me." He stopped pacing and looked at Zimmerman through the bars. "There's only one way I can see our way clear of all of this and that's to storm the saloon. Front and back at the same time. Burn him out of there if we have to. Send in the new men first, then the rest of us go in after if we need to."

Zimmerman shut his eyes. He had already thought

about that, too. "You happen to see where that last shot came from, John? The one that punched through the desk."

"No."

Zimmerman had not thought he did. "It came from the second floor. Before, he was shooting at us from the window just next to the doorway. He's figured on us making a run on him after the horse broke through the place. By now, he's probably got himself a nice barricade at the front and back doors. I was in that saloon just today, and I know the layout. There's a balcony where he could pick off any men who try to hit him from the front. The way he shoots, they'd all be dead before they reached the stairway. There's a back door to the place, but I'll bet my share of the money that he's got that blocked, too. It'd take some doing to open it, but not before he picked off our men." It was a rotten plan before, and circumstances had not changed it any. "We'd just wind up losing a lot more men we can't afford to lose."

Zimmerman may not have liked it, but the more he thought about it, the more he was convinced his original plan was the best one. A man like Boddington would have given up by now. But a man like Halstead would never give up. The best plan was to head to Rock Creek, get their money and fresh horses, and run like hell out of Montana.

Later, he would come back and kill Jeremiah Halstead, but on his own terms and on ground of his own choosing.

"I'm sorry, John, but it looks like making a break for it after dark is our only option right now. I don't like it any more than you do, but I'm playing the only hand we have."

He tipped his hat over his eyes and settled in to get some shut-eye while Hudson continued to rail at him, cursing him for his incompetence. His lack of planning and nerve.

Zimmerman did his best to block out the insults the outlaw hurled at him. He even thought about shooting Hudson to shut him up once and for all. He did not need him any longer, but he did need the men who were still loyal to him. Cree and Mick and Pole and Bug and Cliff. Especially Cliff. The black man was itching for a reason to kill him, and killing Hudson would give him that reason. He would never believe that their leader had been killed by Halstead and, even if the others believed it, Cliff would blame him for allowing him to get killed. He had no doubt he could kill Cliff if he had to, but the others would be trouble.

No, as he allowed sleep to take him despite Hudson's threats, he decided a dead Hudson was more trouble than he was worth.

Besides, like Halstead, he could always kill him later.

Back at the Hotel Montana, Antonio and Robinson once again lifted the heavy beam from the back door.

"Every gun on the street is aimed at Ryan, Boddington, and the doc." Robinson said. "If we're going to make a break for the livery, now's the time."

Antonio slowly opened the door while Robinson grabbed his axe and checked South Street. Besides a few people cowering behind a few buildings, there was not a gun in sight. "It's clear. Let's get moving."

He stepped outside, hoping young Miguel was following him, but saw him embraced by his father. The two spoke to each other in Spanish, before the father kissed his son on the cheek and sent him out the door before slamming it shut.

The boy doubled back when they heard the wails of his mother from inside the hotel, but Robinson held him steady. "She'll be just fine if you make it back alive. Now let's go."

He pushed Miguel ahead of him, knowing the teenager was much faster than he. Robinson moved quickly behind him, keeping an eye out for the sight of a gun pointed in their direction. He might not be able to shoot back, but he could certainly give the boy warning to duck for cover.

"Stay as flat as you can against the buildings," Robinson told him. "And keep moving!"

With every step he took, he braced for the sound of a rifle or the impact of a bullet. They cut through a small crowd of frightened townspeople gathered at the back of the bank, and Robinson told them to head back to the hotel for safety.

He and Miguel paused before the last alley between them and the livery. Robinson stuck his head out to make sure the alley was clear before he motioned for the boy to move. He made it to the other side without incident, and Robinson followed.

When they reached the rear of the livery, they found Doc Mortimer's wagon had been parked against the back door. Robinson reached up, released the hand brake, and motioned for Miguel to help him push the old wagon out of the way.

The wagon creaked but rolled easily for its size. Robinson gently rattled the warped plank door. "Ralph! It's me, Todd and Miguel Reyes from the hotel. Let us in."

Ralph Wheeler pulled the door in, brandishing an old

army rifle. He looked like he had just been roused from a deep sleep, but Robinson knew he always looked like that.

The liveryman had no welcome for them. "Just what the hell are you two up to, sneaking around back like this? Ain't you heard all that shooting just now?"

Robinson pushed past him. "Why do you think we're here. We need the deputy's horse. The mustang he liveried here a couple of days back when he came into town."

Wheeler eyed him carefully. "You picked a hell of a time to take up horse thievin', Todd."

Miguel had already found the mustang and was lugging a saddle to its stall.

"We're not stealing it," Robinson told Wheeler. "We're borrowing it to save Deputy Halstead and maybe the town. Young Miguel here is gonna ride to Helena for help."

"Well, why didn't you just tell me that in the first place?" Wheeler set his rifle against a post and grabbed another saddle. "Set that one you're carrying aside, boy. This is the rig she came in with. You'll want her to be comfortable, seeing as how you're new to riding her and you've got a long way to go. Just be careful with her. She's a mighty spirited one."

"I can handle her," the boy said. "I just need to get her ready to ridc."

The three of them secured and buckled the saddle to the horse. Robinson could tell Wheeler had been right. The mare was spirited and not given to being handled by so many strangers at once. He also supposed the animal sensed the danger in the air.

When they were finished, Miguel slipped his father's rifle into the saddle scabbard and checked that the saddle was cinched tightly enough.

"I'm not sure I like this," Wheeler said as he led the mustang from the stall.

Robinson was beginning to lose his patience with the older man. "Damn it, Ralph. I told you we'll bring her back."

"Ain't talking about that," Wheeler argued. "I'm talking about all the attention young Miguel here will draw as soon as he rides out of here. I've seen all sorts of strangers moving about town since that explosion a while ago. I don't want the boy getting shot at before he has a chance to get away."

Robinson realized Wheeler had a point as he helped Miguel climb into the saddle. "Don't worry about me, boys. This is a mighty fast horse, and they'll have to catch me to kill me."

"No horse is faster than a bullet," Robinson told him. He may not have known much about horses, but he had seen what bullets could do. "We'll need to create some kind of distraction that'll draw their fire, if there's any to draw."

Wheeler gestured to his rifle. "That's a single shot piece I brought home from the war, but I'm pretty fair with it. I imagine I can probably wing someone if they're fool enough to stick their head out far enough."

Robinson knew less about guns than he knew about horses, but even he knew one shot at a time would not be good enough. The men in the jail had repeating rifles and could fire fifteen rounds at Miguel before Wheeler reloaded.

They needed a better plan.

He looked at the back door they had just used and saw that it was too small, even for the mustang to fit through. Since they could not send Miguel out the back way, he could only go out the front.

But something about the back of the livery held some possibilities. Something that could not only help Miguel get free but help him fulfill his promise to Halstead about taking a look around town for him. "I think I've got an idea. Ralph, how's your back?"

"Fair to middlin' I suppose," the liveryman admitted. "Not like I sleep on a feather bed every night. But I'm no cripple if that's what you're askin'. Why?"

Robinson preferred to show him rather than tell him. He wanted to get the boy moving before too long. He wanted to put his distraction into action before he was smart enough to change his mind.

He pointed up at Miguel. "Bring that mustang to the front of the livery, but don't go outside. Wait until I tell you to go before you do it, understand? Not a second before."

The boy nodded that he understood and moved the horse into position. Robinson picked up his axe as he led Ralph out the back door.

He went to Doc Mortimer's wagon that he had pushed out of the way earlier, released the hand brake again, and walked over to the front wheel on the other side. Knowing he would need both hands to move the wagon, he buried the axe deep in the wooden sidewall and grabbed hold of the front wheel.

Wheeler clearly understood what Robinson was up to and took his spot at the back. When the bartender gave him the signal, the two men began to push the wagon forward. It took a bit of effort at first, but they got the big rig moving and turned around the corner toward Main Street.

"Glad the good doctor pays me to keep these wheels slathered with plenty of grease," Wheeler said as he pushed.

Given the circumstances, Robinson was even more glad than he was. "I just need you to help me get this thing rolling, then get back to the livery. I'll handle the rest from there."

Wheeler kept pushing. "I sure hope you know what you're doin', Todd."

Robinson hoped so, too.

As soon as the wagon got close to passing the livery entrance and rolling out onto Main Street, Robinson told Ralph, "Get back. Now!" Then to Miguel, he called out. "Ride, Miguel. Ride!"

The wagon was rolling easier now that it had momentum behind it and had just nosed out onto the thoroughfare when Miguel Reyes and the mustang raced out of the livery. Within a few strides, the horse was at full gallop and speeding away from Silver Cloud.

Rifle shots echoed throughout the empty streets of town as Robinson continued to roll the wagon from one side of Main Street to the other. Bullets pelted the wagon wall as he kept his head down as much as he could whilc he used all his strength to keep it rolling. Every bullet that hit the wagon was another round that did not hit Miguel or him. And judging by the number of shots pelting the wagon, Robinson knew Wheeler had been right. Zimmerman had men all over town.

He flinched when a bullet pierced the wagon wall less than an inch from his head. He saw that he was only a few feet from the far side when he decided he had gotten as much cover from the doctor's wagon as he could hope for. He pulled the axe free from the sidewall and ran toward the side of the feed store in front of him. Bullets peppered the corner of the store, but none of them found their intended mark.

He threw himself flat against the wall of the store and held the axe close to his chest as he caught his breath. The wagon had rolled easy, but it was heavy and keeping it rolling had taken a lot out of him. More than he had expected.

The wagon had also cost him whatever element of surprise he might have hoped to have as he scouted out the town for Halstead. The gunmen were onto him now. What's more, they knew exactly where he was.

Which might not be so bad for him.

He knew they would be coming for him now. It would be foolish to think otherwise. But they would be careful. They would expect him to have a gun. Perhaps a rifle. But not an axe. A man acted differently when he approached a man with a gun. Maybe his element of surprise was still intact after all.

Robinson looked to his left when he heard a boot scrape against the packed dirt of North Street. He saw a long shadow of a man sneaking up on him. A townsman would not sneak up on him without announcing himself, so he knew this man had to be one of Zimmerman's bunch.

Robinson moved as quietly as he could along the wall toward the back of the store and dropped himself into a crouch. He brought his axe back and held it there, ready to swing the moment the man came into view. The long shadow the man cast told him he was close.

Robinson did not have to wait long.

The man rounded the corner, rifle raised to his shoulder.

Already in a crouch, Robinson was beneath the gun as he swung the axe as hard as he could. The blade sunk deep into the man's side, causing him to cry out as he fired into the air.

Robinson tried to pull the blade free, but it was imbedded too deep. He snatched the rifle from the dying man as he got to his feet and pulled him around to his side of the wall. The man tumbled forward and fell awkwardly onto his side, causing the blade to only go deeper. He scraped at the ground with his hands and feet, trying to get up, but his struggle stopped as quickly as it had started.

Robinson set the rifle aside and tried once again to pull the blade free from the dead man's side. He recognized him as one of the new regulars who had drank at The Green Tree. He could not remember the man's name, only that he was a lousy tipper. He must be one of the men Ace had hired.

Robinson was still struggling to free the axe when he heard a man call out from behind the feed store. "You get him, Jasper?"

Robinson cursed his luck as he gave the axe a final tug, but it would not budge. It was in too deep and, with the stranger approaching, he did not have time to work it free.

"Jasper?" the man called out again. "You get him?"

"Yeah." Robinson winced. He had no idea what the dead man sounded like. He grabbed the rifle, and his beefy, swollen fingers were still too thick to work the trigger. He decided to use it as a club instead.

"Good man." The stranger's voice was getting closer. His footsteps faster now that the danger had passed. "Who'd you kill?"

"Dunno." Robinson inched toward the corner and held the rifle like a club as he watched the stranger's shadow approach. "Come look."

The man turned the corner wider than his partner, but not wide enough to avoid the rifle butt connecting with his temple.

The outlaw spun from the impact and dropped to the ground. Robinson stepped toward him and brought the butt down again, finishing the job.

Two fewer men Halstead had to face.

He ducked back behind the corner and stole a quick look down North Street. He did not see anyone else coming, but that did not mean it was safe. Men had fired at the wagon. There were still plenty of places along the back street where a man could hide along the way. If he turned back to the livery now, he knew he might have a chance of reaching the relative safety of the hotel.

But he had not ventured across Main Street to be safe. He was here to let Halstead know what he was up against. And telling him he had killed two men at the end of town would not be much help. He needed to find out what was going on at the general store.

His decision already made for him, he grabbed the rifle like a club once again and began walking toward the general store.

Chapter 26

Mr. Ryan saw the wagon first. "What the hell is that?"

Boddington saw it just as the chatter of rifle fire picked up all along Main Street. Zimmerman had not been lying. He really did have men stationed all over town.

Doc Mortimer, who had been walking ahead of them, put his shoulder into the nearest closed door and forced it open.

With gunfire filling the air all around him, Boddington wheeled Mr. Ryan around and pulled him backward into the building before the doctor shut the door.

It was only then that the sheriff realized this was the Silver Cloud General Store when he saw all of the men and women sitting on the floor along the counters.

A large black man with an eyepatch lowered his rifle in Boddington's direction. "Well, look at what the cat dragged in." He looked at the star pinned on Boddington's vest. "Or should I say the sheriff? I take it you are the sheriff?"

This was not the first time Boddington found someone pointing a rifle at him, and he turned to face the man fully. "You take it right. Now point that cannon somewhere else. We're not going to cause you any trouble."

The outlaw smiled as he raised the rifle and placed the butt on his hip. "Just coming in out of the rain, huh? Seems to be raining bullets out there. What's your friend Halstead up to now?"

"Halstead's in the saloon. Someone's pushing a wagon across the east end of Main Street." Boddington moved to the window to see what was happening outside. The wagon was slowly making its way across Main Street from the livery to the feed store. Whoever was doing it was either incredibly brave or incredibly stupid. Boddington could not decide which. He only wished he was with him, whoever it was.

From behind him, he heard a man say, "Kill him, Cliff. Just kill him and be done with it. If you don't kill him now, you'll have to kill him later."

"Don't know about that," Cliff said. "Zimmerman didn't see fit to kill him down at the jail, so why should I do it here? Maybe he wants him alive for some reason. Besides, he seems tame enough to me. In fact, he looks kind of clumsy. Just look at his nose. Bet he broke it walking into a wall."

Boddington kept his right hand on the windowsill. He knew he could probably draw his gun and fire before Cliff had a chance to lower that rifle. But probably was not good enough for him now. Not with Mr. Ryan in the way.

The man who had told Cliff to kill him came over and gave Boddington a hard shove. "Remember me?"

He shoved the man back and brought back his right hand to punch him. He did not look familiar, not that it mattered. "Let me guess. You're some punk who got his head split open for running his mouth at me."

"Bama Jones," the man sneered. "And before this is

over, it'll be the last name you hear before I send you to hell."

"Knock it off," Cliff said over the sound of rifle fire from outside. "We've got enough excitement going on around here without you two acting up."

Boddington lowered his hand and realized the shooting outside had stopped.

Cliff clearly noticed it, too. "Sounds like whatever it was is over."

A final rifle shot broke the silence.

The outlaw grinned. "Now it sounds like it's really over. Who was it, sheriff? One of your deputies?" He snapped his fingers as if he remembered something. "Oh, that's right. Your boys are in bits and pieces down at the jail. How could I forget that, especially since I'm the one who threw the stick that did it? Those fools went and left the front door wide open for me, too."

Boddington knew Cliff was trying to bait him. The look in his eyes was practically daring him to go for the Colt on his hip.

But Boddington knew when he had been beaten. And there was no way he could clear leather before the outlaw blew him away.

He put his right hand on Mr. Ryan's wheelchair instead. "Now that it's quieted down some out there, I think it's best we get going."

"Quite right," Ryan said. He pointed toward the door. "Doctor, if you please."

Cliff slowly lowered the rifle at Mortimer. "I wouldn't do that if I were you, doc. You wouldn't like what happens next."

The captives in the store moaned and stifled sobs, which

made bile rise in Boddington's throat. He was supposed to be protecting these people, not be helpless right along with them.

Ryan turned in his chair as best as he could to face the outlaw. "What in the devil are you up to? There's no reason why we can't return to my home. We've agreed not to interfere. Zimmerman never would've let us live otherwise."

Cliff cocked his head at the mine owner. "Let's just say I enjoy your company. The twelve of us have been cooped up in here for a while, and we've gotten a bit tired of each other. Having you all in here gives the place some class."

Boddington could practically feel Mr. Ryan's blood pressure rise. "Now, you just listen here, boy."

The black man subtly shifted his aim from Mortimer to Ryan. "Boy?"

"Yes, boy, as I'm practically old enough to be your father," Ryan persisted. "The sheriff and I told Zimmerman we were working on a way to end this without any more bloodshed. We're going to do our best to make Halstead listen to reason. We can't do that if we're cooped up in here with you lot."

Cliff slowly raised his rifle, if only a little.

Ryan continued. "You're in complete control of the town. Anyone can see that. The three of us can't harm any of you. We'd be riddled with bullets if we tried. If you let us go, we can try to help. If you keep us here, we're just another bunch of men you have to keep under the gun."

Boddington could see Cliff turning over the idea in his mind. He was not the typical kind of dead-eyed thug he had gone up against since becoming sheriff. He had a good head on his shoulders, which made him especially dangerous.

He thought Mr. Ryan had the big man turned when they heard a weak voice come from the back door of the general store.

"Bama," it rasped. "Come quick. I'm hurt bad."

"That sounds like Jasper!" Bama was already heading that way before Cliff could stop him.

From what he had been able to hear from his spot at the back door to the general store, Robinson knew now was the time to act. It sounded like there were only two gunmen inside with Boddington, so if he could cut the number in half, he might give the sheriff a chance to do something.

Since Cliff sounded like the leader, Robinson had decided to target Bama instead. He remembered the young cowpuncher from The Green Tree. He had always been a hothead and would be easy pickings if Robinson played it right.

He put a rasp in his voice as he spoke into the store. "Bama. Come quick. I'm hurt bad."

Robinson left the rifle propped up against the wall as he waited for the young man to rush out to help his friend. He had always been able to handle the wiry punk easily enough in the saloon, and now would be no different.

"Jasper!" Bama called as he rushed out the door.

Robinson slugged him with a heavy right that connected solidly with Bama's jaw. The blow should have been hard enough to knock the bean pole cold, but it only served to send him off balance.

Robinson quickly followed it up with an upper cut that

barely missed as the man staggered backward toward where Robinson had placed the rifle.

Bama's legs were rubber and barely held him up. Robinson grabbed Bama by the neck and forced him against the wall, squeezing his throat with all of the strength he could muster.

He felt Bama's cartilage give way, crushing his windpipe.

He placed a hand over the gagging man's mouth as he kept him pinned against the wall. He did not want to risk Cliff hearing the sounds of a struggle and coming to investigate. All of this effort had taken more out of him than he had thought it would. He did not think he had much more fight left in him.

And when all of the life had finally gone out of Bama, he allowed the man's body to slowly and quietly drop to the ground.

He froze when he heard a man's voice behind him say, "Damn, mister. You've sure got a way of killing folks."

Robinson slowly turned and saw a large black man with an eye patch standing just outside the back door of the general store. He was a couple of inches taller and just as broad. He figured this must be the man he had heard Bama call Cliff. He looked more like a mountain.

He judged the distance between them to be about ten yards or so. Not a very long distance normally, but it might as well have been a country mile when facing down an armed man.

Cliff seemed to know what Robinson was thinking by watching his eyes. "You'll never make it, mister. But there's no harm in trying." He placed both hands on his belt buckle. "And just to show you I'm a fair man, I'll even let you make the first move."

Robinson snatched the rifle from the wall and threw it in Cliff's direction as he charged the outlaw with a roar.

Cliff easily sidestepped the rifle just as Robinson plowed a shoulder into his midsection. The bigger man doubled over as he was sent back against the wall. Robinson quickly brought up his head, connecting with Cliff's jaw and snapping his head back with a crack.

Fearing he might go for his pistol, Robinson pinned Cliff's right hand to the wall as he reared back and threw a haymaker with all of his might.

The blow landed solidly on Cliff's left cheek and knocked the big man to the ground.

Refusing to let go of the gun hand, Robinson was pulled down, too, and landed awkwardly on top of Cliff.

But his grip on the gun hand was broken upon hitting the ground, allowing Cliff to pummel Robinson's left kidney with a series of punches that caused him to cry out in agony.

It was only then that Robinson realized Cliff had not been punching him. He had been stabbing him with a small blade. The outlaw must have had it tucked in his belt buckle.

Robinson felt his strength begin to ebb as the pain grew worse. He wanted to get to his feet, to pummel the man who had stabbed him, but the more he wanted to move, the less he could.

He realized the outlaw had wrapped his arm around his neck, preventing him from moving even if he'd had the strength to do so.

"That's it, amigo," the outlaw said into his ear. "You

just stay right where you are and die. Big Cliff's got you. You put up a good fight. No shame in getting beaten. No shame in dying well, either."

When Cliff went out to check on Bama, Boddington knew this was their best chance to get away.

He grabbed hold of Ryan's wheelchair and motioned for Mortimer to open the front door. "Open it, doc. Let's get these people out of here."

Mr. Ryan surprised him by grabbing hold of the wheels to lock himself in place. "Hold on for a moment. I'm not going anywhere."

But Doc Mortimer had already opened the door. Five of the hostages quickly got to their feet and ran out ahead of them. Ryan called for them to stop, but they were too panicked by the prospect of their freedom to listen. They scattered in all directions as soon as they reached the boardwalk.

A rifle shot rang out and took down Margaret Conway, a clerk at the bank. She fell within steps of the front door of the store. The rest of the people had broken to the right and out of Boddington's view. But four more shots quickly rang out, and he knew his ears could tell him as much as his eyes could. He knew the shots were coming from the clock tower of the bank, which gave the shooter a nearly perfect view of the town. The men and women who had fled the general store were dead.

Doc Mortimer must have known it, too, for he quietly shut the door.

Ryan turned in his chair to look up at Boddington. "I don't blame civilians for panicking, Barry, but I expected you to keep your powder dry amidst all this. That man in the tower would've killed us if we'd stepped one foot out there."

Boddington wanted to answer him. He wanted to tell him he was wrong. He wanted to tell him anything that would get them out of that store and back to Ryan's home, where he could take a moment to think straight. Maybe come up with a plan to help Halstead or at least help the town.

But time was the one thing he did not have. Not time to think, anyway. Time to wait under an outlaw's gun. Time to wait to see if he would die. Time to watch a great man like Emmett Ryan held hostage and in danger every moment of it.

His own weakness began to eat away at his guts. What good was a sheriff who could not enforce law and order? The star on his chest did not mean much on its own. It was just a piece of tin without the muscle to back it up.

No matter what Ryan said, Boddington knew he had to do something, and he had to do it quickly. Zimmerman and Cliff and the others could not be allowed to ride into Silver Cloud, blow up the jail, and take over the town. His town. Someone had to make them pay for that and pay dearly.

It was not up to Halstead to do it, either. He was not sheriff of Silver Cloud. Barry Boddington was, and it was high time these outlaws knew who they were up against.

He heard a heavy thud against the rear wall of the general store, quickly followed by the sounds of a scuffle coming from out back. Ignoring Ryan's orders for him to stay put, he drew his Colt and ran toward the back door to see what was happening.

He was surprised to find Todd Robinson, the bartender from The Green Tree Saloon, slumped over Cliff. A large pool of red quickly spreading on the lower left part of the back of his shirt.

Boddington raised his pistol and aimed it at Cliff who was pinned beneath him. "Move out of the way, Todd! I can get him!"

But Todd did not move.

Cliff did. He slowly raised his pistol and aimed it at Boddington. The sheriff fired, trying not to hit Robinson. The bullet struck the ground an inch or so away from Cliff's head.

The outlaw did not even flinch.

And neither did his gun. "You should've listened to your boss."

Boddington readjusted his aim, but not before Cliff fired first.

Chapter 27

From a window on the second floor of The Green Tree saloon, Halstead watched the last escapee from the general store fall in the middle of the thoroughfare. An old man with a limp. The shooter had saved the slowest for last.

And as the last echo of the last gunshot drifted away, Jerry Halstead knew he could no longer stay there. Remaining holed up in the saloon just to keep Zimmerman and Hudson at bay was not solving anything. It was getting people killed.

This was turning into The Fall of Dover Station all over again, where he had no choice but to watch a town he had sworn to protect burn to the ground. He had been forced to hole up in the tiny old jail back then. He would not hide in this rundown saloon and watch the same thing happen all over again.

Zimmerman's cackle filled the uneasy silence that had settled over the town. "Looks like we had something of a jail break up at the general store, Halstead. Can't say as I blame them, though. I know what it's like to be held in a place for so long, all you want to do is get away."

Halstead took a quick look out the window to see if Zimmerman had been foolish enough to show himself. He was still behind cover.

As Zimmerman continued with his taunts from the ruined jail, Halstead decided it was time to move.

He slung his saddlebag over his shoulder and took the two Winchesters with him as he headed across the hall to the rooms facing South Street. There was no point going down to the main floor because he had blocked all of the doorways as best he could and doused the floor with liquor. One stray match would set the whole place aflame in seconds. It was a last, desperate measure he would employ if Zimmerman ordered his men to storm the saloon. He knew it would only be a matter of time before they did, especially as the sun grew closer to the horizon.

"The deaths of those fine people are on your hands as much as mine," he heard Zimmerman say as Halstead opened a window that led to the sloping porch roof at the back of the saloon. "I'm used to living with innocent blood on my hands, deputy. How about you? Do you have the stomach for it?"

Halstead checked South Street to see if anyone was back there. Except for three women hiding behind thc bank, no one was there.

He took off his saddlebag and allowed it to slide down the roof. He was glad when it hit the ground without making much of a sound. It was loud enough to make the three women behind the bank jump, but they quickly calmed down when they saw Halstead stick his head out the window and hold his finger to his lips.

Zimmerman kept up his dialogue. "Guilt's a terrible thing, ain't it, Jeremiah? Can eat a man up if he doesn't know how to handle it. What about you? Have you learned to handle it yet? You'd best get working on it if you haven't already because a lot more people will die here today if you force it."

Halstead allowed the heavier Winchester '86 to slide down the roof first, quickly followed by the lighter '73. Carrying two rifles, along with the pistols on his rig, would make for some heavy carrying, but he saw no other choice. He'd need the '86 for distance and the '73 for closer work.

"You don't have to force it, you know," Zimmerman went on as Halstead climbed through the window and allowed himself to slowly slide down the sloping roof of the porch. He dug in his heels at the edge and saw an outcropped porch beam he could hold on to. It would cut his drop to the ground by more than half and reduce the likelihood he could sprain an ankle or break a leg.

"I intend to keep my promise to Old Man Ryan," Zimmerman said. "You come out, hands up, and I'll let you live. I know you've got a job to do. An oath to uphold. I never held much for oaths myself, but I know they mean something to a man like you. I respect that, which is why I plan on giving you a fair deal. What do you say?"

Halstead grabbed hold of one of the roof beams and allowed the rest of himself to slide off the porch. The wood moaned but held as his feet dangled less than a foot above the ground. He let himself drop and landed softly next to his gear. He was glad to see Col was still where he had tied her and crept over to the mustang to unburden his load.

"There's no shame in it," Zimmerman continued as Halstead slung the saddlebags over his horse and slid the two rifles into their saddle scabbards. He untied her reins and led the animal as close to the buildings as he could get. He had not forgotten about the man in the bank tower and remained close to the buildings as he moved.

Zimmerman went on. "As a matter of fact, we're both surrendering in a way. How do you think I'll feel knowing you're out there dogging my tail every step of the way? I won't be able to put my head down at night without wondering if I'll wake up to see you standing over me."

The three women behind the bank got to their feet and began praying as he drew closer. He held his finger to his lips again and they struggled to remain quiet. He wondered why they hadn't left with Robinson until he saw a little girl of about three peek out from behind her mother's skirts. She looked terrified, which made Halstead's blood boil even more.

"Were any of you in the bank when all of this started?" he asked, ignoring Zimmerman's ongoing soliloquy about death and honor.

The older of the three women whispered, "I'm a clerk here. This back door is open, but there are two men inside, maybe three. I know one is in the lobby and I think the other is up in the tower. We ran out of there when the shooting started and have been hiding here ever since. Mr. Robinson wanted us to go with him, but the little one here was too frightened to go. We feared her crying would call attention to us and we didn't want that."

Halstead heard Zimmerman going on about the honorable surrender at Appomattox as he took a knee to get on the same level as the little girl. She only half hid behind her mother's skirts.

"You like horses, honey?"

She nodded. Her cheeks glistened with tears.

"That's good because my horse likes little girls. Her name is Col."

She looked up at the horse and back at Halstead. "Col."

"That's right. Now, I have to go inside the bank, and I need someone to keep Col from getting scared. Brave little girls make her feel calm and safe. You'd be doing me a real big favor if you kept an eye on her for me. Could you do that?"

She looked up at the mustang again, then at Halstead. "How?"

"By helping your mama and these other fine ladies here take her over to the hotel. You see it? It's just over there. They've got nice people inside who'll give you a nice glass of milk and keep you and Col safe. Can you do that for me? Col would feel a lot better if you did and so would I."

She wiped her tears away with the back of her hand and nodded.

Halstead stroked her cheek and stood up, handing the reins to the clerk. "Stay close to the buildings and head over to the hotel. Antonio and Maria will take you in. Just knock at the door gently and wait. Tell them I sent you."

"I will, sir, and thank you."

He pulled the '86 from the scabbard and urged the women to get going.

The mother of the little girl turned as they left and mouthed "God bless you" as she moved away.

He doubted the Almighty would spare him the time, but he appreciated the sentiment just the same.

He set his '86 against the wall and examined the back door to the bank. It was a single slab of iron with rivets holding it to the frame. There was no handle or knob to use to pull it open. He had not expected there to be one.

He pulled his father's Bowie knife from the back of his pants and worked the edge of the thick blade under the panel. The door moved slightly, and he used the knife as a lever to ease the door open. It opened enough for him to get his fingers inside so he could begin pulling it out toward him. He had no idea if one of the gunmen was nearby, so he opened it slowly, hoping against hope that the hinges were well-oiled.

By the time he got it just open wide enough for him to slip in, he was glad the big door had not made a sound.

He grabbed his Winchester and slipped inside, gently closing the heavy door behind him.

He dropped to a crouch, his knife in one hand and his rifle in the other, as he allowed his eyes to adjust to the indoor darkness. He found himself inside a narrow hallway. One door was on his right and he figured the door at the end of the hallway probably led out to the rest of the bank.

He set the '86 against the wall and shifted his knife to his left hand. He tried the doorknob of the door to his right and saw it was not locked.

He turned the knob slowly and pushed the door in, fearing a creak but not hearing one. Given the ornate decorations of the room, Halstead could tell this must be the office of the bank president.

He also figured the man who was lounging in the chair with his dusty boots on the desk was not the bank president. The rifle on the desk only helped him confirm this.

The gentle snoring he heard told him the man was asleep.

Halstead would see to it that he never woke up.

He crossed the ten feet or so between him and the hired gun as quickly and quietly as he could. He placed his left hand over the man's mouth as he plunged the knife deep into his heart with his right.

The man's legs began to flail, and he gripped Halstead's knife hand as hard as he could. The office chair was on casters and Halstead pulled the chair and the dying man in it away from the desk until they reached the back window. He held the outlaw in place and watched as he slowly gave up the struggle. His legs grew quiet. His grip on the knife weakened. With a final breath, his head drooped, and his body went limp. His hands dropped to his lap.

Halstead withdrew the blade and wiped it clean on the dead man's shirt. The blade had served his father well for many years. He intended on putting it to good use in the years to come.

But he still had the man in the tower to contend with.

He grabbed his '86 and crept to the end of the hallway. He was about to open the door when he stopped.

Why was this man sleeping in the office? Hadn't he heard all of the gunfire out on the street? Why hadn't he joined in? Why had he been sleeping in the first place? He had not looked like one of the Hudson Gang. He must have been one of the new men Ace had hired when he'd first come to Silver Cloud.

Still, even a hired hand should know better than to let his guard down like that.

Unless he had someone watching the front for him. Maybe the clerk had been right. Maybe there had actually been three men in the bank instead of just two.

Once again, Halstead set aside the big Winchester and dropped to a crouch as he slowly turned the handle on the door. If there really was someone on the other side, they would probably expect the man he had just killed to walk through the door. That hesitation would buy him about a second. Seeing an empty doorway might make him curious for another second, two at most, depending on where the gunman was standing.

Halstead gritted his teeth and pulled the door inward. The hinges did not make a sound and neither did he. He found himself behind the tellers' cages. The dying light of day sent long shadows through the bank's windows.

And a man with a rifle standing at one of the teller stations, keeping an eye on the empty street.

He checked the rest of the lobby for other gunmen but saw only the one. A door at the far left of the lobby on the other side of the cages was open. Halstead figured it must lead up to the clock tower and the rifleman above.

But he had to deal with the lookout first.

He ran at a crouch toward where the man was standing, wrapped his hand around the man's forehead, and drew the blade edge across his neck like a fiddler would his bow. Just like his uncle Billy had taught him.

As the man gagged, Halstead slammed the butt of the Bowie knife down on his hand before he could accidentally get off a warning shot. None of this worked without the element of surprise.

His blow missed as the man dropped the rifle anyway to clutch at his bleeding neck.

Knowing the clatter of the rifle might have been enough to alert the man in the tower that something was wrong, Halstead easily lowered the dying man to the floor and kept him there until he had gasped his last.

Sure that the man was dead, Halstead cleaned his blade on the dead man's sleeve and went back to the hallway to retrieve his Winchester.

He found the door to the lobby at the far right of the cages and took an ink blotter from one of the stations to keep the door propped open. If things went bad in the tower, he would need a quick way to escape. Going out the front door would be suicide, leaving the back door as his best chance to make a getaway.

He reached the open door in the lobby and saw three flights of stairs that led upward. They had to lead to the clock tower. He could see the natural light spilling in from the outside.

But he could not see the sharpshooter he knew to be up there.

And a lot could happen on three flights of stairs. One creak of a stair or banister and his advantage would be lost. He would have only one chance to get this right.

For the third time since entering the bank, he set his Winchester against the wall before he began to make his ascent. He tucked the Bowie knife back into its scabbard and quietly drew the pistol from his belly holster. The knife would not do him much good if the rifleman heard him before he reached the top.

Each step he took upward brought him closer to the

rifleman. Each stair could have cost him his life. One crack or squeak could draw attention and put the man on guard. He doubted Zimmerman had trusted such an important position to one of the men Ace had hired. He was going up against one of the Hudson Gang now. A man tried and true and deadly.

With his heart practically in his throat with each step, Halstead eyed the top of the landing. He could hear the man moving around above him now, but he did not think he had been discovered.

One flight down. Two more to go.

Halstead did not know what he would do if he managed to take the tower. He might have a perfect view of the town, but only for as long as he could defend it. Zimmerman's men would be on him in a hot second as soon as they realized their man was dead and now Halstead was in control of the perch. He could not hold them off forever, and they would get him in a rush if they stormed the bank. He had figured out a way in. They would, too.

But as he continued to climb, he decided to put those concerns out of his mind. He could worry about what he would do about holding the tower once he had actually taken it.

If you take it, he reminded himself.

He reached the second floor without a sound. Only one flight remaining.

He kept his Colt at the ready as he ascended the final set of stairs that led to the top. He removed his hat and allowed it to quietly fall to the landing below. Even a split-second edge could make the difference between life and death when he was this close.

He stole a quick look above the floor that led to the

tower. An intricate jumble of spindles and gears sat in the middle of the room with rods that shot out in four directions at chest level to control the hands of the four clock faces on each side of the tower.

The rifleman was looking out the eastern clock face that offered the best view of the general store. One of the panels of the clock face swung in like a door and he was looking outside, probably for the next innocent man or woman to shoot.

The constant clacking of the gears of the clock would make it difficult for the outlaw to hear him coming, but the rods that controlled the clock hands would make it tough to sneak up on him. The narrow room was effectively cut into quarters by the rods. Getting to him would not be easy, but it would be just as difficult for the Hudson man to escape.

Halstead held his Colt tight as he took the final steps to the top landing and took careful aim at the man looking out the window.

The man brought his right elbow back with surprising speed and knocked Halstead's hand aside. He quickly followed it up by slamming the butt of the gun into his chest, sending him tumbling backward toward the stairs.

"I was wondering when you'd show up," the swarthy man said. "Thought you'd get the jump on me, didn't you?" The man tried to bring his foot down on Halstead's arm, but the lawman moved out of the way. "No one's snuck up on Cree. Not ever!"

The outlaw tried to bring his rifle around, but in the cramped confines of the clock tower, it clanged on one of the spokes.

Halstead buried his Thunderer in the man's belly and

fired three times at point-blank range. Each of the bullets passed through Cree and punched holes in the eastern clock face behind him.

The dying man sagged across one of the spokes like a rag doll. Halstead grabbed hold of his rifle before he dropped it.

Halstead used the long gun to help him get to his feet and understood why it was so difficult for the dead man to bring it around. It was a long-bored Sharps. A fifty-caliber, just like the one his uncle Billy used. Just like the one he had taught him to shoot.

He used the butt of the gun to push the murderer off the spoke. He did not want the machinery to act up and cause Zimmerman's men to be curious. The dead outlaw's body dropped to the floor like a bale of hay.

Halstead opened the window panel of the western clock face and saw a clear view of the ruined jail. The entire front part of the building had been obliterated by the blast, but from this angle, he could see that Zimmerman was still talking to him from the cover of the cell Halstead had slept in on the first night he had come to Silver Cloud.

And he had a clear shot at him from here.

The sound of the clockworks prevented him from hearing what Zimmerman was saying, but it did not matter.

He checked the chamber and saw it contained a fresh round. He snapped it shut and took careful aim at Zimmerman. He would have preferred his Winchester '86. He had grown more comfortable with using that gun at distances this great, but he was in no position to be picky. In the time it took him to run downstairs, get the rifle, and bring it back, the outlaw might have moved back under cover.

Instead, Halstead remembered his uncle's training. He brought the rifle butt up tight against his shoulder. He drew a careful aim, shifting higher and to the right of his target to account for distance and gravity.

He let out a final breath. Grew still. And squeezed the trigger.

He watched the fifty-caliber bullet strike Zimmerman in the left arm and spin him like a top before he hit the floor. It had been lower than he had been aiming for, but he knew the big slug had caused plenty of damage. Even above the mechanical sounds of the clockwork, he could hear the outlaw screaming.

Knowing his one shot was gone, Halstead dropped the rifle and bolted down the stairs two at a time. He knew it would be only a matter of seconds before the remaining men from the Hudson Gang trapped him in the bank. He realized the only place he could go was the Hotel Montana. It was only a few doors away from the bank, but with every gun in town aimed at him, it would feel much longer.

Shards of glass rained down on him as the Hudson men began firing up at the clock tower. He practically jumped down the last landing, swiped his hat off the floor, grabbed his '86, and ran for the safety of the cages.

Three men on Main Street spotted him and began firing at him, but the thick glass Boddington had bragged about held, webbing but not breaking until Halstead had reached the door to the cages. The window shattered then, just as he kicked the ink blot free and pulled the heavy door shut.

He dove behind the counter as bullets began to ricochet all around him. He crawled down the hall toward the back door as bullets bit into the ceiling and walls, covering him with wood splinters and dust.

A great blast boomed inside the bank, and he knew at least one of the men had made it inside. That blast had probably destroyed the heavy lock on the door to the cages.

He flipped onto his back and aimed his Colt down the hallway as a hired man ran toward him without looking. Before the man had the chance to aim properly, Halstead killed him with three shots to the chest.

He tucked the empty weapon into his belly holster and drew the Colt on his hip as he heeled his way backward until he backed into the rear door. With his pistol aimed back up the hall, he got to his feet and pushed the heavy door open.

Bullets plinked off the iron as Halstead spilled out onto South Street. The door slammed shut under its own weight.

Knowing it was only a matter of seconds before his pursuers came rushing out the door, he got to his feet and oriented himself. He saw the ladies had tied Col to the post of the back porch of the Hotel Montana and began running in that direction as fast as he could.

He holstered his pistol and shifted to the '86 instead. He skidded to a stop when he heard a pistol crack. He turned and dropped to one knee and brought up the rifle to his shoulder. Two men were charging his way firing pistols as they went.

Halstead aimed just to the left of the man in front and fired. The impact went through the first man's chest and struck the man behind him in the shoulder. The first man fell, but the second remained standing. Halstead levered in a fresh round and fired, hitting him in the chest and putting the man down for good.

Not pausing to admire the shot, he resumed his mad dash toward Col. The closer he got, he saw that the mustang's reins were hanging loose on the ground. She had not been tethered after all.

The horse remained still as he jumped up on the back porch of the hotel for a few steps before leaping into the saddle. The mustang adjusted under the sudden weight but did not move until he gathered up the reins and heeled the animal into action. She responded quickly and they raced around the livery, out onto Main Street, and continued on for a few hundred yards until he was certain he was out of rifle range of the town.

He pulled the animal to a skidding stop, throwing up a cloud of dust that surrounded them.

He finally took a chance to breathe. He had made it. He had lived. He had escaped with his life. All he had to do now was continue riding east and, in a few hours' time, he would find himself in the relative safety of Helena.

Most men may have thought this way. But Jeremiah Halstead was not like most men. And the thought of riding on to Helena had never crossed his mind.

He had not ridden this far to flee.

He had ridden this far to reload.

Deciding he would not need the '86 for what was to come, he stowed the rifle in the scabbard under his right knee. He cracked open the cylinder of his belly gun, dumped out the dead shells on the ground, and reloaded with fresh rounds off his belt before tucking it away. He did the same with the Colt on his hip and slid it back into its holster.

He reached back into his saddlebags and pulled out a handful of fresh bullets, sliding them into the empty slots on his belt.

He had just finished loading in the last one when he saw a rangy man ride out of the livery and come his way.

Halstead reached for the Winchester '73, when he recognized the man as Wheeler, the livery man. He approached with his hands raised and waving in the air.

"It's just me, deputy," Wheeler called out as he rode closer. "Don't shoot. I'm here to help."

Halstead left the rifle in its scabbard as Wheeler approached him.

"The hell you doing out here, old man?" Halstead said. "Looking to get yourself killed?"

"I'm here to help, just like I told you I would," the horse keeper said. "Tell you what I saw and where they are."

Halstead decided that might be helpful. He had not been able to see much from the cover of the saloon or from the clock tower, and there had been a lot of shooting since then. "Tell me."

"I think there's only one man left at the general store," Wheeler said, "but I can't be sure he's still there. A bunch of them rushed the bank, but about five of them broke cover and ran back toward the jail. Robinson didn't come back from the general store, either, and I don't know what to make of that."

"Damn it," Halstead cursed. "I told him not to do anything."

"Given the kind of man he is," Wheeler said, "I'd wager he probably took his pound of flesh before they took him down, if that's what they managed to do."

Halstead could not afford to think about Robinson's fate, but only hoped that if he had died that he had managed to take a few of the Hudson Gang with him. "What about Boddington?"

"Ducked into the general store when all that shooting started earlier," Wheeler reported. "Had Doc Mortimer and Mr. Ryan with him. I ain't seen any of them since, but I heard some shootin' comin' from there, too. Make of that what you will."

Halstead could not make much of it, but it was good to know the general store was a place to watch out for. "Any trouble around the Hotel Montana?"

"None that I've seen. Just a lot of scared folks flocking into the back of the place."

That was the first bit of good news Halstead had heard all day. "Get yourself over there and let them know I'm riding back in. Tell them to be ready to shoot anyone who comes their way who isn't me. Think you can remember that?"

Wheeler sat taller in the saddle. "I'm crazy, mister, not stupid."

Halstead wished he could say the same for himself. "Go on now like I told you. And keep your head down. This isn't over yet."

Wheeler giggled as he brought his horse around. "Hell, deputy. If I thought that, I'd never have wasted the time riding out to talk to you."

Halstead watched the man ride off and took a final look at the town of Silver Cloud. It was still a nice-looking place, despite all that had happened and all that would happen still.

As good a place to die as he had ever seen, he supposed.

He looked up to the sky where he figured his father to be, if he was anywhere. "At least I made it out of El Paso, papa. I guess that counts for something."

He dug his heels into Col and snapped the reins as they made one final charge toward Main Street together.

Chapter 28

Halstead saw a few men scatter from the thoroughfare as he began to race toward town. He had no idea if they were civilians or Hudson men. He did not care, either. He simply wanted news that he was headed back into town to spread along Main Street as fast as it could. He wanted Hudson and Zimmerman to wonder what he was up to.

In fact, Halstead wanted to know that himself. For other than charging through town to see where Hudson's men might be, he had no plan. He hoped to speed down Main Street, draw fire, and pray that Col was fast enough to dodge the bullets that were sure to be fired his way.

But as he raced toward the edge of town, he saw two dead men laying on the ground next to the feed store. He wondered if they might be some of the men Robinson had killed on his way to the general store. One of the dead men had an axe blade sticking out of his side while the other was on his back nearer to North Street.

That must be where the danger was. And if Wheeler was to be believed, that was where Robinson had found himself in trouble.

Halstead broke off his charge down Main Street at the

last second and steered the mustang to the right toward North Street.

He pulled the horse to a halt and grabbed his Winchester '73 as he climbed down from the saddle. Knowing the mustang's nature, he knew she would run as fast as she could down the back street and not stop for any reason until she was in the clear again.

He hated using Col as a decoy, but he would rather her stop a bullet than himself. The fire she might draw would tell him a lot about where the remaining Hudson men were hiding.

He gave her a firm slap on the rump and ran behind her as she galloped at full speed down North Street.

The horse had an easy time of it until she passed the general store, where a couple of rifle shots rang out. The sounds made Col stretch herself out longer as she began to run even faster. Halstead had been watching her closely and did not see any bullets strike her.

But he did see a body slumped against the back wall of the store. And, as he got closer, he saw Todd Robinson slumped on the ground, face down. The left side of his shirt was an ugly dark red.

Halstead stopped running and began to walk slowly toward him. He would have bet a year's salary that whoever had done that to Todd was a Hudson Gang regular. And the same man who had killed him had just shot at his horse.

He was not surprised when the large black man with the eye patch he had seen through his field glasses back at the stand of pine trees strode out of the store, rifle at his side. He had not looked back toward where Halstead was standing. He was looking at where he had expected the rider of the horse to have fallen.

"Where the hell did he go?" Halstead heard him say.

Halstead raised the Winchester to his shoulder and aimed it at the big man. "You missed."

The big man moved his head slightly but did not turn around. "You Halstead?"

"Yep. And you're under arrest. Drop the rifle and throw up your hands."

The deputy could see a grin on the outlaw's profile. "And if I don't."

"You've already got one hole in your head, mister. I don't think you want another."

Cliff nodded down toward Robinson. "I killed your friend. He put up a hell of a fight. Died like a man. Your sheriff friend, too. That ought to count for something. At least let me die the same way. Not like a dog shot in an alley."

"It entitles you to a bullet in the head or a long drop from a short rope." Halstead moved his finger to the trigger. "Your choice."

The moan that rose from Robinson surprised them both.

Halstead grinned. "Sounds to me like you didn't kill him. You couldn't even get that right."

The outlaw shook his head. "Sure would hate to leave unfinished business behind me."

When Cliff began to move his rifle in Robinson's direction, Halstead fired.

The bullet caught him in the center of his broad back and sent him pitching forward in the dirt.

Halstead kept his rifle trained down on him as he

walked toward the fallen man. And, despite his fatal wound, he was still trying to slide the rifle along the ground to aim it at Robinson.

Halstead slowly lowered his boot onto Cliff's hand and kicked the rifle out of his reach.

"A bullet in the back is a tricky thing," Halstead told him. "Could take you a while to die. Tell me if there's anyone else in the store and I'll end it quick."

Cliff struggled to raise his head. "Go . . . to . . . hell."

Halstead lowered his rifle. "See you there." He squeezed the trigger and ended it.

He looked up when he heard a great calamity down by the jail. He saw a man trying to block Col's path. He ran in front of the horse, arms and legs outstretched as he tried to grab hold of her reins. She rose up on her hind legs and kicked out with her foreleg, catching the man in the head. Halstead could tell by the way he fell that he was already dead.

Col resumed her run as a man stepped out from behind the jail and aimed a rifle at her.

Halstead raised his rifle, aimed, and fired.

Judging by the way the man staggered and fired into the air, he knew his bullet had hit its mark, but it had not put him down. The wounded man managed to make it around the corner of the jail as Halstead's second shot went wide.

"Jerry," Robinson moaned. "Help me."

Halstead hollered into the store. "Doc Mortimer. It's Halstead. Get out here, now."

He aimed his rifle at the doorway but raised it when the doctor ran out into the street with his medical bag in hand. He stepped over the dead outlaw and knelt beside the bartender.

"Thank God you're here," the doctor said to Halstead. "That bastard over there wouldn't let me tend to him. Said his moaning was music to his ears. I was surprised he let me take care of Boddington's wounds."

He remembered Cliff had said something about Boddington. "Any other Hudson men in there?"

The doctor shook his head as he tore Robinson's shirt open and began examining his wounds.

Halstead darted inside to check on the sheriff. The hostages gasped when they saw a new man with a rifle enter the store, but quickly calmed when they saw who it was.

He found Boddington stretched out on a makeshift bed of bags of oats. The left side of his shirt had been cut away and a bandage had been wrapped around his left shoulder and left bicep.

The sheriff tried to get up when he saw Halstead, but the deputy took a knee and eased him back down.

He looked at the frightened people in the store. "The men who were holding you here are dead, but you should stay here for a while until I clear out the rest of them, just to be safe."

The people thanked him and asked God to bless him, Mr. Ryan amongst him.

"I've never gone from hating a man to being glad to see him so fast in all my life," Ryan told him. "You're a mighty tough man to hate, boy."

Halstead ignored him and checked Boddington's bandages. Spots of blood were already beginning to spread and judging by their locations on his body, he was a lucky man.

"Cliff do this to you?" Halstead asked him.

"Not a very good shot with a pistol," Boddington groaned. "Aimed for my heart and head and missed both times. Guess I have Robinson to thank for that. He was on top of him when he shot me. Would've finished me off, too, if it hadn't been for the doc and Mr. Ryan here."

Halstead was glad to hear it. "Those black eyes you got from that busted nose I gave you probably made him mistake you for a racoon. Thought you were rabid, being in the daylight like you were."

Boddington laughed, and his wounds immediately made him regret it. "You pick the damnedest times to have a sense of humor, Halstead." He looked out the back door at Cliff's body. "He dead?"

"Yep. And Robinson's still got some life in him."

The sheriff stifled a cough. "What about Zimmerman and the others?"

"I winged him from the tower," Halstead told him, "but I don't know if I killed him. A bunch of them seem to be holed up by the jail. I just hit two more at the end of the street." He did not bother telling him that Col had helped in her own way.

"Guess that means you'll be heading down to the jail to finish them off, don't it?" Boddington asked.

"Don't see any other way around it."

Boddington swung his legs off the canvas sacks and sat up before Halstead could stop him. "Then I'm coming with you."

Mr. Ryan reached out from his wheelchair and took hold of Boddington's right sleeve. "Don't be a fool, Barry.

You're shot all to hell. Let the deputy take care of this. He's better suited to do this on his own than either of us in our present conditions."

But Boddington pulled himself free from the man's grasp. "It's not his town, Mr. Ryan. It's mine, remember? I get a piece of all business here and that means I handle all the troubles, too. I've got two good feet under me and a job to do. And I'm going to do it." He fixed Halstead with a hard glare. "I wouldn't try to stop me if I were you."

Halstead thought Boddington was a fool for trying, but he had no intention of stopping him. He could have asked the Reyes family for help, but they were civilians. He wanted to keep them out of this if he could. He could use the extra gun when going up against Zimmerman and however many men he might have left. Even if Boddington was likely to get killed, it would be one less bullet aimed his way.

"Have it your way," Halstead told him. "Your pistol loaded? Can you handle a rifle?"

"Pistol's fine," the sheriff said, "and they've got a coach gun behind the counter I can use. It'll be up close work, anyway, so it should be enough."

Halstead had to admire the man's spirit. He had come to think of him as nothing more than a bully, but he appeared to be much more than that. His father had written him about how a man's true colors came out when the lead started flying. He imagined he was seeing a glimpse of the kind of man Boddington truly was.

The sheriff held out his right hand, and Halstead helped him to his feet. Other than a wince of pain from the effort, the sheriff stood steady.

"You head down North Street," Boddington told him.

"I'll head down Main. I'll try to flush them out your way while you finish them off from the back. Sound good?"

It sounded far from good. It sounded desperate. But Halstead was in no position to be particular. "Best plan I've heard all day."

Chapter 29

Halstead took an extra box of bullets from the store and reloaded his rifle. He pocketed the extra rounds and began his slow steady walk down North Street while Boddington headed down Main.

"Damn it," he heard one of the men down by the jail yell. "It's Boddington!"

A series of rifle fire picked up from the far end of Main Street, but not a sound from the shotgun the sheriff was toting. He was still too far away for it to be effective, so Halstead hoped the sheriff had found cover somewhere.

He set aside his concern for the sheriff and continued to keep his eyes trained on the line of stores and buildings in front of him. He fought the urge to run toward the jail and aid the sheriff, but he had no intention of running into a bullet.

He saw a man on horseback round the corner of the jail and aim a rifle in his direction. Halstead dove to the side as a bullet struck the wall where he had been standing. He rolled into the prone position, aimed, and fired.

The man on horseback did not move, and Halstead knew his shot had gone wide.

The outlaw fired again, and the bullet landed about a foot in front of Halstead, kicking up dust and dirt that flew in his face and got into his eyes. Halstead shifted his aim again and fired blindly in the direction where he had last seen the rider. He rolled quickly to his left to make himself as difficult a target as he could. He heard two more rounds strike the ground where he had been.

He wiped his eyes on his sleeve and tried to aim at the rider again, but he was already galloping in the opposite direction, his black coat billowing behind him.

Halstead cracked off two more shots, but the rider kept on riding, hunched down in the saddle as he dug his heels deeply into the sides of his mount.

Halstead blinked his eyes clear and shook his head as he got back to his feet and resumed his steady walk down toward the jail.

He was glad to hear the boom of Boddington's coach gun echo through the town, followed by a scream. *Good for you, Boddington. You got one.*

As he got closer to the jail, he saw the body of the man Col had kicked as she fled town. His bug eyes were still wide as his head was at an unnatural angle. *Good girl.*

The back wall of the jail was still intact, and Halstead slid along the back of it. He paused when he got to the corner as he heard Boddington cut loose with the second barrel of the coach gun. He would be down to his pistol now, unless he found a way to reload one-handed.

Halstead could hear raised voices coming from inside the ruined jail but could not tell if one of them belonged to Zimmerman.

He listened to see if he could hear anyone around the

corner, but there was too much noisy shooting on Main Street to tell for certain.

Realizing he could not wait there forever, he came around the corner as he raised his rifle.

A man let out an inhuman scream as he ran straight into him before he could get off a shot. He had a knife raised high above his head.

Halstead used his rifle as a bar against the charging man as both of them fell to the ground. His attacker straddled him as he brought down the knife. Halstead stopped the blow by holding up his rifle crossways, then brought up a knee to flip the man over his head.

As the man tumbled over him and hit the ground, Halstead got to his feet before the man with the knife could recover and aimed his rifle down at him. He recognized the man as Pole and was surprised such a tall, skinny man could have so much strength.

He was about to pull the trigger when a bullet struck him on the left side and sent him sprawling over Pole. His rifle tumbled away as he fell.

Ignoring the searing pain in his shoulder, Halstead flipped on his back as Pole once again fell on him with the knife.

Instinct caused Halstead to bring up his knees and kick the man in the stomach. Pole staggered backward but quickly regained his footing and began to come at him again.

Halstead drew his belly gun and fired three times, hitting his attacker twice in the chest and once in the head.

Pole fell to the side, revealing a redheaded man behind him racking a fresh round into his rifle as he yelled, "Die, you son of a bitch!"

Halstead's first shot hit him in the belly. His second hit him in the chest. The redheaded man dropped his rifle as he fell backward into the compact dirt of Main Street.

Halstead got to his feet, doing his best to ignore the fire in the left side of his chest. He ran as quickly as he could manage to the cover of the back wall of the jail as he opened the cylinder of his Colt and shook the dead shells out. He shifted the gun to his left hand and began plucking fresh rounds from his belt to feed into the pistol. He was surprised that his left hand felt normal and chanced a glance at the wound. He was glad to see a hole just above the star on his coat, for it meant the bullet had gone straight through his body. If it had hit his heart, he would already be dead. If it had hit his lung, he would not have been able to breathe. He figured that meant he would probably live, at least long enough to end this thing once and for all.

His pistol reloaded, he snapped the cylinder shut and chanced another turn around the corner. He left his rifle where it was, knowing it was down to pistol work now.

He stepped over the redheaded man he supposed was Mick and came upon the jagged ruin of the wall of the jail. He saw two dead men in the middle of Main Street. Neither of them was Boddington.

One of them was Brad the bouncer.

"Over here, deputy," the sheriff called out to him.

Halstead stepped away from the jail as he came around the corner and aimed his pistol into what had once been the sheriff's office.

He found Boddington standing in the rubble, aiming his pistol into the cells. "Look at what I found."

Halstead looked over the dead man behind the overturned desk, hoping it was Zimmerman. But it was only the man Halstead had killed when he had shot through Boddington's desk with his '86.

He stepped over the corpse and joined Boddington. He was glad to see John Hudson sitting on the bunk of the same cell he had occupied for the past few days.

All of this destruction, Halstead thought. All of this death and the man had not so much as stepped foot out of his cell.

"Right where we left him," Boddington said as he holstered his Colt. "Guess all that gunfire just plain rattled him."

But Halstead kept his pistol trained on the man. "Where's Zimmerman?"

Hudson did not raise his head to speak. "He went to fetch the horses. Said he'd be right back. Guess he lied."

Halstead figured Zimmerman had been the man who had shot at him from horseback on North Street. Part of him was glad the man was out of his hair for now.

And part of him regretted not being able to kill him.

"Would you look at that?" Boddington said as he stepped into the cells. "The key's still in the door."

The iron door wailed as the sheriff swung it shut with his good hand. He put his hip against it to keep it in place as he turned the key in the lock. He removed the key and gave the door a good shake to make sure it was closed.

He looked back at Halstead and beamed. "Still works, too. They don't make iron doors like that anymore."

Halstead tucked his pistol back in his belly holster. "Outlaws either, seems like."

Chapter 30

The next morning, after Maria made him a breakfast fit for a king, Halstead accepted a hug from his hostess despite her tears. Her embrace around his middle made the hole in his left side ache something awful, but he swallowed the pain for her sake.

"You poor boy," she said in Spanish. "You should rest here for a while. Let us take care of you."

"I'll be fine, Dona Maria," he told her. "Doc Mortimer did a good job patching me up and I promise I'll see a doctor as soon as I get to Helena. You've got my word on that."

She looked up at him, her eyes still wet. "And you'll send back my Miguel when you find him."

"I will if Mackey hasn't deputized him already." He smiled. "Your son is a brave young man."

"Of course, he is," Don Antonio said. "He comes from a good bloodline."

"I don't doubt it." Maria released him reluctantly as he shook hands with her husband. "Thank you for taking in all those people. You saved a lot of lives, my friend."

The hotelier frowned at Halstead's wounded shoulder.

"I only wish you had let us do more. Maybe then you would not have been injured."

"And maybe you would've been." Halstead shook his head. "I couldn't live with that."

The couple walked him to the front door of their hotel where Ignacio stood holding Col's reins. He had been kind enough to ride out the previous afternoon, find the mustang, and bring her back.

"Well, I'll be," Lance McAlister greeted him as he stepped out on the boardwalk. "If it isn't the man who helped me make my fortune."

Halstead could not remember the last time he had smiled so much. "I told you not to bet against me."

"And I didn't," the old gambler said. "Unfortunately, you killed most of the men I bet with, but the sheriff said he'll see what we can do about that by selling what they left behind."

"I hope you get your money," Halstead said as he climbed into the saddle and took the reins from Ignacio.

"And if I don't, I'm just happy you're alive." McAlister reached up and patted Halstead's leg. "Don't worry about Todd. The doc said he can live just fine on one kidney. And I'll see to it he gets the best of care."

Halstead was glad to hear it. Robinson deserved the best and more. "See to it you take care of yourself in the meantime."

Halstead saw Boddington riding toward him with John Hudson atop a bay trailing close behind him. He saw the prisoner had a noose around his neck.

When he reached Halstead, the sheriff handed the rope over to him. "I figured he ought to get used to the feeling of a rope, considering his circumstances. Wrap that end around your saddle horn so it does the job for you in case he tries to run."

Halstead looked at the broken outlaw, who kept his head down. "I don't think I'll have any trouble with him."

Halstead bid his new friends good-bye as he and Boddington moved their horses onto Main Street and began the slow walk to Helena.

The townspeople who had lined the boardwalk began to cheer as the two lawmen rode past with their prisoner. Halstead was not used to hearing cheers and did not know what to do with the attention except wave a little.

"Looks like you'll always be welcome here in Silver Cloud, deputy," Boddington observed. "Might even get yourself a reputation as big as your boss if you keep going like this."

"I hope not," he said, meaning it. Mackey had never liked the name he had earned for himself, and Halstead planned on following in his footsteps. *A popular man is a targeted man.*

They slowed their mounts as they reached the end of Main Street.

"Well," Boddington said, "I'd like to say it's been a pleasure, but I can't."

Halstead could not disagree with him. "That left arm going to be all right?"

"That's what the doc tells me. He also told me to give you his fondest regards. Said he would've been here to see you off, but he's tending to Todd after his operation. You've done wonders for his mortuary business and he stands to earn a pretty penny planting all the men you've left behind. He might make enough to challenge Mr. Ryan for richest man in town."

Halstead laughed until he remembered Cassie. "I guess you'll be burying Cassie soon, won't you?"

Boddington nodded solemnly. "Yeah. The service is tomorrow. I'm sorry you'll miss it. She would've liked you to have been there."

Halstead was not so sure of that but did not argue the point. "Put an extra flower on her casket for me if you think to. I guess I hadn't done much for her in life, but I'd appreciate it just the same."

"I'll be glad to, deputy, if you'll agree to do something for me."

Halstead had not been expecting that. "Sure, name it."

Boddington held out his hand to him. "Should've offered it to you that first night you came here and I'm mighty sorry I didn't. But I'd be honored if you'd take it now."

Halstead shook the man's hand and gladly. "The name's Jeremiah. Jerry to my friends."

"I hope I can call you a friend," Boddington said. "I truly do."

"You can." He broke off the handshake. "Be well."

He put his heels to Col's side and got the horse and prisoner moving toward Helena.

Boddington called after him. "And maybe next time, you'll get around to telling me how your horse got its name."

"Maybe," Halstead called back.

"And tell me why your boss made you stay in town as long as he did."

Halstead intended on finding that out for himself.

Chapter 31

Deputy Billy Sunday let out a long, low whistle that filled the marshal's office. He was building a cigarette in his dark, nimble hands. "Aaron, I believe we've got a very angry young man in our midst."

Aaron Mackey, United States Marshal of the Montana Territory, barely grunted as he continued to read Halstead's report on all that had happened in Silver Cloud.

Halstead said nothing. The pain pills the doctor had given him had dulled his senses a bit, and he was glad for it. He was liable to say something nasty otherwise. And although he had known these men all of his life and had looked up to them for just as long, they were still his bosses, Mackey in particular.

That did not mean he could not be angry with them.

The air in the marshal's office smelled like Billy's stale cigarette smoke and old coffee.

Mackey finished reading the report and shoved it on his desk. Like Billy, he was in his mid-thirties. A lean, clean-shaven man with the deepest, hardest set eyes Halstead had ever seen.

Those eyes looked at him now. "Looks like you were

busy in Silver Cloud. Brought in your prisoner alive, killed off most of his gang, and solved a murder in the bargain. Some men would call that an accomplishment. Might even be proud of themselves."

"Some would," Halstead allowed.

"But not you," Mackey observed. "Go ahead. Say what you want to say before it burns a hole through you." He looked at Halstead's left arm. "You've already got one too many."

Halstead struggled with what to say and managed to come up with, "I'm not pleased, Aaron."

The marshal folded his hands across his flat stomach. "Why?"

Halstead could barely understand the question. "Well, for starters, I guess I'm wondering why I had to stay in Silver Cloud for so damned long."

"Because I ordered you to," Mackey said. Then added, "And because it was the smartest thing to do, given the circumstances."

"Circumstances?" Halstead felt his temper begin to slip away from him and he held on to it tight. "I was already half a day's ride ahead of Hudson's men. I could've let out at first light and been in town before they even reached me."

"Your horses needed rest."

"Not *my* horses," Halstead countered. "I wasn't riding a Clydesdale, Aaron. My mustangs were fresh and ready for the trail the very next day, especially on ground that's as easy as between here and Silver Cloud."

"Easy ground," Billy repeated. "Mighty open ground, too."

"Easy ground where Hudson's men could've overrun

you," Mackey added. "Silver Cloud usually has a full livery. Who's to say Hudson's men wouldn't have traded out their tired mounts for fresh horses and run you down?" He pointed at the report. "Who in town would've stopped them? This Boddington and his deputies don't sound like much to me. I don't know if you've ever found yourself in open ground on played-out horses, Jerry, but Billy and I have. It's not fun, especially when you've got an armed gang bearing down on you and no place to hide."

"Not fun at all," Billy added.

None of this was making Halstead feel any better. "So, you just left me in town as what? As bait? Like a worm wriggling on a hook just waiting for that bunch to take a bite out of me?"

"No," Mackey said. "I expected you to remain in a relatively safe area with the prisoner secured while the dust settled. Your wire said Zimmerman had taken charge of the Hudson Gang. He's known to be a tough man to figure out. There was a chance he might've convinced the others to cut their losses, let you have Hudson, and double back to Rock Creek to get their money."

"Could've gone either way," Billy said. "It just happened to break ugly." He shrugged. "It happens."

"Easy for you to say," Halstead spat. "You two were safe here in Helena while I was the one getting shot at."

The cold stares he drew from both men made his soul run cold. He regretted it as soon as the words passed his lips. His throat swelled up and he lost the ability to speak.

He swallowed hard. "I'm sorry. I didn't mean that."

Mackey leaned forward, glaring at him. "You don't think either of us have ever been shot at? You don't think we've ever gone up against the odds you have? Worse than that? You've got a short memory, Deputy Halstead."

Halstead tried to keep his hands from shaking by gripping the arms of his chair tighter. He had just insulted two men he considered friends. Heroes, even. Men most of the territory considered them legends, and they were right.

Suddenly, Jeremiah Halstead felt very small. "I didn't mean that. I said I'm sorry."

Mackey did not look like he had accepted the apology. "I was waiting for another telegram from you to learn how things were playing out in town. If you'd needed help, we would've been there, personally. Billy and me. But you didn't send a telegram because you didn't have time. That's the way it is in this business, Jerry. Things don't always happen the way you plan or the way you'd like. You found yourself in a bad way and look what happened. Just look at how you handled yourself."

"They're dead," Billy said, "and you're here enjoying a nice afternoon tea with us."

Billy's wide smile told him all was forgiven, but he could not shake the cold feeling that spread through the center of him.

Billy lit his cigarette and got up from the chair. "Cheer up, Jerry." He slapped him on the shoulder as he went over to the stove to get some coffee. "You're alive. You won. Enjoy it."

But Mackey did not smile. "You let me pin that star on your shirt. I didn't force it on you. And that star is more than just a piece of tin. It comes with a responsibility to get the job done no matter what. You're not always going to find yourself so close to Helena. You might find yourself in a bad way far away from here where the nearest help is more than a week away. You needed to learn how to handle things for yourself." He tapped the report on his desk. "And based on what I've read here today, it sounds like you did just that. Don't be mad, Jerry. Be proud and remember what you learned out there because next time, it might just save your life."

Halstead felt like a fool. "Yes, sir."

Mackey kicked the leg of Halstead's chair. "Don't sir me. I'm still young enough to teach you a thing or two." He gestured toward the cup Billy held out to him. "Now, drink your coffee. You've earned it. You did well out there, Jerry. Very well."

Halstead knew that was as close to a smoothing over as he was liable to get from Aaron. He accepted the cup and took a sip, quickly remembering how good Billy's coffee was. "I could've used some of that in Silver Cloud. The food wasn't bad, but the coffee left something to be desired."

"So did the company," Mackey added, "based on your report. Judge Forester is beyond pleased that you managed to bring in Hudson alive despite everything. He might put you up for a commendation of some kind, and I'm inclined to agree with him."

Halstead did not think he was worthy of it. "I didn't get everyone. Zimmerman got away."

Billy carried over a bundle wrapped in brown paper tied with string and let it drop on Mackey's desk with a thud.

Halstead eyed the parcel carefully. "What is it?"

"Open it and find out." Billy got a mug of coffee from the stove, handed it to Mackey, and got one for himself. "Think of it as an early birthday present."

Halstead set his cup aside and went to the desk. He pulled the knot open and tore away the paper.

It was a stack of wanted posters and one glimpse of it was enough to make him smile.

It read:

WANTED
EDWARD ZIMMERMAN
$5,000 REWARD
DEAD OR ALIVE

The sketch of Zimmerman was mighty accurate, too.

Billy had been right. It felt like his birthday and Christmas all rolled up into one.

Mackey grinned at him. "How's that for a welcome home present?"

Halstead picked up one of the sheets and looked into the dead eyes of the man who had escaped him. "Pretty good. It'll be even better if I'm the one who kills him."

Billy hoisted his cup. "Amen to that."

The three men clinked mugs and drank their coffee.

The warmth of the coffee felt good in his belly. Felt good all around.

THE END

TURN THE PAGE
FOR AN EXCITING PREVIEW!

Welcome to Johnstone Country.

Watch Your Back

**Keeper of the peace, enforcer of the law,
Buck Trammel has faced every kind of killer,
outlaw, and prairie rat that's crawled from the
depraved depths of America's western frontier—
with a quick draw and a clean conscience . . .**

SIBLING RIVALRY

"King" Charles Hagen is dead. The empire he carved out of Blackstone, Wyoming, by hook and by crook now lies in the hands of his children.
Caleb Hagen has long stood in his father's shadow, ambitiously plotting, and ready to stake his claim. Young and impetuous Tyler Hagen plans to expand the family legacy across the nation. Christina Hagen's ruthless nature believes the time has come for a queen to reign over the Hagen kingdom.

Only Adam, their estranged brother, has a different plan. His vengeance against their father requires him to tear down everything "King" Hagen ever built, even if that means shedding family blood. But none of the siblings reckoned that crippled crime boss Lucien Clay was prepared to send a murderous pack of gunslingers against them all for control of the territory.

Blackstone has been ruled by lawlessness long enough. The town is Buck Trammel's jurisdiction. And he will protect it as judge, jury, and executioner . . .

**National Bestselling Authors
William W. Johnstone
and J.A. Johnstone**

THE FIRES OF BLACKSTONE

A BUCK TRAMMEL WESTERN

**Coming in May 2022,
wherever Pinnacle Books are sold**

Chapter 1

"Sounds like company's coming, boss," Deputy James "Hawkeye" Hauk said as the train whistle echoed through Blackstone.

"Yeah," Sheriff Buck Trammel said as he set his coffee mug on his desk and got to his feet. "It certainly does." Unlike some residents, he found the new sound of a train whistle echoing throughout town to be charming. But he knew this particular whistle was more than just a train engine letting off steam. It was a warning that trouble was coming to Blackstone.

"Guess I'd better go down to the station to meet it." He took his Peacemaker from his desk and tucked it in the holster under his left arm. It had been a long time since he'd been a Pinkerton, but he'd never gotten comfortable with wearing a gun on his hip. "Head off whatever trouble I can."

He was still getting used to the idea that Blackstone now had a train station. Adam Hagen had built a railroad spur north from the main line in Laramie so he could bring his wood from the mill and his cattle to market in the City.

The short line ran on a regular schedule and at Adam Hagen's convenience. A trip that used to take half a day now took about thirty minutes. Unfortunately, the train not only served to bring goods and people down to Laramie, but to also bring them up to Blackstone. Hence the reason for Trammel's concern.

Trammel looked at the rifles in the rack by the jailhouse door but decided against taking one. It might put people on more of an edge than they already were. He figured his size and the Peacemaker would serve as suitable deterrents.

Hawkeye asked, "Want me to go with you?"

Trammel shook his head as he pulled on his hat. "Best if you stay here for the time being. But get ready to come running if you hear any trouble from the station."

If Hawkeye was disappointed, he hid it well. He took down the double-barreled shotgun from the rack and began feeding shells into the tubes. "I'll be here if you need me."

Trammel bent his head as he stepped out of the jail and onto the boardwalk. "You always are."

At six-seven and two-hundred-and-forty solid pounds, Steven "Buck" Trammel was always conscious of his size. He'd never quite gotten used to the attention he drew whenever people saw him for the first time. Lately, he drew more odd looks than normal for there were a lot of new people in Blackstone these days. The railroad spur Adam Hagen had built as soon as he had gained control of the Hagen empire had brought them here. The building boom that Adam had started had kept them here.

The new Hagen wood mill was almost done and a new street full of houses for the workers was almost finished.

The tents the workers had been sleeping in for the past three months would soon be a thing of the past, and, Trammel hoped, the disorder they brought would go with them. In his experience, a man tended to simmer down once he had a fixed roof over his head. It made him appreciate being out of the rain more.

Trammel stood aside on the boardwalk as a group of ladies marched past them on the way to the new church Adam Hagen had built for the town at the end of Main Street. The gesture had just been a small part of Hagen's plan to wipe every trace of his father from the town and remake Blackstone in his own image.

Trammel figured Adam would have to build a church twice the size of Notre Dame if he were looking to atone for all the sins he had committed in his life.

King Charles Hagen was dead. Long live King Adam Hagen.

"Good morning, Sheriff!" came a familiar voice from the balcony of the new hotel across Main Street.

Trammel stepped out from beneath the overhang and into the thoroughfare. The new Phoenix Hotel loomed larger than its predecessor, the Clifford, which had been burned in a riot the previous year. A few modest buildings had to be torn down for the Phoenix, but those inconvenienced by the construction were moved to newer, larger homes in the bargain. They had offered little complaint. Trammel knew Adam was a lot of things, but he knew how to treat people when he wanted something from them.

Trammel pegged the Phoenix as being more than twice the size of its predecessor. It sported a proper gaming area that rivaled even the finest gambling houses in New Orleans. Dozens of well-appointed rooms were said to put some of the nicest hotels in New York to shame. Hagen had even gone as far as to bring a chef all the way from Paris to make sure every meal was an occasion. Guests flocked to Blackstone from far and wide to see what all the fuss was about.

The Phoenix featured a large porch on the first floor that accommodated plenty of rocking chairs where guests could lounge while they took in the bustling new Main Street. A grand balcony on the second floor served as Adam Hagen's favorite perch from where he could see all that his large inheritance had given him. He was building a town that might one day be worthy to become the capital of the territory.

"Nice to see you, Buck." Adam Hagen toasted him with a cup of coffee. Even from that distance, Trammel could see the intricate pattern on the china that sported a deep red design matching the fiery theme of the Phoenix Hotel. "You're looking well this morning."

Trammel certainly did not feel well. Dr. Moore had pulled four bullets out of his left side after the riot. The wounds still ached whenever it was about to rain.

"You're looking prosperous yourself," Trammel said, "for a man with a price on his head."

Hagen threw back his head and laughed. "People have been trying to kill me for years, Buck, yet here I am."

Here he was, Trammel thought, but he had certainly changed over the years. In the morning light, he could see Hagen had aged quite a bit since they'd first met in Wichita. His fair hair had begun to turn white in places, though Trammel knew he was just past thirty. Hagen kept his beard trimmed and close to his smooth skin. He looked leaner than he used to, and his light eyes were set deeper than they used to be. Harder, too.

And since King Charles's suspicious death, Adam had changed his clothes to a more somber tone. Loud brocade vests had given way to darker colors more befitting a man of property and stature.

Hagen's smiled held as he asked Trammel, "I take it you're heading over to the train station?"

"Somebody's got to go," Trammel said. "Want to head off any trouble before it starts."

"No need," Hagen said. "Ben London and his constables are already there. They'll see to it nothing happens. Let them do their job. It's what I pay them for."

Trammel had been against the creation of a town constabulary when Hagen had first raised the matter at a town council meeting. But given that Blackstone was his town, none of the elders saw fit to oppose him. The group quickly became known as *Hagen's Constables*. Their blue tunics and brass badges made them easy to spot. They existed to serve Hagen's interests, which were not always aligned with those of the town. Trammel and Hawkeye were still the only official law that existed in Blackstone, a fact of which the sheriff had to remind Hagen many times.

But Trammel saw no benefit to continuing that old argument standing in the middle of Main Street, especially now that the second train whistle was much closer than the first. "Enjoy your coffee, Adam. I've got work to do."

"Be sure to give my regards to my family when you see them," Hagen called after him. "We're not exactly on speaking terms these days."

Trammel couldn't blame them. After all, Adam Hagen had killed his father.

* * *

The walk to the new train station at the east end of Main Street took longer than it used to. Even Trammel was impressed by all the changes Hagen had made in a short amount of time.

When Trammel had first come to Blackstone, the place had been little more than a cow town. A place where miners and cattlemen who didn't work for the mighty Blackstone ranch came to find some hint of civilization. The town had been laid out as an "E" back then, with three avenues shooting off from Main Street.

Since the demise of King Charles, Adam had gone on a building spree of epic proportions. Main Street had been doubled in length and now featured two general stores besides the old Robertson's place. Robertson had sold out months ago and moved to Colorado. There were also several claims offices to cater to the miners, three banks, and just as many hotels.

Those who couldn't afford the opulence of the Phoenix could find clean, comfortable rooms at the Occidental, the East Sider, and the Knickerbocker.

Saloons still dominated Main Street, though drunkards had ceased to wander the town per Hagen's orders. The Pot of Gold Saloon still catered to the opium trade, but the Chinese who peddled dragon smoke had taken down their canvas tents in favor of a building that fit in with the rest of the town. Hagen had also made sure they did a better job of keeping their customers inside until they were sober enough to walk around on their own steam.

As he continued walking toward the station, Trammel was happy to see the shingle of Dr. Emily Downs hanging beneath that of Dr. Jacob Moore outside a two-story building. The two physicians tended to the needs of the growing town and were busier tending to colds and flus rather than broken bones and gunshots these days.

He hoped nothing would happen at the train station to change that.

The train station on the far eastern side of the town was a small but ornate affair. Hagen had designed it with intricate wooden fixtures that gave it an elegant look. It also featured a telegraph office. The telegraph lines that had followed the tracks made it easier for Blackstone to communicate with Laramie and the rest of the country. Modernity, Trammel decided, had its privileges.

Wagons and carriages of every sort were waiting outside the station building, ready to take any new arrivals or goods to their destination. A large stockyard had been built at the far end of the tracks for the easy loading and unloading of livestock.

But as he waited for the train to pull into the station that morning, Trammel was less concerned about any four-legged passengers the train might be bringing to town. It was the two-legged variety that worried him.

The locomotive emitted a large plume of steam from its great smokestack as it came to a halt. Black porters jumped from the passenger cars and placed step stools on the ground to help passengers looking to get out at Blackstone.

Trammel walked to the end of the train where he saw the two private Hagen family cars. Their own footmen were already off the train and loading the luggage of their employers onto a waiting wagon.

Caleb Hagen was the leader of the family and looked it.

He was approaching fifty and, although he had been born and raised at the family ranch in Blackstone, he could have been mistaken for a New York banker. His face had some of his late father's sharp features, but too many steak dinners and black cigars and made him thick around the middle. His dark suit had been tailored to hide his girth, but as Trammel had learned, clothes could only hide a man's true nature for so long. He had once handled the Hagen empire's investments and had been proud of his accomplishments until Adam inherited it all and replaced him.

Bartholomew Hagen was shorter than his brother and, if the paintings he had seen at the Hagen ranch house were to be believed, favored his mother. A capable looking man who lacked his brother's height and frame, King Charles had placed his second son in charge of the family's mining interests. From what Trammel had heard, he had done more than a fair job of making the family even richer than they already were.

Like her brother, Debora Hagen Forrester favored her mother's portrait except for her eyes. There she resembled King Charles, right down to the cold, casual glare. Not even the parasol or the fashionable pink hat she sported could soften her look.

Her husband, Ambrose Forrester, was at her side. He had a habit of constantly running his hand through his hair to ensure it remained in place. The fop came from the powerful Forrester family of Colorado, which counted several relatives in state houses throughout the west and one in the U.S. Senate. Other than an impressive last name, Trammel found him entirely forgettable.

Elena Hagen Wain was the baby of the family and Adam's favorite sister. She had married a Philadelphia lawyer who Adam claimed was well on his way to being named partner in the family firm.

Where her brothers and sister were severe, Elena was gentle. Her golden hair and porcelain skin made her look like Adam's twin, though she was much younger and only his cousin. Trammel wondered if her siblings had told her Adam was not really their brother or if they had been uncharacteristically kind enough to hide that fact from her.

Trammel knew if there was one trait the Hagen clan lacked, it was kindness.

The family did their best to ignore Trammel as he ambled over to them where they had clustered together on the platform outside their train cars.

"Welcome back to Blackstone," he told them.

Caleb chewed on a black cigar and scowled up at him as if he was a beggar. Bart and Debora made a half attempt at smiles, but nothing more.

Elena waved and smiled. "Morning, Buck. Nice to see you again."

Trammel touched the brim of his hat. She had still been living with her father when Trammel had brought Adam back to Blackstone. She had been a charming young woman then, and he was glad some things had not changed. "Nice to be seen, Elena. Hope your trip up here was a pleasant one."

Caleb took the black cigar from his mouth as he strode between Trammel and the rest of his family. "I suppose Adam sent you here to spy on us?"

Trammel had not been expecting a handshake. "Your brother and I have an arrangement, Caleb. He doesn't tell me what to do so I don't have to defy him. Makes it easier to keep the peace that way."

"My brother," the banker spat. He looked like he wanted to say more but caught himself. "What are you doing here, then?"

"Making sure your visit starts off on the right foot." Trammel inclined his head to the five men in blue tunics standing next to the station building. "I don't want anyone to make you feel unwelcome."

Caleb looked over at the five constables gathered nearby. "They look more like common thugs to me."

Trammel could not argue with him there. They were all like him, former saloon bouncers who had somehow managed to get badges pinned on their chests. Every one of the ten constables on Hagen's payroll had the same look. Tall, broad, and mean, and they made no effort to hide it.

Big Ben London was the biggest and meanest looking of the bunch. About Trammel's size, the silent Negro looked at the Hagens with cold indifference.

"I'm not with them and they're not with me," Trammel reminded Caleb. "They won't give you any trouble while I'm around."

"No need," Caleb said. "We can take care of ourselves against their kind."

Trammel looked at Caleb's belly and thought otherwise. "Well, with me around, you won't have to."

"That's what's always fascinated me about you, Trammel." Caleb pointed at him with the unlit cigar. "You despise Adam every bit as the rest of us, yet you always somehow find a way to save his life."

"Just doing my job," Trammel said.

Caleb went on. "You should've let that crowd rip him to pieces last year, but you didn't. Hell, you almost got yourself killed in the process. You're not a stupid man.

That's plain for anyone with two eyes to see. Why not just sit back and let nature take its course?"

"On account of I'm not paid to let nature have its way, Caleb. I'm paid to keep the peace here in town, and that's what I'm going to keep on doing until they take this star from me. That's part of the reason why I came over here to see you folks. I'd like to know what you're doing back here."

Caleb sneered. "So, you are scouting for Adam after all."

Trammel shook his head. "You know I'm not. Your troubles with him over your father's estate are your business so long as it stays peaceful. We've had our fair share of trouble in this town, and it's up to me to make sure things don't get out of hand."

Caleb opened his coat. "I'm not armed, Sheriff."

"Men like you never do your own fighting," Trammel said. "I've seen some rough characters milling around town over the past couple of days. Over at the Knickerbocker and the Occidental. I figure they're yours."

Caleb shrugged. "And what if they are? What concern is it of yours?"

"None, so long as they don't step out of line."

"Does the same go for Adam's so-called constables?"

"There's only two sworn lawmen in Blackstone, Caleb. Me and Hawkeye. The constables only have authority on Hagen land and, last I checked, Blackstone is public property. They step out of line? They get stepped on same as everyone else."

Caleb Hagen took his time looking the sheriff up and down. "Is that so?"

Trammel let him look. "It surely is."

Caleb popped his cigar in his mouth and looked away.

"You've got nothing to worry about from me or my family, Trammel. We're as peaceful as Pascal lambs. For now, our fight is in the courts."

"Glad to hear it." Trammel meant it. "Just make sure it stays there. And that your men stay out of trouble while they're here in town."

Caleb nodded toward the constables. "And them?"

"I'll be watching them like I'm watching you. They bother you or your people, you let me know."

Caleb did not look convinced, but he did not look like he wanted an argument, either. "We'll leave it at that, then. Nice seeing you again, Steven."

Trammel touched the brim of his hat. "Caleb."

He stood aside as he watched the family take their time loading themselves into the coaches that had lined up to take them to the Hagen ranch house up the hill from town.

The five constables milled around close to the carriages as the family boarded them but did not say a word. Only Caleb antagonized them by staring at Big Ben as they pulled away.

Trammel stayed on the platform as he watched the servants and a porter load the family's luggage on flatbed wagons. They were trunks and chests and boxes of all manner of size and description. He figured they would be staying at the house for the foreseeable future, which would only make his job even harder.

With the family gone, Big Ben slowly walked back toward Town Hall. The remaining five constables grew bolder around the staff.

"Would you just look at all that finery," the one named Jimmy said to the others. "Why I'd bet everything I've ever owned in the world would just about fit into one of them hat boxes they've got there."

Rand, the second oldest man in the group, added, "Sure must be nice to have money. Look at all the pretty servants they got, too."

The three men who Trammel assumed were footmen stopped loading for a moment before resuming their task. The black porter never stopped.

"Looks like one of them didn't like us calling him pretty, Rand," the one called Eddie said. "We're gonna have to keep our eyes on him."

The man called Smith cackled. "Be careful, Eddie. He might throw his hanky at you."

The five of them laughed, with the one called Red adding, "Now you've gone and done it, boys. They look like they're just about ready to cry."

The three servants stopped loading the wagon and squared up to the constables.

Trammel decided to step in between them before things got out of hand. "That's enough, boys. Let them work and be on your way."

The constables stopped laughing as Jimmy took a step toward Trammel. "This here is Hagen property. We don't have to do a—"

Trammel decked Jimmy with a short left hook to the jaw. He was out cold before he hit the ground.

The four remaining constables took a step backward. Only Rand found the courage to speak. "What'd you go and do that for?"

Trammel looked down at Jimmy. "That man's drunk."

"Drunk?" Red repeated. "Why it ain't even noon yet. He hasn't touched a drop in two whole days."

"He has to be drunk to step to me like that." Trammel looked at Red. "You drunk, too?"

Red held up his hands and backed farther away. "I'm sober as a judge."

"Good, then you boys had best pick up your friend here and get him off the street before I run the whole lot of you in for loitering."

Trammel dug the tip of his boot under Jimmy's shoulder and turned him over in the dirt. "Get going."

Rand told Smith and Eddie to pick up their fallen comrade and carry him away. Red went with them, leaving Rand to bring up the rear.

And the constable was in no hurry to move.

Trammel closed the few feet between them. "Get moving or I won't be as gentle as you."

But Rand kept his hands raised as he backed up. "I'm moving, Sheriff. I'm moving. For now. But there's gonna come a time real soon when I won't have to move until I'm good and ready. None of us will. And that time's coming sooner than you think."

"But today's not the day." Trammel kicked dirt in his direction. "Now get like I told you."

Rand smirked as he slowly backed away until he turned and joined the other constables.

Two of the footmen went back to loading the wagon. One of them caught Trammel's eye. "We could've handled them fellas on our own, Marshal."

Trammel heard a bit of Ireland in his voice. "It's *Sheriff* and while I'm around, I'll do the handling. Get back to work."

And although the constables were gone, Trammel waited until the luggage was loaded up and on their way to the house.

There was no sense in courting trouble as he knew there was more to come.

CHAPTER 2

"I'd like to thank you for taking the time out of your busy schedule to see me, Mr. Clay," Bernard Wain said.

"So do it," Lucien Clay replied.

The younger man appeared stuck for an answer. "Do what?"

"Thank me." Clay smiled. *The richer they were, the dumber they were.* "You said you'd *like* to thank me for taking time out of my schedule to meet you. I said you should do so."

Wain laughed, though it was clear he still did not understand what Clay had meant. "Thank you."

"That's the spirit. Isn't it funny the way people talk these days? You say you'd like to thank me when all you had to do is cut to the core of it and thank me. English is a strange language, but it's the only one I know, so I guess I'm stuck with it."

The criminal watched the lawyer smile again as he sipped his whiskey. Whiskey that Clay had poured him personally from his private stock.

Lucien Clay could remember a time when he enjoyed

receiving visitors, especially high-born visitors who came to him hat in hand.

But that had been in the time he now thought of as "Before." Before Buck Trammel had shattered his jaw with a single punch, causing him months of ceaseless pain and agony. Before the headaches set in and blurred his vision. Before the jaw healed crooked, ruining his face and marring his speech.

He had gone to Colorado to see a specialist, who told him the blow seemed to have caused some damage to his brain. The same punch that had broken his jaw had also cracked his skull. At least it explained the pain and the blurry vision. The doctor said the only way for it to heal properly was to break his jaw again so it could be reset. It would require more weeks of bedrest. More endless soups and broths that had turned him into little more than the skeleton he was now.

He thanked whatever gods existed for laudanum. It was the only thing that worked to dull the pain in his jaw, but not the damage to his ego. Only Trammel's corpse could cure that particular ailment.

Spending six weeks away from town was impossible. The buzzards had already begun to circle when word of his injuries leaked out the first time. It had taken a lot of killing just to preserve what he had managed to hold on to.

If he were to spend six weeks in Colorado, he knew he would return to find himself penniless and homeless. Men like Mr. Bernard Wain of Philadelphia would have no use for him then.

The decision had been made for him. He would live with the pain and the deformity. And trust Dr. Laudanum to take away his agony, even at the cost of his soul.

"I heard you were quite a character, Mr. Clay." Wain smiled. "I'm glad I wasn't misinformed."

Clay decided to have some fun at the man's expense. Telling him he was gullible would be one thing. Proving it to him would make the lesson stick and remind him of his place in the matter.

"What does that mean?"

Again, the lawyer came up short. He squinted his bluish eyes. His fleshy cheeks grew pink from embarrassment. "Excuse me?"

"You said I was quite a character," Clay repeated. "What did you mean by that?"

Wain blinked twice. "Your manner, sir. Your discourse. Your way of looking at life."

"And death," Clay added. "Because death *is* what you've come here to discuss, isn't it, Mr. Wain?"

The lawyer put his glass of whiskey on the desk. "Not in so many terms, but—"

"Of course not." Clay was glad to interrupt him. "But it's the crux of the matter, isn't it? The reason why you're really here. People like you don't come to me to loan them money or help them find workmen to build them a house or even for advice about how to run a saloon. People like you come to me when they're in trouble. When they think I can help them get out of it. And most of the time, that solution involves someone getting killed. You being an in-law of the aggrieved Hagen clan, I'd bet my last dollar that you're here about Adam." Clay cocked his head to the side and ignored the nagging pain that radiated from his jaw. "You want me to kill him for you, don't you?"

Wain cleared his throat and looked away. "You're quite direct, sir."

"Killing a man's just about the most direct thing in the world, Mr. Wain. Make no mistake about that. No shame in wanting it done, either, so there's no reason for you to look away from me. Unless you find it hard to look at me in my present condition."

Wain still did not look at him, and Clay couldn't blame him. He caught his own reflection in the mirror on the wall behind where his guest sat. Clay had always been a trim man, but his clothes hung loose on his emaciated frame. The months of broths and brews had served to keep him alive, but barely. The swelling in his jaw decreased a little every day, but his mouth was still crooked, causing him to occasionally drool on himself. His speech was slurred as if he was on his way toward being drunk, so he compensated for it by speaking slowly. The laudanum dulled the pain, but he never drank enough to allow it to intoxicate him. That didn't mean he was not in its grip. There was no question he was hooked, but he told himself he had it under control.

Wain finally looked at him. "I don't avert my eyes because of your condition, sir, but for the purpose of my visit."

"No need to be bashful about it," Clay told him. "Everybody finds themselves in a tough spot at one point in their lives, even rich folks like you. I'll make it a bit easier for you. Your court case against Adam isn't going so well, is it?"

"No," Wain admitted. "It isn't."

"The judge doesn't think King Charles's signature was forged on the will, does he?"

"Two judges, actually." Wain's eyes narrowed. "How did you know?"

Clay did not grin lest it cause him pain. "I still have my sources in this territory, Mr. Wain. Adam hasn't been able to shut me out completely."

"But he has shut you out, hasn't he?" Wain persisted. "You had some kind of deal with him that he has reneged on?"

"Now you're thinking like a lawyer," Clay said. "Yes, we had an agreement, a contract, even, but not the kind any court could enforce."

"But one that should be enforced between men of honor."

"Honor? No. Men of blood? Yes." Clay shifted uncomfortably in his chair. "I tried the honorable route a couple of times. All it got me was a lot of dead men. The last of them, Pete Stride, just got hung yesterday morning for his trouble." Clay drank some whiskey to dull a different kind of pain. "Stride was a good man. I hated to lose him like that."

Wain frowned at his whiskey. "May I ask why each of your attempts on Adam Hagen failed? Surely it wasn't for a lack of cunning on your part."

Clay could tell the tenderfoot was working up to something. And he would enjoy watching him do it, even though he was sure it wouldn't amount to much. "I didn't fail due to any lack of cunning or planning. Every plan I put in place to corral Hagen would've worked if it hadn't been for that bastard Trammel."

Wain took his glass of whiskey again as he sat back in his chair. "What if I knew of a way to remove Trammel from the equation? That is to say, get him out of the way, so to speak."

Clay felt a spark of hope and anger go through him. "I

know what an equation is, you damned pup. And don't go thinking moving Trammel aside is an easy task. He's tougher than he looks."

"That's quite a statement," Wain said. "I've seen him, and he looks quite formidable."

Now that Clay had taken Wain's bait, he was interested in getting in the boat. He could always jump back into the water later. "What are you cooking up, and what does it have to do with me? And if you try to get cute about it, I'll have you thrown out of here on your ear."

Wain seemed to grow more at ease. Clay knew they were entering his part of the forest now. "Adam believes he has beaten his family at their own game. We know he forged my father-in-law's signature on the will that left the Hagen empire to him. My late father-in-law hated Adam. He would've seen him dead before he left him a penny. But there are ways around that. Ways that require a pen and influence rather than guns and bloodshed. In short, Mr. Clay, you've tried to remove Adam in your own way and have come up short every time. I ask you to allow me and my family to try a different tactic. One that is more subtle and, perhaps, more effective."

Clay was interested. Only a fool wouldn't be. But he wasn't convinced just yet. "Adam Hagen and Buck Trammel aren't subtle men. Adam's not as smart as he thinks he is, but he's clever. He's used your family's money to buy him a lot of influence throughout the territory. Trammel might not like his opium and other businesses, but he always winds up backing him in the end."

Wain was not put off. "Adam has hired on his own constable force since we were here last, hasn't he?"

"Ten thugs with uniforms are still thugs," Clay told

him. "And now that he's got Big Ben London with him, he's going to be even tougher to take on than ever."

Wain smiled. "Which has robbed Sheriff Trammel of some of the influence he's enjoyed in the past, yes?"

"The constables keep a tight lid on things before it gets to him, so I guess you could say that." Clay was growing tired of talking around things. "What are you working up to?"

Wain swirled the whiskey in his glass. "Perhaps the good sheriff is discontented with his diminished role and would be amenable to a promotion of sorts?"

"Promotion?" Clay repeated. "What kind of promotion?"

Wain shook his head. "Not until you and I reach some sort of understanding, Mr. Clay."

Clay was beginning to like this young man. He was not as innocent as he looked. "What kind of understanding?"

"I'd like you to throw in your lot with my family," Wain explained. "You agree to use your remaining influence to help us, and we agree to help you. Once we get back the empire my father-in-law built, you not only retrieve all you have lost at Adam's hands but all that he has built since. I believe you're particularly interested in the opium trade he has taken over from you."

Clay shifted in his seat again, though this time, it wasn't due to discomfort. "Since we're talking plainly here, you should know I still get a cut of everything that happens in Blackstone. Adam might've cooled to me recently, but that's one thing I have in writing."

"Thirty percent if I recall," Wain said. "A decrease from your original agreement of fifty percent. I take it that reduction was a result from his belief you had acted against him."

Clay was impressed. "I see that I'm not the only one with sources of information."

Wain shrugged it off. "My family and I are prepared to make it one hundred percent, once you help us get rid of Adam when the time comes."

For the first time in months, Clay could not feel his jaw throbbing. "That's an awfully big number to throw around. Say it again and I'm liable to hold you to it."

"The town means nothing to the family," Wain told him. "All we want is the estate, of which the town is a small and troublesome part. Agree to help us and the town is yours to do with what you like. You can keep it as it is or turn it into the biggest den of vice this side of the Mississippi for all we care. We only want the ranch and the mines, though we're prepared to allow you to keep a share of the mines in the area at thirty percent."

Clay studied this well-dressed pink man across the desk from him. He was young in years but not in spirit. His fancy clothes and elegant manners and five-dollar words aside, he knew what he was saying. And he understood the man to whom he was speaking.

"You're sure about that? You speak for the rest of the Hagen family?"

"I've already spoken to them," he said. "You have my word and their word as well. We can't afford to put anything in writing now, of course, but I'll gladly shake on it. And before you threaten me, please rest assured that I understand the nature of our agreement. Our lives will be forfeit should we fail to live up to our end of the bargain and none of us are fond of the prospect of dying out here in the middle of nowhere."

Clay sat back in his chair, studying the man. "You're serious."

"You're a serious man, Mr. Clay." He extended a pink, smooth hand across the desk to him. "Do I have to spit in my palm first or do we have an agreement?"

Clay shook his hand, embarrassed by how frail his own hand looked compared to the lawyer's. "We have a deal."

"Splendid." Wain finished his whiskey and set it back on the desk. "I think this calls for another drink to celebrate our new partnership, don't you?"

Clay pulled the cork out of the bottle and poured a good amount into each glass. "When does this grand scheme of ours begin."

Wain took his glass and inhaled the whiskey, smiling at the aroma. "That's the beauty of it, Mr. Clay. The wheels of progress have already begun to turn."